Missing Thread

Missing Thread

The Georgia Series, Book 3

June V. Bourgo

Acknowledgements

The writing of this story was a different and more difficult process than the two previous books in The Georgia Series. Winter's Captive and Chasing Georgia leaned more to the physical and emotional endurance necessary to ensure Georgia's survival; while Missing Thread encompasses her strength of character and tests her ability to overcome adversity in a mental capacity.

I would like to thank Anne Marsh, whose creative insights and opinions are always helpful and so appreciated.

Research for this story took me in many directions and introduced me to worlds and people I would normally never encounter. A big thank you to Susan Goddard of the Acquired Brain Injury Supports at VCH Home Care Services and the University of British Columbia's Centre for Brain Health for their time and patience in answering all of my questions.

A huge shout out to the Federal Bureau of Investigation, Public Affairs and Community Outreach, New Orleans Division, as well as FBI Headquarters for providing me with procedural information and how the various security agencies in the United States are linked together. I enjoyed their southern Louisiana hospitality and being referred to as Miss June. Any errors in the book in reference to any of the security agencies are solely mine.

A special thanks to two of my grandchildren, Braelynne and Brody, who provided a realistic child's perspective of how Georgia's children, Shelby and Kaela would deal with the challenges of Georgia's plight.

Interviewing them was such a pleasure for me but their mature and serious answers to my questions showed an intuitiveness and understanding that truly amazed me.

I must acknowledge my husband, Dennis Bourgo, for his love and constant support on a creative and personal level. He always keeps me grounded and well fed.

And to my Next Chapter team, thank you all for helping to make my book the best that it can be.

DEDICATED TO ALL THE PEOPLE IN MY FAMILY CIRCLE

Archer	*Keeley*	*Nelson*
Bake-Powell	*Kinzer*	*Newman*
Banks	*Lavoie*	*Palahicky*
Booth	*Legros*	*Pallick*
Bourgo	*Letourneau*	*Rogers*
Bowlby	*MacWilliam*	*Saunders*
Davies	*Mcconnachie*	*Shuker*
Fede	*MacDonald*	*Smith*
Gregorchuk	*McLain*	*Thompson*
Harrison	*Markwart*	*Wood*
Jarvis	*Marsh*	*Wright*

PART ONE

"Even in its darkest passages, the heart is unconquerable.
It is important that the body survives,
But it is more meaningful that the human spirit prevails."

Dave Pelzer, A Child Called 'It'

Prologue

Friday, Lake Charles, Louisiana

FBI Probationary Agent Benjamin Samuels, of the Federal Bureau of Investigation sat in his van staring at nothing. He glanced at his watch for the third time in the past ten minutes. A sigh escaped his lips. Time was moving slowly. *Boring.*

The house he was watching had been still for hours. He reached over to the passenger seat and opened the cooler bag. *Hmm... tuna sandwich, apple, a bag of peanuts, a couple of ding dongs, and some bottled water.* He grabbed a ding dong, downed it in three bites and washed it down with coffee from a thermos.

He changed the CD that was playing to a more upbeat sound and drummed his fingers on the steering wheel to the beat of the music. He sang along with the song and threw in some ad libs of his own. *Anything to help pass the time.*

It was a dead end street with lots of bushes. He was parked down the block from the home that was his assignment, well-hidden in an old overgrown driveway. There were no houses directly in front of him and he had a clear view of the old cottage and the driveway that ran up the side of the property. The black pick-up parked there, hadn't moved since yesterday, according to the nightshift agent. Ben's dayshift started four hours ago.

Ben heard the gurgling of his stomach and felt a sudden burning in his chest. *Indigestion. Shouldn't of had that left over chili for breakfast.*

He'd been late rising this morning and the chili was the only quick food he could find in his near empty fridge. Ben reopened the cooler bag and grabbed a bottle of water. He drank half the bottle, while rubbing his abdomen.

It wasn't the FBI's case originally. It came from out-of-state. He didn't have all the details, except that it was a joint venture between the FBI and US Border and Customs Protection, reporting directly to a committee of Homeland Security. The subject under investigation had returned to Lake Charles, Louisiana to attend to his mother's affairs. She'd died a week ago. The field office in New Orleans had been contacted. They covered sixty-four parishes in Louisiana, divided up under six satellite offices. Lake Charles was one of the six resident satellite offices in the state. New Orleans had passed the case on to his boss, Cam Hutchins, Resident Agent in Charge.

Ben's job was to watch and record the subject's activities. So far, nothing of interest had occurred—a small funeral attended by the deceased woman's son, who was their subject, with a few Bingo lady friends, and a couple of neighbors; a quiet reception at the house; and a visit to a lawyer. Garbage bags had been put out on pick-up day and some cardboard boxes were delivered to a thrift shop. All had been confiscated by his agency, unbeknownst to the subject. All very mundane. The man had a return plane ticket to New York state and would be leaving in a few days. The field office would forward a report of their surveillance to the powers that be back east and the role his office played in the case would wrap up.

His radio crackled. "Agent Samuels? Motz here. Do you copy?"

The agent picked up his radio and addressed the SOG Specialist. The Surveillance Operations Group was contracted by the FBI to provide trained personnel to assist their Agents in surveillance ops. This arrangement freed up time and manpower for other FBI projects. "I'm here. What's up? Over."

"I'll be out of the car for five minutes. Pee break. Over."

"Ten-four. Out."

Aaron Motz was parked out of sight one block over; ready to pick up the tail should their subject be on the move.

Ben felt a discomfort pass from his stomach into his intestines. He squirmed in his seat and drank more water. *Damn chili.*

As a probationary agent, he'd been with the bureau for ten months. He knew he had to cut his teeth on jobs like this. He'd spent his whole life wanting to be a part of the FBI and here he was. All he had to do was pay his dues and find ways to deal with the humdrum side of the job. These days would pass and he had big dreams for his future with the Bureau.

A few gas bubbles welled up inside his chest and he burped them out, bringing some relief to his indigestion. But he sensed he was in trouble as the discomfort grew in his lower abdomen. A glance around the van confirmed that in his rush to get to work this morning, he'd left an all important item at home—a roll of bathroom tissue. *Shit.* Ben groaned. *Great choice of words, Einstein.* It wouldn't be the first time he'd retreated behind bushes or down laneways while on surveillance. It was a hazard of the job. Nature had her own schedule. Ben had no problem relieving himself in this manner, but no way would he succumb to this particular urge without that precious square of paper. And it had started to rain.

He glanced at his watch and noted ten minutes had passed since his conversation with Motz. "Motz, you there? Over." *Static and more static.* "Motz? Over." *Damn.*

Flatulence gurgled through his intestines until the gas escaped, forcing him to roll down his window for some fresh air.

He stared at the house down the street and came to a decision. One turn of the key in the ignition and the van started. He turned right onto the street and drove in the opposite direction of his charge towards the gas station two blocks down.

A few minutes later, he was back with a fresh thermos of coffee and feeling all the better for it. Ben turned around in the abandoned property and reclaimed his position in the bushes. Motz confirmed he was back in place. He released his seat belt and adjusted his seat for better comfort. *Might as well be comfortable.* Ben opened the thermos and poured some coffee into the lid.

He searched out the house down the street. "Oh fuck…" His hand holding the coffee to his lips froze. His eyes searched up and down the street.

"Ooh no… no…" He pounded the steering wheel with his other fist. "You're in deep shit now." The black pick-up was gone, leaving the gravel driveway empty, except for tufts of overgrown grass blowing in the breeze.

Fifteen minutes…fifteen fuckin' minutes. That's all I was gone. Ben stared at his cell phone charging in the cigarette lighter. He had no choice but to call it in. All he could think of was how he'd blown such an easy assignment. *All because of some spicy chili.*

The call was picked up by a receptionist. "Resident Agent Hutchins, please," he said in a defeated voice. He punched the steering wheel one more time. *Hutchins' gonna be pissed.*

Chapter 1

Two days earlier, Wednesday afternoon

The plane dropped, tilted sideways and rose up hard. Coffee flew out of the cup in Georgia Charles-Dixon's hand, landing on the front of her white shirt.

"Damn." She set the cup back onto the tray and dabbed at the stain with a napkin. The plane took another dive and she put the lid on the cup and secured it in the slotted tray.

The seat belt light bonged and flashed as the P.A. system came to life. "Ladies and gentlemen, we are experiencing some air turbulence. Please remain in your seats and fasten your seat belts. Thank you."

Georgia glanced nervously at her husband in the seat beside her as she engaged the seat belt. She knew turbulence was a natural phenomenon and with all the air miles she'd clocked, she should be used to it. *Fat chance.*

Sean took a hold of her hand and squeezed it. "Relax. It's nothing to worry about." His soft soothing voice made her feel better.

She looked through the window and saw nothing but forests below. They were somewhere over northern California. Soon they'd be landing in Los Angeles. Her thoughts focused on their trip. Sean would remain in L.A. for three days on movie business. She was catching a connecting flight to Houston, Texas to appear as a guest speaker at a Writer's Convention. She had come to enjoy speaking at events. They brought her to places she would never have visited and introduced her to many interesting people. But, lately, they'd become a chore.

The plane shuddered and shook as they hit another air pocket. "Uhh ..." Georgia sucked in her breathe, her body tensing against the back of the seat.

Sean leaned closer to her and tightened his grip on her hand. "Are you okay?"

"Yes, of course. I'm being silly. I've never been fond of flying, but since I've become a parent, I'm more aware of my mortality."

"I think parenthood does that to a lot of people, especially mothers."

"It doesn't help knowing the girls were upset we left them with Grams." Georgia thought about her daughters, Kaela and Shelby. They'd just celebrated their ninth birthday.

Sean loosened his grip on her hand. "It's the first time that we left them without one of us being there."

Kaela was her birth daughter from a previous marriage. Shelby was Kaela's half-sister. The girls were born a couple of weeks part, the result of her ex-husband's affair during his marriage to Georgia. Both women became pregnant around the same time. Georgia adopted Shelby when her ex-husband and his second wife had both died only months apart. Two and a half years ago, Georgia married Sean and he adopted the girls as his own.

They were a family.

Georgia sighed. "I knew Shelby might be upset with both of us away. But it's been four years since she lost her birth parents."

"We can't keep her in a cocoon forever, hon. Sooner or later, she needs to accept that we're not going anywhere."

"You're right. I've been thinking that with the girls in school full-time, I'd like to get involved with something else part-time."

"Like what?" Sean asked.

Georgia laughed, which turned into a snort. "I haven't a clue. But I'm thinking this will be my last speaking engagement to do with my past and my books."

"I thought you loved all of this. You've kept it pretty low key since the girls started school."

"I do love it. But I want to do something more meaningful. I'm tired of talking about me."

"That I understand but what you've been doing has inspired other people."

Georgia nodded her head. "I suppose. I guess I'm bored and I need a new challenge. My life needs to move forward as well."

"Then you must find one."

"Hmm … I'm not sure how."

Sean brushed her hair out of her eyes and kissed the tip of her nose. "Then let it find you. When it does, you'll know."

The turbulence stopped and the rest of the flight was without incident. Georgia watched as they flew out to sea and changed their approach back to the coast. Ten minutes later they departed from the plane at LAX and headed to the ticket counter to check Georgia in for her connecting flight to Houston.

Sean walked her to the security check point. "Call me when you're settled into the hotel." "I will." Georgia slipped her arms around his waist and placed her head on his chest.

He held her tight and whispered, "I love you."

She lifted her head and looked into his eyes. "I love you too."

Sean tilted his face and kissed her good-bye. "Have fun, hon."

Georgia watched him walk towards the exit door to a waiting taxi. As if sensing her gaze, he stopped and turned. Sean gave her a wave and disappeared outside. She sought out the end of the security check line and took her place. It took her twenty minutes to get through the line and walk the distance to the waiting lounge. No sooner had she settled into a seat, when her cell phone rang. It was her grandmother's number in Gibsons. She smiled, knowing it would be her daughters.

"Hi Mommy." It sounded liked Kaela but her voice sounded muffled.

"Hi sweetheart. How was your day at school?"

"Okay I guess. Darcy Brooks got caught throwing a spit ball at me. He's such a dork and … oops… Shelby, stop it."

Georgia could hear both her daughters in a fit of giggles. "You there?"

"Yes, Mommy." A crunching sound came through the line."

"You're eating in my ear, Kaela. Do you know what that sounds like at this end?"

"Sorry. Grams made us chocolate chip cookies. Shelby made me laugh and a piece fell out of my mouth." More giggles. "Where are you, Mommy?"

"I'm in L.A. airport waiting for my connecting flight to Houston. Won't be long now."

"Is Poppy with you?" Kaela asked.

"No, he's on his way to his hotel." Georgia smiled. The girls had decided when Sean became their adoptive father, they would call him Poppy. The name had stuck and Sean couldn't have been prouder.

"Okay. We just wanted to check in with you. Shelby wants to say hi. Love you, Mommy. Bye."

"Love you too, sweets. I'll talk to you tomorrow. Bye."

Georgia waited for her other daughter to say hello. Shelby took the phone, dropped it with a clatter. Another fit of the giggles came through the phone.

Shelby finally spoke. "Hi, Mommy."

"Hi sweetheart. Good to hear you two are in happy moods. How was your day?"

"I got an A in my short story about my favourite animal."

"Good for you, Shelby. You worked hard on that piece. I'm proud of you. So what are you guys up to tonight?"

"Grams is taking us out for pizza. Grampa Frank is coming too."

Georgia's eyebrows shot up. "Grampa Frank? Sounds like fun."

"Mommy?" Silence. "Are you and Poppy still coming home on Sunday?"

"Yes, hon. We'll be there Sunday."

"I miss you already. Oh…Grams is calling us. Grampa is here."

"You'd better go then. I miss you too. We'll talk tomorrow okay? Enjoy your pizza."

"Love you." Shelby blew a kiss in the phone.

"You too, hon. Bye now."

Georgia put her book down and looked out the window of the plane that was taking her to Houston. A smile formed on her lips as she thought about her conversation with her daughters. Kaela hated talking on the phone and always kept it short. Shelby on the other hand would have talked longer if they didn't already have dinner plans. Further dialogue with her daughter would have brought the child's neurosis to the surface and Georgia knew she'd have felt guilty for leaving her. She was grateful that Grams and Frank were keeping the girls busy.

Shelby had come a long way since losing her parents at age five. Georgia was now Mommy to her and she adored Poppy. The sisters, two weeks apart in age, looked like their father and many people who didn't know the family thought they were twins. Georgia believed this had helped the girls bond and become close very quickly. Having to explain that her ex-husband had an affair and impregnated his legal assistant around the same time as his wife became pregnant always raised eyebrows and brought more questions. But then the pair had become ill and died and Georgia took custody of Kaela. New people in their lives assumed that the girls were twins and Sean's children. They didn't bother to explain unless something came up in conversation.

The thought of Grams and Frank made her smile grow wider. Grams was her maternal grandmother. Frank was Georgia's ex-father-in-law. It seemed to her they had been spending some time together lately. *Hmm...no, what a ridiculous thought. Grams is at least eight or nine years older than Frank.*

The seat belt light flashed and Georgia prepped for the landing. As they began their descent into Houston Airport, a nagging feeling deep in her chest that started small grew to a level of anxiety. A pounding at her temples caused her head to ache. The inside of the plane disappeared before her eyes. She envisioned darkness and the pounding water in a heavy rainstorm that bounced off the near invisible asphalt. As quickly as the vision appeared, it was gone. Georgia swallowed hard and took deep breaths to keep herself calm. They landed and taxied the runway but a feeling of dread stayed with her. She stood and followed the line of passengers off the plane.

Something's going to happen. A premonition?

Chapter 2

Two nights later, Friday evening, suburbs of Port Arthur, Texas

Dylan Ortega's wife was angry. He noted her wild brown eyes flashing darker and braced himself for the backlash he knew his wife was about to bestow on him. Too late, he realized he'd pushed Camila to the point of no return.

"You're the man of the house? *You* make the decisions? You've been out of work for six months, Dylan. Our savings are gone, our mortgage is starting to fall behind, and the bills are next."

Dylan bristled. "It's not my fault that I was laid off. I've tried to find other work... *any* work."

"I know that. But it hasn't happened and now you're mad because I found work? Now is not the time for your e*stupido* male ego," Camila yelled.

His face reddened at her insult. "I'm angry because you didn't discuss it with me before you took the job."

Camila marched right up into his face and put her hands on her hips. "Why would I? I've tried to have this discussion with you many times. You always say my place is at home raising the kids. It's your job to work to take care of us. Well, I'm not going to lose everything we worked so hard for without at least a good fight."

"And what about the kids? Who's going to be here for them?" Dylan flashed back.

"You, that's who. When they're in school, you can look for work. You only need to be here after school until I get home." Camila crossed her arms and jutted her chin out. "I guess you'll have to stay out of the bar for awhile."

It was Dylan's turn to lose control. "You act like I'm in the bar all the time. That's not true."

"Don't deny it. I know you meet the guys every day for beers. You're spending less time at home, and throwing money away in the bar that we can't afford."

"I'm here tonight aren't I?"

Camila laughed sarcastically. "Oh get real. The only reason you're home tonight is because of this horrid storm. Half the area is without power which probably includes the bar."

Furious with her accusations and the truth of her words, Dylan looked for an outlet for his anger. He wanted to smash his fist into her smug face, but he'd never ever laid a finger on Camila and he never could. He picked up a brass ornament on the coffee table and threw it past her head and into the wall, leaving a ragged hole in the plaster.

Camila screamed. "*Bastardo!* The kids gave me that for Mother's Day."

Dylan turned on his heels and left the room. His need to get out of the house overwhelmed him. As he grabbed his truck keys and jacket in the hallway, he heard Camila's softened voice.

"Please...don't go out in that," she pleaded.

He left anyway, slamming the door behind him.

The rain pelted against the windshield. He headed along the roadway towards the Neches River. Once out of the residential area, the road was dark. The torrential storm made it difficult to see beyond a few feet. *Camila was right. No one in their right mind should be out in this.* Knowing, once again, that his wife's wisdom outweighed his stilted thinking in more ways than one, his anger was fuelled even more. He took the curve ahead at a speed that matched his level of anger and found himself behind a car travelling at a slower speed. To avoid hitting the car from behind, he pulled into the oncoming lane.

His wheels hit a puddle and skidded towards the car on his left causing it to move over onto the gravel shoulder. An adjustment brought his truck under control and he pumped the brakes to slow down. Through the rear view mirror he saw the car had stopped. *Probably scared the hell out the driver.* A shudder passed through him at the thought of what could have been. *The smart thing to do, would be to turn around and go home.* Dylan shook his head. He wasn't ready to face Camila. He needed some time and space to think things through and calm down. Dylan drove on into the storm.

Chapter 3

Friday evening, Bridge City, Texas

The frantic *whap whap* of the wipers against the windshield matched the pounding beat of Georgia's heart. The water ran down the glass in torrents, making visibility near impossible. She'd left the lights of Bridge City, Texas behind her moments before. Lightning strikes lit up the dark night sky, while deafening claps of thunder added to her already frayed nerves. *Why did I insist on driving tonight?*

The weather report predicted rain, not this sudden torrential storm. She adjusted her seat to support her back muscles; aching from leaning forward to peer through the distorted glass. The lights from an approaching semi truck blinded her momentarily. The tires of the truck hit a dip in the road full of water and splashed it onto her windshield. "Uhh ... damn," she gasped. Visibility was lost and Georgia felt the car hydroplane. She steered out of a skid and tapped the brakes lightly to slow her vehicle down.

A green light up ahead flashed *Cafe*. She drove the car off of the highway and into the parking lot. "Phew." A deep breathe escaped through clenched teeth and she leaned her head back against the headrest, releasing the pent up tension in her shoulders. One glance through the car window told her there was no sense waiting for the rain to let up. Georgia grabbed her purse, opened the door, and stepped out into the pelting rain. By the time she reached the door to the coffee shop, her clothes were soaked. Her wet hair dripped water down her face and off the tip of her nose.

"Oh my, what're doin' drivin' on a night like this?" The waitress led her to a table and brought her a hand towel from the kitchen. A teenage couple sat at a corner table whispering to each other, oblivious to anyone else. The door opened and a man entered in much the same state as Georgia, rounding it out to four patrons.

"What can I get ya, hon?" the woman asked her.

"Coffee, black, please."

The waitress scurried to the kitchen for another towel for the stranger.

Georgia pulled out her cell phone. No signal. *Great, the weather probably took out the tower.* She placed her cold hands around the cup for warmth. The man ordered a coffee and a donut. With little to do, the waitress wandered over to Georgia's table, her face shrouded with a look of concern.

"Where ya headed?"

"Houston," she said.

"Bad night for it. Maybe y'all should wait 'til mornin'."

"I have a flight to catch to L.A. I would have changed flights if I'd known this storm would turn for the worst. I'm about half-way. I might as well travel on."

"Y'all not from around here, are ya?"

Georgia smiled. Her lack of a southern drawl was a dead give-away. "No. I'm from Vancouver, Canada. I had business in Houston and today I went to Lake Charles, Louisiana for the day.

"Beautiful city that Vancouver. I visited there for the Olympics. Refill?"

"Yes, please." She glanced around the cafe, enjoying the warmth exuding from a woodstove in the corner. The lone male caught her attention and he nodded at her; a slight smile creased his mouth. Georgia nodded back. She took a few sips of her coffee. As comfortable as it felt here, it was time to get back on the road. She left money on the table and stood.

The stranger spoke to her as she passed. "Killer night."

Her eyebrows shot up. "Let's hope not."

A slight smile curled his lips for a second time. "Sorry, bad choice of words. Have a safe trip."

"You too."

The waitress met her at the door. "Now, hon, y'all take care out there, hear?"

"I will. Thank you."

There was no traffic on the road and it seemed darker than ever. "Everyone's too smart to be out here. Not like me," she muttered. She drove her way through the bridge systems over waters running to the Neches River which connected with Sabine Lake, eventually emptying into the Gulf of Mexico. A direction sign told her Port Arthur lay fifteen minutes ahead. Houston was a little over an hour away. The final bridge over the Neches River came into sight. Georgia noticed a vehicle behind her, closing the gap at a high rate of speed.

"What the..."

Considering the road conditions and limited visibility, whoever sat behind the wheel was definitely driving recklessly. It caught up to her back end in no time. Judging by the height of the headlights, it appeared to be a pick-up truck. High beams shone in the rear view mirror, adding to her already compromised vision.

"Jerk." She reached up to the mirror and flipped the knob but the lights still blinded her. "Asshole," she cried out. One quick slap of her hand pushed the mirror upwards, forcing her to rely on the side mirrors.

She concentrated on the road and the bridge looming ahead. The pick-up pulled out into the opposing lane. The vehicle didn't pass, but stayed right beside her. "What the hell?" Suddenly, the truck swerved towards her car, forcing Georgia to veer to the right. The tires on the right side of the car hit dirt and she started to skid. As she attempted to steer the car back onto the paved road, the pick-up moved into her lane and swerved towards her again. "What are you doing?" she yelled, frightened.

They'd reached the bridge span. With no place to go but into the concrete abutment where the bridge joined the bank, Georgia tapped her brakes and held on to the wheel, hoping to stop in time on the dirt shoulder. The pick-up stopped on the roadway at the entrance to the bridge blocking her way back to the pavement. She spiked her breaks to stop in time, but the wheel on the right passenger side caught a patch of mud and the car slid sideways. "Oh my God..." she screamed. Georgia cleared the bridge column, but the car kept sliding right over the embankment. Her body froze. The whole thing played out in slow motion. She heard the motor rev of the pick-up and the squeal of its tires as it sped onto the bridge deck and disappeared into the night. The front passenger side of her car hit a large rock, while the momentum of the still moving car forced her side to spin forward and up into the air. The vehicle flipped a couple of times as it careened down the bank and into the Neches River.

Because the car flipped side over side, Georgia's head flew to the passenger side with the first roll and back towards the driver's door, hitting hard against the window post before the air bags deployed. Her lungs gasped for air amidst the sharp chest pain she felt from their impact.

Blood ran down her face, filling her eyes, and mouth. She spat it out and shook her head to overcome the sense of disorientation.

The car landed in shallow water initially, but was tilted to the right and slid into deeper water. Georgia panicked. "Oh no, I've got to get out." She remembered reading in the car manual that one had so many seconds to open windows and doors before the power pack shorted.

She reached up and turned on the interior light, pushed the side air bag out of the way and hit the electronic window buttons. Cold air and freezing water poured into the windows. She pushed the seat belt release, but it wouldn't budge. "Uhh ... no ... no ... come on," she cried, pounding the button. Georgia shifted in her seat to see what the problem was. The water was up to her waist, distorting everything under its wake. She felt around with her fingers and realized the seat belt casing was buckled. Her heart pounded, but she wouldn't give up. The water rushed in faster now as the car sunk lower.

With numbing fingers, she held her breath and slid under the water to grab her purse on the floor of the passenger side. Her head popped back up. "Uuuh...that's cold," she gasped. The water was up to her neck at this point and she tilted her head back as her fingers searched for scissors in her make-up bag. Her body was numb from the cold water. *Thank God for sharp scissors.* It took a bit of effort, but she managed to cut through the belt and release herself. A small pocket of air remained at the roof of the car. Georgia took a few seconds to calm herself, sucked in a deep breath and pushed herself through the open window into the murky water as the car sunk into the dark depths.

Disoriented by the cold water and her head injury, Georgia didn't know which way was up. She looked up and down in the dark water. Surprisingly, the headlights and interior lights were still on and she could see them slowly moving away from her, confirming which way she must swim. Her lungs were bursting as she forced herself up, slowly releasing the diminishing air in her lungs. She hit the surface and sucked in air and water, causing her to cough and sputter.

Georgia tread water for a time, spinning in circles, not sure in the darkness where the shoreline lay. Her teeth chattered from the bitter cold water and rain pelted on her face, blinding her further. She finally made out the lights on the bridge and knew which way to swim to shore. She floated on her back to catch her breath and rebuild her energy. A moment later, the gravity of this decision hit home. Too late, the current of the river caught hold and pulled her out into the channel. "Help," she screamed. The water became choppy and as hard as she tried to swim back to calmer water, the river pulled her back. "Help...somebody help me." The current pulled her under at times, and when she resurfaced, the waves slapped her in the face, making it difficult to gasp for air without taking water in too.

Georgia gave a courageous fight, but it wasn't enough. The river, with all the force of nature, sought the path of its destiny as it had always done, taking her along with it.

The battle was lost.

Chapter 4

Dylan proceeded at a sensible speed down the road and turned off the highway onto a secondary road. He followed it until he reached an open area with a dirt road leading to the banks of Sabine Lake. A favourite make-out spot for local teens, Dylan smiled. He and Camila had shared their first kiss right here ten years previous. The area was dark and empty tonight, matching the feeling in his heart. He parked facing the lake and turned up the radio. With his head resting back against the head rest, he stared out at the lake. The headlights picked up the turbulence of the dark water crashing against the banks, fuelled by the force of a strong wind.

He thought about the innocence of their courting days, their marriage, and the birth of their two boys, now seven and nine. *How young and naive we'd been.* A sardonic laugh, starting deep within, escaped through his lips, building its momentum until he shook with laughter, taking him to the point of tearing up. Dylan gave his head a shake, took a couple of deep breaths, and was back in control.

He stared out at the water in a stupor, afraid to move and break the feeling of numbness he felt and welcomed. Even the beat of the rhythmic salsa playing on the radio, usually a sound that stirred his Latino blood, went unnoticed. His eyes focused on a spot where the Neches River entered Sabine Lake. The churning water of the whirlpool mesmerized his vision and comforted him. *Strange, but I don't have the need or desire to examine the feeling.* Round and round the swirls went, pulling his focus into their deep recesses.

Something's not right. Then he saw it. He frowned and leaned forward, staring out the windshield at an object caught in the center of the whirlpool. The wipers afforded him a quick glance at whatever it was, each time the blades cleared the pools of water running down the glass. Dylan opened the truck door and stepped out. He stood in front of the truck and shielded his eyes with the palms of his hands to keep the rain from blocking his vision.

"Holy shit..." In an instant, he knew it was a body. Dylan kicked his shoes off and ran towards the bank's edge, pulling his jean jacket off as he went. Without so much as a thought, he dove off the grassy knoll and into the lake. The cold water hit him like a hard wooden board and stung his skin. He pushed it from his mind and swam as fast and hard as he could towards the whirlpool. He'd been a champion swimmer in college and knew no fear of the water. With one reach of his arm, he grabbed hold of some clothing and pulled the body towards him. There was no time to check the status of the person. It was imperative to get himself and the body, dead or alive, out of the icy water. Assuming there was life still in the person he had in his grasp, Dylan turned the body over and held the face out of the water with one arm and swam with the other.

The current was strong and he struggled to hold onto the body and keep the face above the water.

By the time he pushed the body up and onto the bank, he was forced to take a moment to catch his breath and rebuild some strength. Finally, he pulled himself out of the water and collapsed. Time was of the essence. Dylan pushed himself up and rolled the body over onto it's back. It was a woman. She wasn't breathing and he couldn't find a pulse. A quick listen to her chest, told him her heart was still beating, albeit, a slow, faint beat. He applied the breathing technique over and over until she sucked in a huge breath and coughed water out of her lungs. Dylan rolled her onto her side so she wouldn't choke on the water. She didn't regain consciousness but she was breathing. He felt a pulse in her neck. A deep gash on the left side of her head began to bleed profusely. Without cell service, he'd have to take her to the hospital himself. He carried her to the truck and placed her in the passenger seat, propping her up against the door. A sweater belonging to Camila was shoved behind the seat. Dylan used it to tie around her head to try to slow down the flow of blood. His teeth chattered as he started the fifteen minute drive and he turned the heat in the cab on high.

Dylan drove as fast as he dared. He headed towards the Medical Center of Southeast Texas in Port Arthur, a physician-owned hospital with state-of-the-art technology. It was in the process of being built when their first child was born but Camila had their second son at this hospital. He pulled into the emergency entrance honking the horn. He jumped out and ran around to the passenger side. Dylan gathered the woman into his arms and rushed through the hospital doors, almost running into a police officer. The officer yelled for the nurse, who grabbed an empty bed set against the wall in the hallway. The policeman helped him place the woman on the bed. The nurse told Dylan to follow her and they hurried past half a dozen people sitting in the waiting room and through the door to triage. The triage nurse called for help to move the woman from the bed onto one behind a curtain. Dylan sat down in a chair beside the bed, shaking from the icy water, his wet clothes stuck to his chilled skin.

The officer stood beside him. "Car accident?"

"No," Dylan answered in a shaky voice.

The nurse took over the questioning as she felt the woman's pulse. "Tell me what's happened here."

"I was down at the lake … seen her floating in the water. I swam out and brought her in." The nurse and the officer exchanged glances. "She wasn't breathing, but her heart was beating." Dylan shook his head to clear his thoughts. "I applied CPR and brought her straight here."

"Did she regain consciousness at all?"

"No."

"You're covered with blood. Are you hurt?"

"No, it's her blood, from her head." Dylan did feel weak and couldn't stop shaking.

"All right, but you're most certainly suffering from hypothermia. I'm going to get you out of your wet clothes and into a bed. We'll need to check you out."

Dylan felt confused. "I'm okay."

"What's your name?"

"Dylan Ortega." He noticed the police officer pulled a pad out of his pocket and wrote on it. "Do you know this woman?" he asked.

"No."

The nurse put a hand on his shoulder. "Well, Dylan, you're showing signs of hypothermia. We're going to get you into a bed and treat your symptoms. Okay?"

Dylan hadn't the energy to protest. Bed sounded like a great idea. He stood up and his legs gave out. The nurse grabbed hold of him to keep him from hitting the floor and the officer went for a wheel chair. He was lowered into the chair and taken to a bed across the room. The nurse assigned another to his immediate care and went back to the rescued woman.

The new nurse helped him undress, don a hospital gown and climb into bed. She placed his discarded clothes into a plastic bag. He saw her pull the curtain back and hand the bag to the police officer. *What's up with that?* Feeling too tired to care, Dylan closed his eyes. Seconds later the nurse was back with a hot blanket out of the warmer. She hooked him up to a heart monitor and took his vitals. A clerk came in with a clip board to get his personal information. Dylan felt so disoriented that he couldn't remember much of anything about his insurance, his home address, or much else. He did remember that his wallet was in the truck between the seats. The clerk asked the officer to retrieve it. They set up an IV to get warm fluids into his body and placed a heating pad under his back and another one over his chest.

"Dylan? I'm from the lab."

He opened his eyes. A young woman stood holding a basket with empty vials.

She gave him a big smile. "I'm going to get some blood samples for a lab workup, okay?"

"Okay."

Drowsiness overtook him, but just before he fell asleep all hell broke out in the emergency room. The head nurse began yelling instructions. "All staff, STAT. Call Dr. Hoffman." Dylan heard feet running past his curtains. A male voice joined the fray. "Fill me in."

The head nurse spoke. "Female drowning victim, pulled from the water not breathing no pulse, heart rhythm yes. CPR applied with success, never regained consciousness. Arrived ten minutes ago, pulse 40, BP 80/40, body temp 88, suffered cardiac arrest seconds ago."

Dylan's heart jumped to his throat. *No... she can't die. Not after all I did to save her.* His head began to swim. Voices came and went, it was hard to decipher what they were saying when instructions were being yelled back and forth between the staff, but the odd word popped into his consciousness, *defibrillator, clear, again, clear, reset, clear.* As quickly as the bedlam started, it became very quiet. Dylan fought to stay awake and strained to hear something... anything... nothing came back to him... sleep claimed him.

Chapter 5

Friday evening, Los Angeles, California

The number rang and rang, just as it had done the other dozen times Sean called Georgia's cell phone. A frown creased his forehead. *Why isn't it going to voicemail, or telling me that the cell customer I'm calling isn't available?*

He called operator assistance and asked for the telephone number of her hotel in Houston. Ringing through to the desk, he asked for Georgia's room. There was no answer to that phone either. Sean hung up and looked at the time on his cell phone. It read 11:05 p.m.

"Humph ..." *Maybe she's out with members of the conference and her battery's dead. Maybe she went for a walk.* Sean laughed. "Maybe this and maybe that," he said aloud. He hadn't exactly been available for her call earlier that morning. *If she's out enjoying herself socially, good for her.* He settled into bed, his hand going out to the empty mattress beside him. *God, I love the woman.* Although the past few days in Los Angeles had been exciting for him, working with the production company that was to produce his next book series into a mini-series, he missed her. He'd come to depend on her not only as a life partner, but as a creative partner in his writing career. They made a good team. And then there were his daughters. Their family unit was strong and full of love.

Sean rolled onto his side and pulled the unused pillow towards him. It gave him some comfort as he wrapped his arm around it and pulled it tight. His face lit up with a happy smile, knowing in the morning that Georgia would be flying from Houston to join him.

Sean stared at the airline representative in disbelief. "All I'm asking is if my wife checked in for her flight and if she got on the plane?"

The woman straightened her shoulders and stared him down. "I told you, sir. I'm not allowed to give out that information."

"I've shown you my identification. What more do you want?".

"I can't verify that you're who you say you are, sir. We have to re-spect the privacy of our passengers. Please move along, others are waiting to be served."

The agent pursed her lips together and raised her eyebrows, a look that aged her considerably and told Sean that nothing he said would budge this woman. He softened his tone, but spoke firmly. "Then, I want to talk to someone who can help me. Please get your supervisor." A look of annoyance crossed her face, but Sean stood his ground. "I'm not budging until I talk to someone with authority." She turned on her heel and disappeared through a doorway.

People behind him were whispering and shifting uncomfortably. He turned to the line-up he'd created. "I apologize for holding you up, but my wife is missing and I'm seeking some help." Some of the people looked sympathetic, while others glared. But the buzzing stopped.

The airline employee returned with a tall, older gentleman who opened a gate in the counter and smiled. "Sir, would you care to come with me, please?"

Sean followed the man behind the counter and through a doorway to the back. He took him into an office and offered him a seat.

"I'm Bob Rogers, Agent Supervisor." He reached across the desk and offered his hand before he sat down.

Sean shook his hand. "Sean Charles-Dixon."

"As the agent told you, it isn't our policy generally to give out information on our passengers..."

"I know that..."

Mr. Rogers put his hand up to stop him. "...but, I can see how distraught you are. Why don't you tell me what the problem is."

"My wife flew to Houston three days ago to speak at a convention. I stayed here in L.A. on business. She was due to fly in this morning on flight 2423. I didn't see her disembark with the other passengers."

"Perhaps, she missed her flight. Does she have a cell phone?"

Sean took a deep breath. He'd been through all this with the agent, but he didn't want to get on the bad side of this man. "Mr. Rogers, the last time I spoke to my wife was Thursday evening after she returned from a banquet. Yesterday, she had a free day and chose to spend it in Houston because I was tied up here in meetings all day. She left me a message yesterday morning that she was renting a car for the day. She didn't return to the hotel last night or turn in the rental. The hotel told me this morning that her things are still in her room at the hotel, her bed untouched and her cell phone rings unanswered, with no voicemail interruption or message to say she's not available." He paused to catch his breath.

"Does she know anyone in Houston that she may have stayed with?"

"No one. Whenever we're apart, we always talk at least once a day. I met her flight this morning because I didn't know what else to do. All I want is for you to confirm that she didn't check in for her flight and that she isn't scheduled for a later one." He looked at the supervisor pleadingly.

Mr. Rogers stared at him with compassion. "I can understand your concern for your wife's safety. Would you mind showing me some identification?"

Sean showed him his passport. "There's something else. My wife is well-known, a bit of a celebrity. There are books and movies about her. Three years ago, she encountered a situation with a celebrity stalker, in which she ended up in the hospital and he ended up deceased. It's hard for me not to worry about her well-being."

The man looked like a light bulb had gone off above his head. "That's it. I thought there was something familiar about you. I know who you are, sir and who your wife is. Let me get that information for you."

Sean let out a sigh of relief and leaned back in his chair while the supervisor left the office.

Ten minutes later, he returned. "I'm sorry. Your wife didn't check in this morning for her flight, nor is she booked on any of our other flights today and tomorrow."

Sean's heart pounded. "Somehow I knew that, but I needed you to confirm it." He ran his hands through his hair and tried to sort his thoughts. *Don't panic.* He took a deep breath.

"What can I do to help you?"

He looked up at the man. The calming, sincerity in his voice gave him focus. "I need to get to Houston as soon as possible. Can you help with that?"

"I'll take care of it myself. Do you have a bag or luggage?"

"No. Everything's back at my hotel. I can get what I need in Houston."

"Do you have a vehicle in the parking lot?"

Sean shook his head no. "I came by cab."

Within the hour, he sat in a first class window seat watching the city disappear below as the plane made its ascent. The stewardess offered him a drink and he ordered a double single-malt scotch. He downed it in a couple of gulps and waited for it to hit his bloodstream. When it did, he put his seat back, closed his eyes, and thought out a plan.

One hour and fifty minutes later, he watched as they descended into Houston ... calmer, stronger, and ready to find his wife.

Chapter 6

Saturday morning, Medical Center of Southeast Texas, Port Arthur, Texas

Dylan opened his eyes to find Camila sitting in a chair by his bedside. She was leaning back in the chair with her eyes closed. Not sure if she was awake or sleeping, he stayed quiet and studied her. Wisps of dark hair, pulled back in a ponytail, had escaped and lay in tangled curls around her face. *So beautiful.*

His eyes searched his surroundings. He was no longer in the ER but in a private room. The window blinds were closed, but he could see daylight filtering around the edges. The steady beep of the heart monitor caught his attention first. He was being fed oxygen through a clear plastic mask over his nose and mouth. An IV remained intact through the top of his hand, and a blue plastic peg sat on the end of his forefinger, measuring his oxygen level. Wires from the pads attached to his chest and abdomen poked out from under the blanket and ran to the monitor.

His thoughts filled with the memories of the night before, making him shudder. "Uhh..." He felt cold ... not as cold as then ... but chilled, and unaware he had let out a moan.

"Hi, baby."

Dylan locked eyes with Camila. Gone was the anger and rage of last night. Her eyes expressed love, compassion, and tears. He tried to answer but a lump had formed in his throat, forcing him to choke on the words. Instead, he squeezed the hand that reached for his.

"You gave me quite a scare, Mister Superhero." Camila stroked his cheek with her free hand.

He tried to talk but the mask interfered. Pulling it down to his chin, Dylan whispered, "I'm sorry."

Camila smiled and shook her head no. "You're going to be okay, that's all that matters."

"What time is it?" he asked.

She looked at her watch. "Seven a.m."

A cute petite blond with short spiky hair and expressive blue eyes entered the room. "Good morning, I'm Tracy, your day nurse. Good to see you're awake. How are you feeling?"

"Cold."

"We can fix that. First, let's get your vitals, and second, a couple of hot blankets. You'll be snug as a bug in no time."

A few minutes later, she returned. True to her word, the hot blankets helped.

Dylan snuggled his arms under the covers, leaving one hand out to hold onto Camila's. "Mmm, thank you."

"We aim to please." Nurse Tracy chuckled. "The lab vampire will be in soon to suck some blood out of you. We'll be doing regular checks on your blood gasses today. The Doc will be in as well to check you out and have a chat." The nurse pointed to the monitor, "See this number here? That's your oxygen level. It's being monitored by that little blue doohickey on your finger. You need to keep it around ninety-seven. It's dropped a little since I was here the first time. So, I want you to monitor it and if it drops to ninety-two, back on with the mask. Okay?"

"All right."

"Good man. One last thing. We have to wait for the Doc to see if our hero is ready to eat some hot liquids. Meanwhile nothing by mouth. We'll keep you fed by IV." Nurse Tracy turned to leave.

"Nurse? The woman ... did she ... " Dylan's voice cracked. He didn't want to say the words.

"She's alive. Still unconscious though. She's in ICU."

"Do you know who she is yet?"

"I'm afraid not, but don't worry about her. She's in good hands. You need to relax and get some rest."

The lab technician came a few minutes later.

"Where are the kids?" Dylan asked Camila.

"At your parents. I'm going to try calling them on a land line. Cell service is still out. I'll be right back."

Dylan looked at the monitor. It registered an oxygen level of ninety-three. He slipped the mask back over his mouth and nose and closed his eyes. The events of the previous night crowded his mind, including his fight with Camila. It was all too overwhelming. Those thoughts were pushed away and he fell asleep.

When he awoke, Camila was back in the arm chair by the bed reading a magazine. The red numbers on the monitor glowed ninety-seven. Dylan removed the mask. "Did you reach your parents?"

His wife looked up in surprise. "Yes, power's on."

The doctor arrived at that moment. "Good morning, Mr. Ortega. I'm Doctor Saunders. How are you feeling this morning?"

"Exhausted and a little chilled, and I have a headache."

"We'll put you on some Tylenol for that headache. I've looked at the results of all your tests. The good news is that you're progressing well. I'd like to try you on some hot broth and sweet liquids for breakfast. If you tolerate that we'll try some cream soup for lunch. No tea or coffee okay?"

"How long will I be in here?"

"If you do well today, we may send you home late afternoon, tomorrow morning at the latest. Rest up until lunch and this afternoon, we'll get you up and walking. Any more questions?"

"No, and thank you."

Doctor Saunders smiled and put out his hand. "You're welcome and I'd like to shake the hand of a hero. What you did was very brave."

Dylan shook the doctor's hand, but felt embarrassed. "Anyone would have done what I did."

"I don't think so, given the time of year and the weather conditions. You'd better get used to the attention, the press is going to be all over this. I'll check in with you at the end of my shift." He nodded at Camila and left the room.

Nurse Tracy brought him his Tylenol and removed his IV. "You're to stay in bed until after lunch, but if you feel up to it, I can remove the catheter. When you need to pee, ring the buzzer. I'll put you in a wheelchair and help you to the biffy. How's that sound?"

"Please remove it, I hate the catheter."

Alone again, Dylan stared at his wife. "We need to talk … about us… "

Camila placed a finger on his lips. "Shhh, we've been under a lot of stress and we've both said some awful things to each other lately. Now's not the time. You need to get your strength back first, then we'll talk. I just need to know one thing, do you still love me?"

His eyes filled with moisture. "I've never stopped. And do you still love me?

Camila leaned forward and brushed his lips with hers. "More than ever."

Dylan began to shake, tears ran down his face, and he sobbed. All the stress he'd been carrying the past months, compounded by the events of the past twelve hours, culminated to the point where he couldn't hold it in any longer. The sweet compassion of his loving wife and probably the effects of the tranquilizers he'd been fed through the IV, allowed him to let it all go.

Camila climbed onto the bed beside him and held him in her arms. They laid together in silence, and for the first time in a long time, Dylan felt the comfort of the familiar bond they'd shared.

"Mr. Ortega?"

Camila quietly rose from the bed and sat in the chair.

"I'm sorry to bother you. I'm Detective Jarrod Brown and this is Detective Scott Calloway. We'd like to get a statement from you about the incident last night."

Camila's Latino blood flared. "Must you do this now? My husband needs to rest."

"It's okay, Camila. Not a problem, Detective."

Detective Brown turned to Camila. "I'm sorry, Mrs. Ortega, but the more we can learn about the events of last evening, the sooner we may identify the woman he saved. She may have family wondering where she is."

Mixed emotions passed over Camila's face. "Of course, I'm sorry."

"Camila, hon, could you put the top of the bed up a little so I can see the detectives better?"

While his wife raised the bed, Detective Calloway studied her. "Perhaps, Mrs. Ortega, you could accompany Detective Brown outside. He has some questions for you."

Now it was Dylan's turn to become annoyed. "And why would she want to do that? She knows nothing about the events of last night."

Detective Calloway, a short, stocky middle-aged Caucasian stared him down. "She can supply a time frame, such as when you left the house."

"You make it sound like I'm a suspect."

Detective Brown took over. He was a taller, African-American with soft brown eyes. "I think the detective is afraid Mrs. Ortega might take offense at some of our questions, sir."

"Or your answers," Detective Calloway added.

Dylan's eyebrows shot up. He wasn't sure where this was all leading He looked at Detective Brown. "I don't know why you would be asking me any offensive questions, but I'm sure whatever you intend on asking me is in the line of duty. My wife is smart enough to understand that." Turning his attention to the other man, he shot back hard. "As for my answers, my wife is welcome to hear them. I have nothing to hide from her. And I want her here with me."

The two detectives glanced at each other. Detective Calloway cleared his throat. "All right, Mr. Ortega. Suit yourself."

Chapter 7

Saturday afternoon, Hyatt Regency Hotel, Downtown Houston, Texas

"I'm sorry, sir, you're wife hasn't returned as yet."

A sinking feeling hit the pit of Sean's stomach. He ran his hand over his chin and let the words of the hotel manager sink in. "And the car rental company? She hasn't contacted them?"

"No, sir, not that she was expected to. We made the arrangements for the car to be delivered here for her yesterday morning. She was to turn it in at the hotel last night on her return."

"I see. I'd like to check in to the hotel and my wife's room, please."

"Certainly."

Sean registered and received a key. "Can you tell me where the closest Police Detachment is?"

"If you go out these doors, turn right, walk to the corner which is Polk Street, turn left, walk two blocks down to Travis and turn left again. It's right in the middle of the street and the convention centre your wife attended is right across the street from the police department."

"Thank-you."

Sean went up to the room first. He noted Georgia's toiletries in the bathroom and her suitcase on the stand in the closet, with a few clothes still hanging on the rack. He tried her cell phone once more to no avail. He returned to the bathroom to wash his hands and splashed water on his face. The frightened look that stared back at him from the mirror startled him. "Where are you, hon?" he whispered, in a tight voice. With grim determination, he strode out of the room.

It was less than a five minute walk to the police department. There was no missing the twenty-eight floor white columned building. It took up nearly the whole block between Polk and Dallas Streets. Sean entered the building and stood in awe. An information index showed that the building housed a crime lab, a finger-printing lab, a tactical command centre, and a voice/data centre. There were Strategic, Investigative, and Field Operations; all broken down into various manners of theft, vice, and victim crimes. Sean didn't know where to start. The main foyer was packed with people, and he was jostled as they pushed past him. He noticed a glassed-in information counter. There were three line-ups leading to officers behind the long marble counter. He joined one line and waited his turn.

"How can I help you, sir?"

"I want to report a missing person; my wife."

"How long has she been missing?"

"About thirty hours."

"Do you suspect foul play, sir?"

"Well … I don't know. She was here as a guest of the Writers' Conference across the street. I was in L.A. on business."

"So you're both non-residents?"

"Yes, we're Canadians from Vancouver."

The officer's attitude softened. He shuffled under the counter and pulled up a form. "Fill this out and slip it through the slot to my left. Have a seat and someone will process you. Please, understand it may be awhile."

"Thank you."

Sean filled out the form and sat on a chair. About an hour later, his name was called. A petite woman with short dark hair led him through a doorway and into a small room.

"Detective Castle will be with you shortly." The woman left him alone.

The only furniture in the room was a small desk with three metal chairs. A mirror was built into the wall. *An interrogation room. I wonder if someone is watching me.* He paced the room, stretching his cramped legs from sitting so long.

A few minutes later, a tall, lean man with short blond hair entered the room. "Sean Charles-Dixon?"

"Yes."

"I'm Detective Brian Castle." The two men shook hands and the baby-faced man who looked no older than twenty-five took a seat and gestured for Sean to follow suit.

"So I understand that you and your wife flew to L.A. four days ago and your wife flew here for a convention. Why don't you start at the beginning of your trip to the U.S, detailing as to what your business was in L.A., why your wife came to Houston, etc., leading up to all that happened the past four days, as you know it?"

Sean relayed the information to the detective, who wrote notes in a small black book.

"Does your wife know anyone in Houston?"

"No, only the organizers and attendees she would have met at the convention."

"Is it unusual for your wife to disappear without calling you?"

"Totally. Whenever we're apart, we usually talk daily and if we miss each other, as we did the past day and a half, we always leave a message."

"I see. Do you still have the message she left yesterday morning?"

"I do ... do you want to hear it?"

The detective took a tape recorder out of his pocket. "I'd like to tape it if you don't mind."

"Certainly."

Sean put the message on speaker and the sound of Georgia's voice brought a lump into his throat. His hand went to his mouth and he shook his head and looked up distraught into the striking blue eyes of Detective Castle, who'd been studying him intently. "Please ..." he begged, hoarsely. "Find my wife. She's been through so much in the past. This is a happy time in our lives."

The policeman's eyebrows rose a little. "We're going to do the best we can to find her, Sean. You say she's been through a lot. Why don't you fill me in on her past?"

Sean heaved a deep sigh and went back eight years previous to Georgia's kidnapping and escape into the wilderness. He told the detective about her survival and her giving birth alone, and the book and movie of her life that followed his discovery of her that spring at his cabin.

"Three years ago, her ex-husband died and so did his second wife. They had a daughter. The two girls were two weeks apart in age. Georgia and I were married and she adopted the half-sister, and I adopted both girls."

"I've heard of your wife's story," Detective Castle said.

"There's more. During all that happened three years ago, Georgia had a celebrity stalker. He kidnapped her and the kids. She managed to set the girls free and eventually she escaped … but not before she killed him."

"I remember that. He was a serial killer from Nevada. She did the world and all women a favour, but you didn't hear that from me. Do you have a picture of Georgia?"

"I have some in my cell phone."

The detective pulled a card out of his pocket and handed it to Sean. "Could you email me one?"

"Certainly."

"Does your wife have any identifying marks like a tattoo or birth mark?"

Sean's head flew backwards. *Identifying marks?* The question hit him hard.

The detective studied his shocked expression. "I'm sorry, but it's important for us to know."

"Uh … yes. She has a tattoo of a raven on the outside of her right ankle and a scar on her left inner ankle about four inches long from an accident at the cabin, and another scar on her right upper thigh." He leaned forward and put his head in his hands.

"Are you staying at the Hyatt Regency?"

Sean looked up at the Detective. "Yes, in my wife's room, Room 621."

Detective Castle's eyebrows shot up. "Have you been in the room?"

"When I checked in, I went up to the room for all of five minutes. Why?"

"Did you touch anything?"

"No. I took note that her things were still there. Oh ... I did wash my hands and face in the bathroom. Then I left to come here."

"I'd like to go back to the hotel with you and check the room out myself. But first, I need you to write down the names of those you were in contact with in L.A. and their contact numbers if you have them."

Sean frowned. *Why were they wasting their time on me? Am I a suspect in Georgia's disappearance?"*

As if the detective could read his mind, he continued. "At the moment, you're the only link we have to your wife, Sean. The sooner we can corroborate your whereabouts, the sooner we can get on with the search for your wife."

"Of course. I understand."

The policeman left and returned with a pad and pen. Twenty minutes later, the pair left police headquarters and walked back to the hotel.

Chapter 8

Saturday afternoon, Medical Center of Southeast Texas, Port Arthur, Texas

Detectives Calloway and Brown sat down at the table in the conference room, joining the medical staff and social workers caring for the unknown patient.

Doctor David Edwards introduced his team.

Detective Calloway took the lead. "Dr. Edwards can you update us on Jane Doe's condition, please?"

"She's critical but in stable condition in ICU, still unconscious and we're concerned about concussion. She was in a state of hypothermia when she came in but her blood readings have levelled out. There's a contusion on the hairline on the left side of her head which required six stitches. Various bruises on her arms and legs. There's bruising on her chest consistent with a tightened seat belt and blunt force of an inflated air bag."

"So her injuries would indicate that she was in a car accident of some kind?" Detective Calloway asked.

"From all appearances, I'd say yes." Dr. Edwards confirmed.

"There were a few accidents in the area last night in that storm. However, all the people involved have been accounted for," Detective Brown said. "She was found in the water at the entrance to Sabine Lake. Her car may have gone into the river and she was carried downstream by the current. So what do we know about her? Does she have any kind of identification on her?" Detective Brown asked.

Detective Calloway interjected. "Hmm … no one would have been out last night without a jacket. According to the man who pulled her out of the water, she wasn't wearing one then. Any identifying marks?"

It was the head nurse's turn to reply. "No identification. She has a scar on her left inner ankle, another one on the outer right thigh, and a black raven tattoo on her outer right ankle."

"Can you give us a physical description of her?" Detective Brown asked.

Doctor Edwards picked up the chart on Jane Doe. "She's Caucasian, about 5'5", 112 pounds, brown eyes, long brunette hair. I'd say she's in her early thirties."

"I'd like to send in one of our forensic staff to take her fingerprints. We can run them through the database to see if she's in the system," Detective Calloway said.

"We can accommodate that," Doctor Edwards said. "Anything else, Detective?"

"How long do you think she'll remain unconscious?" Calloway asked.

"There's no definitive answer to that. Usually they wake up within 48 hours. But not knowing what is happening with her brain at this point, it's a guess."

"Does anyone else have anything to add?" Calloway asked.

The medical staff looked at each other in silence. Doctor Edwards addressed the social worker. "Donna? We haven't heard from you yet."

"I have nothing. I'll work closely with Samantha but there's not much for me to do until our patient either wakes up or someone shows up who can identify her."

"I think that's it for now." Calloway said. "We'll send out patrols to search the banks of the river from Port Arthur to Bridge City for any signs of a vehicle entering the waterway."

The meeting ended and the Detectives took their leave.

"What now?" Detective Brown asked.

"Back to the office. We'll get forensics down here and set up the patrols. It'll be interesting to see if we have any missing persons reported."

Chapter 9

Saturday afternoon, Medical Center of Southeast Texas, Port Arthur, Texas

Her eyes opened to a white brightness; a blurred iridescent vision that hurt not only her dilated pupils but shot excruciating pain through her already aching head. She snapped them shut with a sharp intake of breath that triggered an intense pain through her chest. The steady beep of a machine with a pounding resonance echoed in her ears. Nausea welled in her stomach, and the taste of bile burned her throat. Her foggy brain tried to focus but before she could force her eyes open again, she slipped away ... leaving the pain and confusion behind.

Georgia floated along the pathway, light as a feather, and was reminded of her raven companion, Feathers. A smile played at her lips as she recalled running in the meadow with her black bird flying above her, only to dive and summersault in front of her. The guttural roll from deep in his throat had become a comfort to her.

She took in the smell of the bloomed multi-coloured flowers and bushes, the sound of the birds singing their song, and felt the warmth

June V. Bourgo

of the sun on her face. Nearing the end of the path, she saw Nonnock sitting on the wooden bench and joined her.

"It's been a long time. I'm so happy to see you again," Georgia said. She took in the long, grey hair falling smooth and shiny in waves, over the same white eyelet lace dress the native spirit had worn many years ago when Georgia had seen her for the first time. "You're a long way from your native Tahltan lands."

Nonnock crinkled her nose, a sparkle emanating from her pale grey eyes. "It's not so far in spirit form."

Georgia loved the iridescent light that shone in Nonnocks' eyes. She remembered the native spirit's tale so many years ago of her Tahltan mother lying with a white trader. This explained the spirit's pale gray eyes.

"Do you remember the first time you saw this garden?" Nonnock asked.

Georgia looked at the blue waters of the pond in front of them and watched the bugs skipping over the surface. "Yes. It was during my time lost at the cabin, after I'd escaped the bank robbers. It was a cold, snowy winter full of depression and fear of my pending childbirth. You brought me here to calm me and you showed my spirit how to travel to my parents' home to see that they were well. The garden is just as beautiful now as it was then."

"Your life was spared back then so you could provide life to your daughter and all went well. Your fears were unfounded."

"I learned so much about myself during that time and my fear of the unknown. The choices I've made in my life and the paths I've walked all came from that winter of awareness."

"Six years later when you encountered your stalker, once again you survived. It was your destiny to provide a home for your daughter's half-sister when her mother, Julie, died. You have provided well for them both."

Georgia smiled at the thought of her ten-year-old daughters. "They're beautiful girls, so alike physically; yet, so different internally.

45

They've found their way through all that they've suffered too. I'm very proud of them."

She stared at the fish rising from the pond to feed on the insects. *All those bugs flying about, skimming the surface; oblivious to the fact that their lives were about to change. Change? No, their lives as they knew it were about to be over. No guarantees and no warning. Just like that ... gone.*

She turned to Nonnock and smiled. "But this time ... you've come to take me with you."

The warning buzzer went off at the nurse's station and all hell broke loose. The head nurse called out to one of her staff. "Page the resuscitation team and Karen, you come with me." They ran down the hall and into the patient's room. Nurse Kelly took one look at the woman known as Jane Doe and knew she'd gone into cardiac arrest.

The hospital intercom bell sounded. "Paging Dr. Edwards and Dr. Benadie. ICU STAT. Dr. Edwards, Dr. Benadie, ICU STAT."

"Start chest compressions," Nurse Kelly said as she wheeled a crash cart beside the bed and turned on the defibrillation machine and prepped the paddles. By the time she took the patient's vitals, Dr. Edwards came in with the rest of the resuscitation team. She filled him in with what she knew so far. Nurse Karen backed away to let the head nurse stand beside the patient.

The doctor stood on the opposite side of the bed next to the crash cart and listened to the patient's heart with a stethoscope. "Prep her for defib," Dr. Edwards said.

He moved forward with the paddles and placed them on the woman's chest. "Stand clear." Dr. Benadie set the dial. The shock was applied. The patient's back arched and her chest jolted up.

In-between the shocks, Nurse Kelly continued chest compressions until Dr. Edwards asked her to stand clear. The process was repeated, with increasing levels of electricity. They stopped to assess.

"IV Epinephrine 0.5 mg, every three to five minutes, followed by 300 mg of Amiodarone," Dr.Benadi ordered. He opened a drawer in the crash cart, retrieved the drugs and passed them to Nurse Karen who set up administration.

Nurse Kelly sucked on her bottom lip. She'd been in this situation many times over the years. *It's taking too long. It's not working.* She looked at the face of the patient. As pale and frail as the woman looked, she was a beautiful woman and far too young to leave this plane.

With each chest compression, her mind screamed out to the woman. *Fight ... fight ... fight ... goddammit.*

Chapter 10

Saturday afternoon, Hyatt Regency Hotel, Houston, Texas

Detective Castle stood in the hotel room writing notes. He glanced at the man staring out the window to the street below. A gut feeling told him that Sean Charles-Dixon had nothing to do with his wife's disappearance, but there was a lot of follow-up work to be done to add fact to his intuition.

He'd ruled out the room as a crime scene. Nothing was out of place or appeared to be cleaned up. Mrs. Charles-Dixon's clothing and toiletries appeared as any woman would have left them while out of the hotel for a spell. Whatever happened to her, it didn't happen in this room.

"Do you know what clothes your wife packed for the trip? Perhaps we can determine what she was wearing when she disappeared."

A pensive Sean turned to the closet and suitcase. " We packed our own suitcases side-by-side on the bed back home, but I didn't really pay attention to her clothing. But unlike some women, she's a minimalist. Only packs what she feels she needs."

The detective watched him walk across the room. "The pantsuit hanging in the closet was for her speech at the convention. The dress beside it was for the dinner banquet on the last night." Sean stared at the suitcase and shook his head.

"How many pairs of shoes did she pack?"

Sean pointed to a pair of black stilettos on the floor of the closet. "Those were for the dinner. Here's her walking shoes. She must be wearing her brown leather boots. They aren't here. They're an ankle boot with a zipper on the inside of the foot and a two inch wedge heel."

"What did she wear on the plane to L.A.? Do you see those clothes here?" Detective Castle probed further.

"Blue denim skinny jeans. She always wears jeans for comfort when flying," Sean appeared excited that he was actually contributing. "They're not here, nor is her turquoise suede jacket, bomber style. In fact, in the picture I emailed to you, she's wearing that same jacket."

"Good. What about jewelry?"

Sean held his left hand up. "Our wedding bands are matching."

The detective looked at the white gold band, centered with the head of a yellow gold raven and a sparkling diamond for its eye. He pulled his cell phone and took a picture of the ring. "Your wife appears to have a propensity for ravens."

"The raven is important to my native heritage and to my wife's experiences."

"I see ... well, I'm heading downstairs to interview the chamber maid and then back to the office to do some follow-up with the car rental company. My partner should be back from court by now and we'll get started on this right away."

Sean stared at the detective. "What can I do to help? I can't just sit around here wondering where she is."

Detective Castle felt for the man. "There's a few things you can do. Stay close to the hotel in case she shows up. Contact family and friends to see if she talked to them in the past couple of days. She may have given them a clue as to where she intended to go with the rental car."

Sean sat on the bed in despair. "I hate calling her family with news of this kind. Especially after all they suffered in the past."

"You don't want them to hear about this on the news, Sean ... and it will make the news, especially as an out of country visitor and one with your wife's notoriety."

His shoulders dropped. "You're right. I'll get onto it right away." He stood and extended a hand to the detective. "Thank you." The two men shook hands.

"We'll be in touch. I've got your cell phone number and the hotel number. You've got my card. Call me if you hear anything or think of anything that could help us locate your wife."

By the time Brian Castle interviewed hotel staff and returned to his office, his partner was sitting at his own desk reading files. "You're back. How'd it go in court?"

"Great. I'm all done. The case is a strong one so the prosecution should have no trouble winning this one. Where ya been?"

"At the Hyatt Regency. Missing person case. I'm glad you're back to help me here."

Detective Alan Blake sat back in his chair and put one foot up on his desk. He rested his arms across his pudgy belly. "Fill me in."

Brian sat down at his own desk opposite Alan's and opened his file. He noted a pile of missing person notices in his in-basket and passed one over to his partner. His assistant had been busy while he was away. "Georgia Charles-Dixon, a Canadian from Vancouver, BC, thirty-eight, married to Sean Charles-Dixon, a novelist. He was in L.A. on movie business and our missing female, also a writer, was a guest speaker here in Houston at a Writer's Convention across the street."

Alan let out a whistle. The forty-year-old detective shifted in his seat. "She's a looker."

"She's also a celebrity. Lots of info about her and her husband online. She survived a kidnapping eight years ago in British Columbia and spent the winter lost in a cabin. Gave birth alone to a daughter. The cabin belonged to Charles-Dixon. He found her in the spring. They wrote about her experience together, made a movie about it, and three years ago they married. But not before our absent celeb was stalked by Benjamin Pearson, serial killer. He beat her up pretty good, but our survivor got the upper hand and shot him dead."

"I remember that story. She was lucky to get away from him alive. What else you got?"

"She had a free day yesterday. The hotel arranged a car rental for the day. She left the hotel with the car but never returned last night. She was to catch a flight to L.A. this morning and the chamber maid entered the room, assuming she'd checked out. Her bed was turned down by the evening staff with a chocolate on the pillow, unused. Her clothes are still there and her toiletries."

Alan reached for his cup and took a sip. He wrinkled his nose and put it down. "Yuk. I hate cold coffee." "Anything unusual about the room?"

"No. It's clean. I think she left with the rental and never returned."

"What's your take on the husband?"

Brian removed his jacket. He tapped a pen on his desk in thought. "My gut says he has nothing to do with this. He appears genuinely distraught. Talked to her the night before last. She left him a message yesterday morning saying she was free for the day. I taped it. When he couldn't reach her last night, he went to the L.A. airport this morning to see if she was on the flight. He caught the first plane here, checked into the hotel and came to us first thing. He's checked into her room and making calls to family to see if she's contacted any of them."

"So, where do we start?"

"We need to contact the car rental company. See if they've heard anything about the vehicle. Find out if the car has GPS and do a trace. The husband gave me a list of contacts in L.A. to verify his where-abouts. We need to check him out and verify his flight info with the airlines."

Alan pulled his foot off of his desk and sat up straight. "I'll start with the rental company."

"Okay, I'll do L.A. and get Sarah calling local hospitals to see if they had any accident victims admitted yesterday. I never told the husband that we had one hell of a storm last night."

An hour later, the two men compared notes.

"They rented the last car available to the hotel. A 2012 Nissan Versa, white, 4-door, black interior, no GPS unfortunately. It's not a standard feature as the Versa is Nissan's entry-level car. They've heard nothing from our missing person," Alan provided.

"L.A. contacts for the husband checked out. Solid tight alibi. I talked to a Supervisor at the airlines he travelled with to Houston. Apparently, Mr. Charles-Dixon made quite a scene at the passenger agent's desk when she wouldn't confirm if his wife checked into her flight here in Houston."

Sarah poked her head into their shared office. "I've checked twenty-five hospitals so far. Nothing. Some of the hospitals told me a man has already called them looking for his wife, Georgia Charles-Dixon."

"Thanks, Sarah. Keep going," Brian said.

Sarah pulled a face. "I hope you realize there's one hundred and seven hospitals in metro Houston. It'll take awhile." She left.

"Well, our husband is doing all the right things. Maybe she ran off," Alan mused.

Brian shook his head no. "It doesn't fit. She has two daughters at home. And why wouldn't she take her things from the hotel with her?"

"Just a thought. Do you know the name of her cell phone provider? We need to get a print-out of her calls. Hopefully, we can track her whereabouts by her phone."

Brian handed him the file. "It's in my notes. I'm heading across to the Convention Centre to chase down the writers' conference organizers. One of them may know something."

Chapter 11

Sunday morning, Police Headquarters, Port Arthur, Texas

Dylan sat in the interrogation room waiting for the two detectives who'd interviewed him at the hospital the morning before. He'd been discharged from the hospital the afternoon before with normal test readings. The detectives asked him to come in this morning and sign his statement.

The door opened and the two men came in and sat down opposite him.

"Good morning, Mr. Ortega," Detective Brown said. "You're looking better today. How are you feeling?"

"I'm fine, thank you." Dylan looked at Detective Calloway and nodded. He didn't like the burly man who nodded back. The man left him with the feeling that he didn't believe his story.

Detective Brown handed him a sheath of papers. "We'd like you to read over your statement and confirm that it's accurate."

Dylan took a few minutes to read it, aware of the stares of the two men in front of him. He put the pages down and glanced up. "It's just as I told you."

He reached for a pen sitting on the table in front of him to sign the document but Detective Calloway's hand flew forward and picked it up first. He rolled the pen between his fingers. "Is there anything you want to add to your statement, Mr. Ortega?"

Dylan looked into his steely eyes. "No, it's accurate."

"Because if there's anything you haven't told us, now's the time," he added.

"What else would there be to tell?" he asked, confused.

"Oh, I don't know. There's lots of questions surrounding this woman. Like why was she out there on such a dreadful night? How did she get there? And how did she end up in the water?"

"I can't answer those questions, sir."

"We searched the parking lot and embankment where you say you parked. There's no tire marks from your truck or any other vehicle for that matter in the mud. There are no reports of missing persons in the area and we're searching the road back along the waterway for abandoned vehicles or skid marks into the river. So far nothing."

Anger started to build in Dylan. "Were you out in that storm Friday night? Of course you won't find tire tracks. That downpour would have washed them away." He leaned across the table and stared the detective down. "Are you implying that I had something to do with what happened to that poor woman?"

"Did you?" Detective Calloway challenged.

Dylan brought his fist down hard on the table. "No, I did not. I saved that woman's life and you want to throw accusations at me?" Realizing his temper wouldn't help the situation; Dylan sat back in his seat and willed himself to calm down.

Detective Brown took a pen out of his jacket pocket and placed it on the papers. "No one's accusing you of anything. If you'll sign the statement, Mr. Ortega, that will be all for now."

Dylan left the police station in a mixed state of depression and anger. When he reached home, he went straight to Camila and took her in his arms, holding her tight.

"Are you alright?" she asked. She pushed back from him and looked into his face.

"Now I am." He led her by the hand to the couch and pulled her onto his lap.

"What happened?"

"I got the distinct feeling the police think I had something to do with what happened to that woman. Can you believe it?"

"You're kidding, right?"

He filled his wife in on his conversation with the detectives.

"Estupido, idioto gringos," Camila spat. "You're a hero and they treat you badly."

"It doesn't matter. I only care what you think." He nuzzled his wife's neck.

"But what if she doesn't wake up and dies?" Camila pushed him back. "It won't be over."

"They can think what they like, but they can't prove anything because I've done nothing wrong. I'm a male who carried an unconscious, bleeding woman into the hospital. The last one in their minds to be with her. They're doing their job." He pushed her hair from her eyes and kissed her on the nose, letting his fingers caress her cheek. A sigh escaped her lips and he could feel her body relax. "Let's hope she wakes up soon and settles the matter."

Camila leaned into Dylan and kissed him lightly on the mouth at first. The kiss took on urgency and he lost himself into the passion of the moment.

A few minutes later, his mind took over. "Where are the kids?" he asked, hoarsely.

"Your parents. They'll be home at dinner."

Dylan slid Camila onto the couch, stood, and pulled her up to him. "I think I need to rest." He paused and gave her a seductive smile. "But first, I want to make up for all the grief I've given my wonderful wife these past months. I'm going to take my beautiful Camila to our bed and make wild, passionate love to her."

His wife threw her head back in laughter.

He picked her up in his arms and headed for the stairs. "Come with me and we'll make the world right again."

Chapter 12

Sunday morning, Hyatt Regency Hotel – Houston, Texas

There was a long silence at the other end of the telephone. Sean thought the call with Robert Carr, Georgia's father, had been disconnected. "Hello?"

"I'm here, Sean."

"I'm so sorry that there's nothing new to tell you. I haven't heard from the police today."

"These things take time ... I guess." Robert's voice trailed off.

Sean didn't know what else to say. "I've been calling hospitals. I'm sure the police are too, but I need to do something. My God, there's over a hundred hospitals in this city."

"Now listen, Sandra and I are booked on a late night flight this evening. We have a stop-over in L.A. We'll see you tomorrow."

"Are you sure? There's nothing any of us can do here but wait."

"We'd rather wait there than here. And you shouldn't have to go through this alone. We want to come."

"In that case, I really could use your support. Give me your flight information. I'll be there to pick you up."

He wrote down the arrival time and said goodbye.

Sean stood in the shower, eyes closed with his face uplifted into the hot, steamy water cascading from the showerhead. Robert Carr had always been a resilient man, but the frailty of his voice resonated through the phone lines. There was nothing new to tell him or Georgia's mother. Sean had been strong for their sake and now that he was alone, he relived the pain he'd heard in the voice of a broken man. It shook him to the bone. The memories flooded back of how hopeless he'd felt when Georgia and their daughters had been kidnapped by a stalker three years previous. *How could she disappear again? Why was this happening? Hasn't this family suffered enough?* Sean pounded the shower stall wall with his fists, until his anger dissipated.

He turned the water off and towel dried, taking his time with his shaving and toiletries. Anything to keep him distracted. He'd gone to the hotel lobby the afternoon before and bought what he needed in the hotel boutiques, along with some new clothes. Certainly not his normal choice for shopping, knowing he'd paid way too much for the goods, but he didn't want to leave the hotel. After he dressed, he sat back down at the desk and called the car rental company again to see if the car had been returned. The voice he talked to oozed with sympathy but he felt sure they must be tired of his calling. He didn't care. *Try living in my shoes.*

Calls to a dozen more hospitals proved fruitless. Sean gave up for the moment and pulled out the business card of Detective Castle.

The phone at the other end rang repeatedly until finally, a receptionist answered. "Houston Police Department. How may I help you?"

"Detective Castle, please."

"One moment, please."

A brusque voice answered. "Detective Castle here."

"Good afternoon, this is Sean Dixon-Charles."

"Aw … Sean. How are you holding up?" a softened voice asked.

"Terribly, to be honest. I wondered if there was anything new you could tell me." Sean wondered if Detective Castle would tell him even if there was something.

"We've been talking with people your wife was in contact with at the conference. We haven't learned anything helpful as yet."

"Georgia's parents will be here tomorrow. They're flying in from Vancouver."

"That's good. Family support is important."

"Yes, it is." Sean didn't want to let the detective go but knew he was being silly. He had nothing to tell him. "I should let you get back at it. I've been calling hospitals. Nothing so far, a good thing I guess."

"Absolutely, Sean. Keep at it and keep busy. We do have an all points bulletin out on the car. As soon as we have any news, I'll call you."

"Thank you." He ended the call.

Sean stared at the yellow page listings of hospitals in front of him. He looked for his place on the page to begin calling once again. He felt his eyes begin to water and his vision blurred. One swift swipe of his hand sent the telephone book flying off the desk and skidding across the floor.

He stood and went to the window. The streets were busy with pedestrians, vehicles racing while busily changing lanes, and honking horns. All strangers, in a strange city, a strange country, none of them knowing him or Georgia ... or caring.

Where are you my love? Are you hurt? Are you de ... No! His hand covered his mouth. *You're alive. I know it. I'd know otherwise ... wouldn't I?* He didn't like where his mind was going and shut it out.

Sean thought of their daughters, Kaela and Shelby. They'd decided as a family not to tell them at this point about their mother's disappearance. The girls, ten years old going on twenty, were staying with their grandmother in Gibsons attending school. *They're beginning puberty, so young. But it seems to be the norm for young girls these days. They need their mother.* His thoughts wandered back to bad thoughts. *How would they cope if they'd lost her?*

Sean steeled his shoulders. "I'd know if you were ... " He cut himself off, took a deep breath, marched across the floor and retrieved the telephone book.

"Poor fellow," Brian said. "I feel for him." He leaned back in his chair and stared at the telephone.

"Watching other people's pain is the bane of our job. But we can't let it drag us down. So where were we?" Alan asked.

"Some of the attendees at the conference haven't made it home yet, still on route. They probably can't help us anyway. Any of the local people I've reached have nothing to tell us. The rest weren't home, call backs. Has that cell phone list showed up yet?"

"No. Should be here later today."

Brian called his assistant in.

"We've passed the missing for forty-eight hours period. I think it's time to get the posters out and notify the press. Let's get her photo on the local news tonight."

"Okay," Sarah said. "I'm done calling all the hospitals. No Georgia Charles-Dixon or Jane Doe's."

"I didn't have the heart to tell the man we'd done the hospitals. He needs something to keep himself busy," Brian said, with a sigh.

"Anything else?" Sarah asked.

"No, that's it for now." Brian turned to his partner. "What are we missing?"

"Well ..." Alan paused. "We can't match any accidents to her or her car; she's not in any of our hospitals. Husband checks out clean. That leaves two choices. Hypothetically, she either met someone and ran off with him; or she met with foul play somewhere in her rental car. Either way, we just haven't found out about it yet."

Brain reclined his chair and lifted his feet onto his desk in his favourite pose. "Hmm ... she rented a car for a reason. Maybe she isn't even in Houston. What local attractions do we have nearby that a tourist would want to visit?"

"Huh! Let's see. She could have gone north to the lakes, or west towards Louisiana, or south to the Gulf of Mexico. Who knows?"

Brian stood and grabbed his jacket. "You've mentioned her stepping out before. I'm going to have a little chat with Sean about his marriage, just to satisfy my gut feeling that you're barking up the wrong tree. Why don't you see if you can hurry that cell phone list up?"

"Sure thing. And hey, I'm just trying to cover all the bases here. We missed lunch by the way. Want me to order in a couple of subs for us?"

"Great idea, you know what I like."

Chapter 13

Sunday afternoon, Houston, Texas

A few minutes later, Brian was in the hotel elevator heading to Sean's floor. The man who opened the door to his knock looked tired. Brian could see the concern and fear in his eyes.

"Detective? Please, come in."

"I don't have anything more to report, Sean. I came by to see how you're doing and I need to ask you a few questions."

"Please, sit down." He gestured to the couch, sitting in an arm chair opposite.

"This is a little personal but I'd be remiss if I didn't ask." Brian tried to sound casual and friendly.

"Okay."

"I know you told me that you and Georgia check in with each other when separated, which tells me you're close. I can see for myself how much you're concerned over Georgia's disappearance."

"We're very close. Our relationship is special."

"Are there any problems between you? I mean more than the usual push pull of any marriage."

Sean looked puzzled. "No. We're fine. We pride ourselves in making sure a line of communication is always open. Why are you asking me this, Detective? Am I still a suspect in Georgia's disappearance?"

"No. Your alibi in L.A. checks out. Can I ask you one more thing? Have you or Georgia ever cheated on one another?"

Sean looked indignant. "Absolutely not. Georgia and I have each had a previous marriage where our spouses cheated and left us for someone else. We've had our share of pain from that kind of situation. If I'm not a suspect, then why these questions?"

Brian took a deep breath. "We need to eliminate the possibility that Georgia may have gone off with someone she met."

"What? Georgia? That's the most ridiculous thing I've ever heard. Anyone who knows Georgia would laugh if you asked them that question."

"And how can you/they be so sure of that?"

Sean now looked exasperated. "Before we were married, Georgia thought I was cheating on her with my ex-wife. I wasn't, but it crippled her from trusting in me because of her ex's infidelity. Once we worked through it, we promised each other that if either of us felt the need to be with someone else we would be upfront about it, not sneak around behind each other's back. Georgia takes our marriage vows very seriously...and so do I."

"Good enough." Brian's cell phone rang. The call display revealed his partner's number. "What's up?"

Alan's voice came through the line. "You'd better get back to the office pronto. I think we've just got a break in the case."

"I'll be right there." He stood. "That's all for now, Sean. I'm sorry if I upset you but as I said, we need to eliminate all the possibilities."

"I can understand that but it's hard you know. She's out there somewhere and she may need us. I hate to see you wasting time on things I know are off base."

Brian put his hand on Sean's shoulder. "Stay strong. We're working hard on this and we'll find her."

Back at the office, Brian hurried over to his desk. "Whatcha got?"

Alan held up some papers and shook them. "Cell phone call list. Our missing person only made two calls on her cell phone on Friday. One was from the Beaumont area to her husband's cell phone. You were right, she wasn't in Houston. You'll never guess where she made the second call."

Brian threw his jacket across the back of his chair and sat down. "Where?" he asked, breathless.

"Lake Charles, Louisiana. The call was to someone living there, a Samuel Parsons."

Brian felt the adrenalin rush and excitedly searched through the file on his desk labelled Georgia Charles-Dixon. "Parsons ... Parsons, I know that name." He found what he was looking for and studied it a moment. His finger punched the paper. "Ah-ha ... here it is. Margaret Parsons, Lake Charles, Louisiana. Telephone number 1-337-555-5110."

"That's the one. Who is she?"

"One of the writer conference organizers. She wasn't at home when I called." Brian leaned forward and grabbed his telephone, punched the numbers and waited. He tapped his fingers on his desk. This could be the break they'd been waiting for.

A female voice at the other end of the line broke through his muse. "Hello?"

"Hello. Is this Margaret Parsons?"

"Yes it is."

"I'm Detective Castle with the Houston Police Department. If you have a few minutes, I'd like to talk to you about the writer's conference you attended here in Houston."

"Ohh? Is there some kind of problem?"

"We're hoping you can help us locate someone. The conference had a guest speaker last Wednesday and Thursday, Georgia Charles-Dixon."

There was a pause at the other end. "Yes, that's right. You're looking for Georgia?"

He ignored her question for the moment and asked another. "We understand she travelled to Lake Charles on Friday morning and made a telephone call to your residence. Did you speak with her?"

"More than that, Detective. I spent the rest of the day with her. May I ask what this is about?"

"Can you tell me what brought her to Lake Charles?"

"Well because I invited her. Georgia and I hit it off at the conference and at the banquet dinner on Thursday night, she mentioned that her husband would be tied up with meetings in L.A. the next day. I invited her to join me in Lake Charles to do some sight-seeing and enjoy some good old Louisiana hospitality."

"Ms. Charles-Dixon hasn't returned to her hotel here in Houston, nor did she catch her flight to L.A. to meet her husband on Saturday morning."

There was a sudden intake of breath on the other end of line. "Dear God. But where can she be?"

"That's what we're trying to determine, Mrs. Parsons. Can you fill me in on what you did together, along with a time frame for Friday?" Brian scribbled down notes as the woman fed the information to him. "So she had dinner with you and your family about five o'clock and what time did she leave your home to drive back to Houston?"

"She left just before seven that night. She should have been back at the hotel by ten o'clock. She wanted some time to shower and pack up her things before bed. There was a hell of a storm that night. Oh dear...I hope she didn't have an accident."

"Is there anything else you can tell us? Like what route she would have taken?"

"As far as I know she was going to go back the same way she came, Route 10 straight from Lake Charles to Houston."

"Thank you, Mrs. Parsons. You've been a big help."

"I wish I could do more. You will let me know when you find her. I'll be worried sick until then."

"I definitely will and thank you." Brian hung up the phone and slapped his hands on his desk. "Yes ... now we're getting somewhere."

"And?"

"The little lady left about seven Friday night on Route 10 heading to Houston. At least we know to concentrate our efforts along that two hour stretch of highway."

"Wasn't there a huge pile-up on Route 10 that night, east of Beaumont? That may be the place to start." Alan turned to his computer and pounded the keys.

"I'd heard something about it. I've been so other directed the past couple of days, I haven't watched the news."

"Here it is. Ten cars, two fatalities, six injured, speed and weather a factor; victims were taken to the area hospitals with various injuries."

"I hadn't realized it was so serious. My gut feeling says that this has something to do with our Miss Georgia." He hit his intercom and called Sarah into the room. "Can you call the Beaumont Hospitals and do a check on the victims' names from that Route 10 pileup Friday night? And get the Beaumont Police on the line, as well as the Lake Charles FBI Field Office."

"At least there's only three hospitals in Beaumont. Will do." Sarah turned to leave but poked her head back through door. "And eat your lunch, it's almost dinner time."

"Yes, Mom."

A few minutes later, Brian was put through to the Beaumont Police Department. He hit the speaker button so Allan could hear the conversation. He filled the other agency in on their case. They had no reports on a Georgia Charles-Dixon or a Jane Doe. They, also, told him Route 10 had been closed for several hours to clear the accident scene.

"What about westbound traffic to Houston?" Brian asked.

The officer on the other end gave them a new possibility. "They were re-directed to Route 87 south to Bridge City. Not that there were many people out in that storm. It was pretty quiet. Some turned around and went back from wherever they came from."

"What time did the pile-up occur?"

"About 7:30 p.m. They redirected traffic shortly after that.

"Thanks for your help."

"Anytime."

Sarah popped back in. "Our MisPer is not one of the accident victims."

"Thought as much. The Beaumont Police didn't have her name in their files. Thanks, Sarah."

Alan leaned over the desk, grabbed a sub sandwich and threw it over to Brian. "Eat before you pass out from hunger."

"Yes, I'm way overtime. So the traffic was redirected to Bridge City. Not a great piece of road in a bad storm. I'll stuff my mouth while you re-iterate where we're at."

"Assuming she reached the accident scene without mishap and was redirected to Bridge City, we now have her on Highway 87 south a two hour trip to Houston. We have our search area," Alan said.

"Mmm ..." Brian paused to swallow a bite of ham and bread and hit the intercom button. "Back to the phones for you, Sarah. Every hospital from Bridge City to Houston."

"Will do," she said.

Sarah put the call through from the FBI Field Office in Lake Charles, Louisiana. Alan took the call while Brian finished his lunch.

"Detective Alan Blake here. We have a missing Canadian visitor. She travelled to Lake Charles from Houston on Friday. We've accounted for her time until seven o'clock Friday evening when she started driving back to her hotel in Houston. She never made it. We're bringing you in because she crossed state lines and we don't know if she's still in Louisiana or back in Texas." The detective wrote some notes while listening to the FBI contact. "You bet, right away. We'll wait to hear. Thank you."

He hung up the phone and looked at his partner. "Once we forward all our info, they'll assign a case agent and let us know when he'll be here."

Chapter 14

Sunday afternoon, Medical Centre of Southeast Texas – Port Arthur, Texas

Molly Sanchez stood up from the reception desk and stretched. She took her headset off. "It's quiet at the moment. I'm going to get some coffee. Want some?"

The young woman sitting beside her glanced up at her with fear in her eyes.

"It's okay, hon, you're doing great. If anyone comes in, ask them to be seated until I come back. If the phone rings and you don't know what to do, take a message or ask them to call back in five minutes."

"Okay …" the girl said. "Cream and sugar, please."

She watched Sally walk away. She hoped it would remain quiet until her trainer returned. This was her first shift and she felt a little overwhelmed. She tried to relax and almost did, until a call came through the switchboard. Her hand clutched her chest, and she could feel her heart pound. She stared at the phone listening to it ring. "Oh my god … you can do this. Her finger reached out gingerly for the button and stopped in mid-air. She took a deep breath and pounded quickly on the flashing light.

"Southeast Medical Centre," she croaked.

"Hello. This is Sarah Kincaid from the Houston Police Department. I'm checking to see if you have a patient there by the name of Georgia

Charles-Dixon. Would have been admitted in the past couple of days through emergency."

The intern didn't catch half of what the woman said because she was so nervous. "I'm sorry, what was the patient's name again?"

"Georgia Charles-Dixon."

The girl turned to the computer screen and entered the name. Nothing came back. "No, she's not here."

Another line rang. The girl jumped back.

"Any Jane D ..."

The panicked girl interrupted her, "One moment, please." As soon as she hit the second line, she realized she'd cut the first party off. She hit the first line again. "Hello?" There was no one there. "Oh shit ..." *I should have hit the hold button. Now I've cut them both off.*

She sat back in her chair, and glanced around. *At least no one saw.* She searched the database for any patients with the first name of Jane. There were none. She relaxed.

A few minutes later, Molly returned. "Any calls?"

Lie. "One for a Georgia Dixon who wasn't listed."

Molly handed her a cup of coffee. 'There you go, hon, you did good."

Chapter 15

Georgia stared at her native spirit, waiting for an answer.

Nonnock frowned. "What are you asking of me?

"Have you not brought me to my beautiful garden to take me with you?"

Nonnock placed her hand over Georgia's. "No, child. I came to make sure you don't give up and to tell you that you must go back."

Georgia shuddered, remembering the throbbing hurt she'd experienced. "There's a lot of pain back there and I don't know why?" She looked at Nonnock, confused. "Do you know?"

"You were in a car accident."

"I was? I don't remember it."

"That's because you hit your head hard and almost drowned. Do you not wish to return to your family?"

Georgia felt confused. "Of course, but it's so peaceful here with you...and free of pain."

"You've been given back your life yet again because there is more for you to do for the peoples in your realm. But first, you will have a great battle to fight. Your soul is intact but not your physical being."

Georgia bit her bottom lip. "You're scaring me. What kind of battle?"

"When we first met at the cabin ten years ago, you were afraid of everything, including the unknown. Do you remember this?"

"I do. And your guidance and wisdom led me through it all."

Nonnock squeezed her hand tighter. "When you return, you will struggle with the greatest unknown and the biggest battle of your life. You have a natural survival instinct that served you well in the past. You must fight hard to find it again."

The sun broke through the branches of the trees around the pond. She watched the rays glittering on the surface of the water. The flickering light almost blinded her. Georgia sighed. "I've packed a lifetime of good and bad experiences into my time on earth. More than a lot of people. I was hoping my family and I could settle into 'normal' for the rest of it. But you're telling me that's not to be."

"To meet your purpose, you must persevere. It's never an easy road. If you return to the beginning, where your journey began, instinctively you will find your essence once again."

When Georgia turned back to Nonnock, she was gone.

She felt herself being pulled through a haze. Her eyes were moving, but she saw nothing and realized she was fighting to open them. Distant voices echoed in her ears, too far away to make any sense. Not that she cared. The more cognizant she became, the more the excruciating pain in her head pounded until the thunderous pitch was unbearable. A cry escaped her lips and her eyes finally shot open, only to be shut instantly, as the glare of the overhead lights intensified the throbbing ache.

A voice spoke to her. "You're in the hospital, hon. You're safe here."

She squinted through half-closed eyes. "The light," she croaked. "it hurts."

The woman walked to the wall, flipped a switch and returned to her side. "Is that better?"

"A little."

"Do you remember what happened to you?"

As hard as she tried, her mind was a blank. "No."

"What's your name?"

A frown creased her forehead. Panic started to well up deep inside her chest. "I ... I don't know."

The woman wrote something on a chart. "Can you tell me where you hurt, hon?"

"My head and my chest."

The nurse spoke in a quiet, calm voice. "Good. Now on a scale of one to ten, one being the least and ten being the most, how bad is your pain?"

Her mouth felt dry, making it hard to talk. She tried to concentrate on the question. "It hurts to think. Umm ... my chest is a six and my head ten times ten."

"Okay, I'm going to check your vitals and get the Doctor in to see you, now that you're awake." The nurse wrote on her chart and gave her a big smile. "Don't you worry none. We're going to take real good care of you and figure out what's going on. And we'll get you on some pain meds."

Left alone, she looked at her surroundings, careful not to jar her tender head. It was a small room with one bed and a bedside table. One armchair sat under a window. There was lots of equipment all around her. An IV was taped into her left hand. She attempted to turn sideways to read the red numbers on the machine she was hooked up to, and was overcome with dizziness and nausea. She straightened out her head and fought the urge to vomit. *I don't know what the numbers mean anyway or even what that thing is for. And why can't I remember my name?*

A few minutes later, a man came in wearing a white coat. "I'm Dr. David Edwards." He pulled an overhead lamp down towards her face and turned it on.

She grimaced and sucked in her breath. "Ow ... "

"Sorry. I'd like to have a look in your eyes and then I'll turn the lamp off."

To add insult to injury, the man turned on a small flashlight and proceeded to look into her pupils at a closer range.

"It appears you've had an accident and hit your head. Nurse Kelly tells me you're a little confused, which is to be expected."

"Is that why I don't know my name?"

"Probably. You have a contusion on the left side of your head, which required six stitches. You have a concussion. All of which is causing the extreme pain you're suffering. I've prescribed some medication to make you more comfortable and I've ordered a CAT Scan."

Whatever that is. "Where am I?"

"You're in the Medical Centre of Southeast Texas in Port Arthur."

Port Arthur? "Where's that?"

She noticed Doctor Edwards and Nurse Kelly exchange glances. "Port Arthur is in the state of Texas, east of Houston," the doctor said.

She'd heard of Houston but none of these places meant anything to her. Her heart started to race. "I don't know my name, where I am, or how I got here ..." her voice trailed off, as she tried to quell a state of panic.

The Doctor pulled the armchair over to the bed and sat down. "I know you're feeling scared right now. But I want you to understand that you've experienced a serious head injury. We need to do more tests to better understand what's happening with you. But memory loss is not an uncommon symptom and can be temporary. What you need to do is stay calm and get lots of rest."

"How long have I been in the hospital?"

"Today is Sunday. You came in two nights ago."

She blinked. " Two nights ago? How did I get here?"

"A man rescued you from Sabine Lake. He gave you CPR and saved your life, a real hero. You were unconscious until a few minutes ago. Now, you need to rest. I'll be back to see you later today."

The nurse returned with a tray containing a needle and two paper cups. "Take this," she said, dropping a white pill into her hand.

"What is it?"

"An anti-anxiety drug and muscle relaxant." She handed her the other cup full of water and picked up the needle. "And this is hydromorphone for your pain."

She watched the woman insert the needle into the IV tube. "Julie was on hydromorphone."

Without missing a beat, the nurse asked, "Who's Julie?"

Julie? For the life of her, she didn't know where the name had come from. Nurse Kelly emptied the needle into the tube and turned to face her.

"I have no idea who she is," she said with a sigh.

The woman smiled at her. "That's okay. Something popped through from the depths of your memory. It should happen more and more until one day you'll wake up and remember everything. Meanwhile, we need a temporary name for you. Since you were found in Sabine Lake, how about Sabina?"

"It's a pretty name."

"Then, Sabina it is. You sleep now. These drugs should kick in pretty quickly."

Alone in her room, she tried to remember something about her life and the woman she'd suddenly mentioned. *What was her name? Oh God ... I've forgotten it already. Who is she? Who am I?*

Chapter 16

Monday morning, Police Headquarters, Houston, Texas

Calls had been pouring in since last night's news broadcast. Detectives Brian Castle and Alan Blake had spent the morning fielding the calls. Most of them were from people attending the convention who reported seeing Georgia there, in a restaurant, a store or walking on the street, but all were incidents that occurred before the woman had gone missing. It was a time consuming job and a waste of precious time, but nonetheless a necessity. Every call had to be followed up. One never knew if the next lead would be the one to blow the case wide open. Then there was the media frenzy. Once again Georgia Charles-Dixon was news. The police chief was holding a news conference in about an hour to deal with them.

Sarah poked her head in. "Port Arthur Police Department on line two."

Brian hit the button. "Detective Castle, how can I help you?"

"Good morning. This is Detective Ian Calloway with the Port Arthur Police Department. Your department ran a missing person report on a Houston news station last night. A nurse at the Southeast Medical Centre here in Port Arthur says she resembles a Jane Doe who came in Friday evening. We had the news station forward a photo to us. She may be your MisPer ."

"Was she in a car accident?"

"We don't know the circumstances. She was pulled out of Lake Sabine by a man who happened by and saw her floating in the water. No ID on her. The woman was unconscious until last night. However, she has no memory of who she is or what happened to her."

"Can you give me a description?"

"She's looks to be in her thirties, long brunette hair, hazel eyes."

Brian gave Alan a promising look. He rustled through his notes to find Sean Charles-Dixon's description of his wife. "What was she wearing? Any identifying marks or jewelry?"

"She was wearing blue jeans, white t-shirt and brown leather boots, a wide, white gold band in native motif on her wedding finger, with a yellow gold raven, a raven tattoo on her right ankle, and a scar on the left ankle and one on the right thigh."

A broad smile crossed Brian's face and he gave Ian a thumbs up. "Sounds like our girl.

"Can you send us the info you have on her?" Detective Calloway asked.

"Soon as I hang up. We'll be there in a couple of hours with the husband." Brian added.

"I'll contact the hospital and try to arrange for the Doctors to be present when you arrive. Write down my cell number and call us when you're close. My partner and I will meet you there."

Brian hung up the phone and pumped his fists into the air above his head. "Yes!"

Alan couldn't help but chuckle at his partner's enthusiasm. "Judging by your excitement, I take it we've solved our case? At least the missing person part of it."

"Yup, some dude pulled her out of Lake Sabine Friday night. She was in a coma until last evening and woke up in the Intensive Care Unit. Apparently with amnesia. Their Jane Doe fits the description from clothes to physical appearance and markings, right down to the wedding ring."

Alan stood up and reached across the desk and gave his partner a high five. 'All right!"

Brian picked up the phone and dialled Sean's cell phone number. "We'll let the doctors fill him in on the amnesia part." He paused while the phone rang at the other end. "Sean ... Detective Castle here. Great news. We believe we've found your wife and she's alive."

Brian heard an intake of breathe at the other end of the phone before Sean responded. "Thank God. Is she all right?"

"Well, sir, she did have some sort of accident and is in a hospital in Port Arthur ... about an hour and a half east of here. We don't have all the details but we'll pick you up and take you there straightaway. We need a definite identification from you."

"Absolutely. I'm ready."

"See you in ten minutes." Brian was about to hang up and remembered something. "Oh, what about Georgia's parents? Weren't they due to fly in this morning?"

"They were. The flight was cancelled due to bad weather in the Vancouver area. I'm waiting to hear when they've rescheduled. I'll call them and give them the news."

"Okay. See you soon."

The two detectives let their superior know where they were headed. As they passed by Sarah's desk, Brian handed her his file. "We think we found our MisPer at the South East Medical Centre. Could you please forward the file to Detective Calloway in Port Arthur right away?"

"Sure." Sarah looked puzzled. "That's strange because I talked to them yesterday and she wasn't registered."

"She's a Jane Doe. Woke up with Amnesia," Brian said.

"Oh...I remember now. I asked if there were any Jane Does but was cut off." Sarah's face reddened. "I meant to call back but got other directed. Sorry ... " Her voice trailed off.

Brian felt annoyed but said nothing. He felt sure the patient was their MisPer and he was pumped. He'd have a chat with her later. "Can you call the FBI Field Office? They have an agent on his way here. Ask them to redirect him to the hospital in Port Arthur."

Sarah nodded. "Don't forget this..." She handed them a brown paper bag filled with the usual sub sandwiches. "Your lunch just arrived. Remember to eat it."

A couple of hours later, Sean and the Houston detectives stood outside of Georgia's room in ICU with Dr. Edwards. A gasp could be heard as Sean identified her through the glass windows. She was sleeping peacefully but with her face turned towards them he could see the bruising on her face.

"Is this your wife, Sean?" Dr. Edwards asked.

He nodded and a quiet croak escaped his constricted throat. "Yes."

Dr. Edwards led them to the conference room where they joined the Port Arthur detectives and the Lake Charles FBI agent and the rest of Georgia's medical team.

The detectives introduced themselves. The FBI agent spoke next.

"I'm Special Agent Benjamin Samuals with the Lake Charles FBI Field Office."

Sean looked surprised. "FBI?"

"I was called in because your wife crossed state lines and was a missing person, sir. However, now that we've found her and the assumption is that she crossed back into Texas before her accident, Port Arthur enforcement will lead the case and keep us informed.

Dr. Edwards made the introductions of her medical team. "As you know, I'm Georgia's Neurologist. Doctor Nuri Benadie is a Neuropharmacologist. Our head nurse is Kelly Franco, Tara Viera is the ICU nurse, Samantha Cole is a psychiatrist and our crisis worker, and last is Donna London, one of our Social Workers.

The Port Arthur detectives explained how Georgia was found in Lake Sabine, administered CPR and brought to the hospital. Team leader, Dr. Edwards took charge of the meeting again.

"I'll update you on your wife's condition and our treatment plan. Georgia was in a coma when she arrived here Friday night. She experienced cardiac arrest in the ER that evening and again Saturday afternoon. On both occasions defibrillation was successfully administered. She was moved to ICU in stable but critical condition. There's a hairline contusion with stiches and some facial and body bruising consistant with that of a car accident." Dr. Edwards paused and looked at his notes. "The good news is that your wife woke up last evening and she is off the critical list. She has a concussion which is causing severe headaches and she's experiencing memory loss. We're keeping her comfortable with pain and anti-anxiety medications."

Sean tensed and sat forward in his chair. "Memory loss? What does that mean?"

"Some patients can suffer retrograde amnesia caused by a trauma to the head. Usually that means her memory from the time of the injury to the present is lost. Generally, it clears itself as her injuries heal or she may never remember the actual accident itself. However, in your wife's case, she has no memory of who she is or where she is."

"So her situation is unusual?" Sean asked.

"From the perspective of memory loss from accident trauma, yes. We don't have all the answers yet. A cat scan was administered yesterday which was insignificant. Due to the extent of her memory loss, we've scheduled an MRI for later today. Do you have any more questions?"

Sean shifted uncomfortably, unsure of what to ask next. He rubbed his forhead with his fingers. "Umm...apart from the memory loss, is she going to be okay?"

"Her prognosis is very positive. Once we get her headaches under control, a physiotherapist will start work with her. And hopefully we will have some answers for you after the MRI."

Sean nodded. "When can I see her?"

"As soon as we finish this meeting, I'll take you to see her. We're keeping her in ICU until we finish our tests. You can stay with her as long as you wish. Donna?"

The social worker turned to Sean. "Do you have somewhere to stay here in Port Arthur, Sean?"

"Not yet."

"We have a lodge behind the hospital beside the cancer unit. Mostly out of town cancer patients stay there who come for treatment. I checked this morning and they do have a room available. I reserved it for you in case you needed it."

"That would be great. Thank you."

"They provide three meals a day, a lounge with a kitchenette where they leave snacks and meal leftovers. You can make tea or coffee at any time. There's a couple of computers and a phone at your disposal if needed and a laundry room. And a living room with television."

Sean was surprised at how organized the medical team were. "I appreciate being close to the hospital."

She passed him a business card. "I'll let them know you're going to be staying with them. When you're ready, give me a call and I'll take you over and introduce you to the Manager. I'm here until 4:00 p.m. today."

Dr. Edwards looked around the table. "Anyone have anything else to say?"

Detective Brown cleared his throat. "When could we talk to the patient, Doctor?"

"We're keeping her pretty sedated for a couple of days. With the memory loss, she won't have much to say at this point. Perhaps Wednesday?"

"We can wait. Just want to introduce ourselves, Doc."

Detective Castle spoke. "Detectives Brown and Calloway will be taking over your wife's case, Sean. It's under their jurisdiction now and our part's done. We'll be on our way back to Houston."

Sean stood and shook hands with the two Detectives. "I can't thank you enough for everything you've done. Thank you for finding my wife."

"Just doing our jobs. We wish your wife a speedy recovery. Good luck to you both." Detective Castle said.

Everyone stood except Dr. Edwards and the crisis worker. The Port Arthur Detectives spoke briefly to Sean. "We haven't found her rental car as yet. But assuming she went into the water, we're down to a twenty minute time frame. We'll keep you informed as we progress." Detective Brown said.

Sean nodded. "Thank you."

Special Agent Samuels took his leave as well, wishing Sean and Georgia all the best.

Sean resat with Samantha Cole, the crisis worker and the doctor. She began. "I'd like to go over a few things with you about Georgia's state of mind. You can expect she's feeling scared and overwhelmed at the moment. The anxiety drugs will help to keep her calm. However, you must be prepared for the fact that she won't know who you are. Your natural instinct will be to kiss her or at the very least hold her hand to reassure her she's not alone. But as a stranger to her she may not respond to touching the way you'd expect. So go easy with her."

Hearing her words made his heart ache. "I understand."

"As upset as you might feel, it's important that you stay detached physically. Reassure her with smiles and talk in a quiet, calm voice. We'll take it a day at a time, okay?" She handed him a business card. "Call me anytime. I'll make myself available."

"Okay."

Dr. Edwards led Sean back to Georgia's room. She was still sleeping. After checking her chart, the doctor took his leave. "I'll let you know the MRI results as soon as I have them."

Sean moved the arm chair beside the bed. Thought better of sitting too close to her and moved it back a little ... but just a little. *I have no idea what to expect sweetheart. But I'm here and so grateful that I found you. We'll get through this together.*

He settled into the chair and watched her while she slept.

Chapter 17

Georgia stared at the man sleeping in the armchair. His dark hair had fallen across his eyes. His full lips were slightly parted. In his relaxed state, his facial expression was that of an innocent boy. But he was no child. *Who is he?* Her eyes took in the length of his slim body with his long blue jeaned legs stretched out and crossed at the ankles. *No white coat, not a doctor. Not that a doctor would be sleeping in my room.*

The man shifted in the chair and his hand slipped off the arm of the chair and into his lap. That's when she noted the ring on his finger; a white gold band with a yellow gold raven, a small diamond for an eye. Her eyes moved to her own hand and the identical ring she wore. *Matching rings ... wedding rings?* The fact that she didn't know who she was had her confused and a little frightened. But if this stranger was her husband, someone she was intimate with and she couldn't recognize him? *It's downright terrifying.* Her chest constricted and her stomach rolled over. She felt the urge to vomit. Her hand rose to her mouth and she swallowed hard to control the reflex.

A nurse came into the room. "Good afternoon, sleepyhead," she said with a warm smile. "I'm Tara, your ICU nurse. How's your headache and pain level?"

"Still bad and an eight."

"Any dizziness or nausea?"

"Yes to both."

"Okay. I'm going to take your vitals and get you some more meds. You're going for an MRI in about half an hour."

While the nurse wrote down the results of her findings, Georgia glanced towards the man in the chair who was beginning to stir. "Who's he?" she asked in a quiet voice.

The nurse shifted on her feet, looking uncomfortable. "His name is Sean Charles-Dixon. I'm going to page the doctor and let him know you're awake again."

Left alone with the stranger whose eyes popped open sent Georgia into a panic. She instinctively knew this man called Sean was an important figure in her life and it scared the hell out of her that she didn't recognize him.

His eyes locked with hers. The moment seemed to linger on and on. His dark eyes were filled with compassion and concern. He sat up straight in his chair and gave her a warm smile.

"Hi, you're awake." The softness in his voice and his quiet reserve calmed her pounding heart.

"Hi." Georgia wasn't sure how to begin a conversation and fell silent.

The man leaned forward. "How are you feeling?"

"The headaches are the worst." She paused and glanced at the ring on his finger. "The... the nurse says your name is Sean."

A momentary look of disappointment crossed his face. Georgia guessed it was because she didn't recognize him. He recovered quickly and threw another big smile her way. "Yes. I'm Sean."

She was afraid to ask the next question but swallowed hard and blurted it out. "Do you know who I am?"

"Yes. Your name's Georgia, Georgia Charles-Dixon."

Her brows knitted together. "Georgia?"

He nodded. "That's right. A beautiful name."

Georgia recognized the last name as the same as his. Her hands shook but she knew she had to keep going with the questions. "We have matching rings. You and I...are we...?" She trailed off afraid to say the word.

Sean stared at the floor, his face contorting with different emotions. He sucked in his lips and nodded. "We were married two and a half years ago but knew each other for six years before that."

There it is. Married! Her chest felt heavy, as if she was pinned with a rock. *How can I not recognize a man I'm married to?* She sucked in a breathe and held it, forgetting to breathe.

Sean reached out to take her hand and she pulled it back with a cringe. Just as quickly, he pulled his hand back.

He looks as frightened as I feel. "I'm sorry," she managed to whisper.

He gave her a thin smile. "It's okay. This must be really hard for you." He hesitated. "Please … don't be afraid. I want to help you in any way I can."

Georgia stared at him without answering. Once again she felt awkward in his presence. *How could he help me? I can't even help myself.*

Luckily, Dr. Edwards entered the room with another woman. "So you're awake." He looked from Georgia to Sean. "And you too," he added with a warm smile. He focused his attention on Georgia. "The orderly will be here shortly to take you down for an MRI. Meanwhile, this is Ellie Simmons, your physiotherapist. She's going to get you up on your feet and walking. When we get the MRI results, I'll be back."

The rail-thin woman with long blond hair approached the bed once Dr. Edwards left. "Hi, Georgia. We'll take this slow and easy." She pulled the covers back. "Let's get you onto your side. I'm going to move your legs off the bed and lock my arm under yours. Now…I'm going to slowly pull you into sitting position. There you go. Stay there and get your balance."

Georgia felt a sudden rush of dizziness and closed her eyes. "Wow."

"You alright?" Ellie asked.

She opened her eyes and nodded with determination. "Yes."

Ellie reached for the walker she'd brought into the room with her and placed it in front of Georgia. She locked the wheels. "Okay. Grip the handles and pull yourself up. I'll be right here holding onto you. Here we go."

The room started to spin and Georgia held on tight to the walker. Her legs felt rubbery.

"Take a deep breath and wait until you feel able to move."

Georgia did as she was told.

"Again … breathe deep. Better?"

"I … I think so."

"You're doing great, hon. I'm going to put another gown on you in reverse. Don't want to give the other patients a heart attack exposing that cute little tush of yours."

Georgia glanced at Sean who had a glint in his eye and an impish smile. Her face reddened. He obviously already knew what her back side looked like but he was a stranger to her.

Ellie held the open arm of the gown by her right hand. "Release your grip and slip your hand through." She threw the gown across Georgia's back and rested it on her shoulder, moved to the other side and they repeated the action. "Alright then." The woman bent down and released the brakes. "You're all ready for the hundred yard dash. Here we go, hon."

Georgia moved forward gingerly, resting with each step, fearful of falling. Eventually, they reached the door and headed into the hallway. Ellie only took her halfway along and turned her around. "You're doing great but let's not overdo it." They inched their way back to her room.

"I'm going to leave you sitting in the chair, hon. The orderly will be here to take you down any minute."

Georgia sat down and sighed. "I feel like I ran a marathon."

"That was a great accomplishment. You should be proud. I'll be back tomorrow morning to get you exercising and walking further. Now if you want to walk at all before then you can. But not by yourself." Ellie gave Sean a glance up and down. "You get your hunk of a husband here to help you. Okay, hon?"

Sean laughed and again, Georgia felt her face get hot. "Don't worry. I won't let her walk alone."

"And if you want to start using the washroom here in your room that's okay too. But get the nurse to help you. Got it?"

"Yes. Thank you."

Ellie no sooner left and the orderly arrived with a wheelchair.

"Hi. I'm your orderly, Wade. Let me to help you into your chariot." He turned to Sean. "I'll have her back in about twenty minutes."

Sean smiled at her. "I'll be here."

"Hang on, pretty lady. I'm late and we're going to be travelling at warp speed."

They arrived at the treatment room in record time. Georgia's wheelchair was whisked into the room and placed beside a narrow platform that didn't look wide enough to lie on. She glanced at the top of the bed at the cylindrical structure. She couldn't remember if she'd ever had an MRI before, but she knew once on the platform, she would be moved inside the structure. Her breath caught.

"Don't worry. It'll be over in no time." Georgia turned and noted a technician standing across the room. "Are you claustrophobic?"

Georgia thought about it. "I ... don't remember. Judging on how I'm feeling about this contraption, I'd have to say yes."

A nurse entered the room and the two positioned her on the platform on her back. Her breathing became shallow and she started to panic. The nurse patted her arm. "Close your eyes and take deep breaths. When you hear and feel the platform move, put yourself in another place. Somewhere you love and feel safe."

Georgia concentrated on her breathing to keep herself calm. She blocked out the sounds of the machine and tried to imagine herself somewhere else. But where? She had no memories of home, or familiar places. As quickly as those thoughts entered her head, her mind went blank and she envisioned a white mist.

There was no weight to her body and no pain. She floated through the mist easily, watching as it dissipated until she found herself in a beautiful garden. The smells of the flora and fauna pleasantly filled her sense of smell. She passed through the prolific landscape, marvelling at the turquoise water and skitter bugs on the surface. Frogs croaked and birds chirped in song. She lifted her face to the sky and felt the warmth of the sun on her skin.

A voice beckoned her. "Hello, Georgia."

She dropped her head and looked into the iridescent grey eyes of an elderly native woman. The woman stood before her with long grey hair, wearing a white lace dress and barefoot. Georgia smiled and cocked her head. She no idea who this woman was but her presence embraced her and she felt calm. "Do I know you?"

"Yes, child. You have forgotten me but hopefully one day soon your memories will return."

"What's your name?"

"Nonnock. I'm the spirit of a First Nation Tahltan elder. We go back a long way together." She cocked her head as if listening to someone. She started to move away.

"Please don't go. I have so many questions."

"I must leave. They're calling you back. Remember, you must go back to the beginning of it all."

A mist began to form and the woman disappeared into a dense white fog. Her voice echoed in Georgia's mind. "You have a great battle to fight, child. I'll be waiting for you."

You must go back to the beginning of it all."

"Georgia ... Georgia ... "

A hand was shaking her shoulder and Georgia opened her eyes to the nurse and technician standing beside the platform.

"Great visualization. You fell asleep," the technician said.

"I guess I did. I was dreaming," Georgia said.

They helped her up and into the wheelchair and a few minutes later the orderly took her back to her room. The nurse settled her back in bed.

Sean excused himself. "I have to register at the lodge behind the hospital. They have a room for me there. I'll be back as soon as I'm settled in."

This suited Georgia. The afternoon had been an exhausting one. She felt the need to be alone and assess all that had happened. Thoughts surfaced of the woman called Nonnock. It had all seemed so real and not a dream at all.

Georgia Charles-Dixon. At least I know my name.

She closed her eyes and promptly fell asleep.

Chapter 18

Tuesday

Georgia sat in the chair staring at Sean who was sitting on the edge of her hospital bed. "My parents?".

"Yes, they were supposed to arrive in L.A. yesterday but their flight was delayed. They arrived this morning and caught a connecting flight to Port Arthur. They'll be here soon."

This new development left her feeling anxious. She was becoming comfortable in the presence of her husband. His quiet, unassuming nature kept her calm and even though he was a stranger to her, she was grateful that she had someone to support her. He hadn't told her much about her life and she sensed he was holding back, perhaps afraid of overwhelming her. She didn't ask for the same reason.

Samantha Cole, the crisis worker arrived and introduced herself to Georgia. The three of them talked about Georgia's condition.

"Have you told her much about her life, Sean?" she asked.

Sean squirmed. "I wasn't sure what I should tell her. I don't want to upset her with things she doesn't remember."

"Understandable."

"Her parents are arriving soon. I was about to tell her about them."

Samantha looked at Georgia. "Are you ready to hear about your family and your life?"

"Umm...yes. It's scary but perhaps it will help me to remember."

The crisis worker gave her a huge grin. "That's the spirit. Right answer. I have no doubt that your memory will return. I've seen this a couple of times in the past with patients. And Sean, the more you tell her can only help her." She turned back to Georgia. "Embrace it."

The physiotherapist arrived to take her for a walk and to do some exercises.

Half an hour later Georgia was back in her room with Sean. Samantha took her leave with the promise of returning that afternoon. Sean sat in the chair. "So tell me about my life." She hesitated, then added: "Our life."

"Okay." He opened his mouth to speak and hesitated. His right eye started to twitch.

Georgia's chin dropped. A feeling of déjà vu swept through her. "I've seen that before." She stared hard at Sean trying to remember when.

Sean's eyebrows shot up. "Seen what before?"

"Your right eye was twitching. It...seemed so familiar." Georgia shrugged. "That's all I've got."

He straightened up in the chair and beamed. "You always said that when I'm stressed out or angry my right eye twitches. Not exactly what I'd like to hear for your first memory of me but hey, I'll take it."

They both laughed.

"I wasn't quite sure where to begin that's why I stopped talking. Let's start with you. I'll give you basic information, not too many details, unless you question me further on something. You grew up in West Vancouver, British Columbia."

"I'm a Canadian?" Georgia asked.

"Yup a Canuck, me too. Actually, I'm part Tahltan, First Nations but that's for later. You have an older brother Kris, in the Air Force, a maternal grandmother, and paternal grandparents. You were married once before me. You divorced after ten years. We met." Sean shifted in his chair.

She watched his eye start to twitch and knew he was holding back some details which was okay. All the ins and outs could come later.

For now she wanted to get the essence of her life and who her family was. "Please, continue."

"I'm a novelist. I have a number of series out and some have been made into movies. That's what this trip to Los Angeles was about. Movie business. You flew on from L.A. to Houston to speak at a conference."

She threw her head back. "What kind of conference."

"A Writer's Conference."

"Me? I thought you were the writer?"

"You've written a few books too and helped me with a couple of movie scripts based on my books."

"If I was in Houston attending a conference, what was I doing driving in a rainstorm that night back to Houston? Where was I coming from?

Sean filled Georgia in on the details of her day in Louisiana and how she detoured off of the main highway back to Houston because of an accident. He told her about the man who found her in the water and brought her to the hospital.

"Have you met him?" she asked.

"Not yet but I intend to at some point."

"Yes, we must find him and thank him. I owe him so much."

She rolled from her side onto her back and hit the button to raise the back into sitting position. "So I'm a novelist too."

Sean shifted again before he spoke. "No, your books were non-fiction."

"Oh ..." She was about to ask about the subject of her books, but Sean pushed on, cutting her off.

"Your father was in the army and stationed in Germany. You and Kris lived on the base with your mom and went to school there. Your grandfather was a General. Both of them are retired now."

"But my brother joined the Air Force. Wonder how that went over?" They laughed.

"From what I understand, your brother left college and joined up behind their backs. It caused a little friction for awhile but everyone forgave him eventually."

"What about your family?" Georgia asked.

"I'm an only child. My grandfather was First Nations Tahltan living in Dease Lake. He was a fur trader and later became a guide to gold seekers heading to the Yukon. He married a white school teacher and they had my dad who married a woman he met in college, my mother. They live in White Rock, just south of Vancouver."

Georgia was struck with another thought. "You said yesterday that we married three years ago, but knew each for six years prior." She feared asking the next question.

"That's right."

She swallowed hard. "No children?"

Sean's right eye started to twitch again. She watched him suck in his lips and knew the answer instinctively. Yes, she had children. Her body turned cold and she shivered. "How many?"

"Two. Girls," Sean said in barely a whisper. She could see he was studying her and gauging her reactions. A look of love and concern.

Georgia knew she had to know the truth but this one was the biggest revelation of all. 'Wow ... how could I not know I'm a mother?" It came out in barely a whisper. Her hands went to her abdomen and she stared at her torso. "I mean, I carried them inside of me all those months. Gave birth to them." She noted Sean had moved over and sat on the edge of her bed. She saw his hand slide across the blanket towards her, stop, and withdraw. Georgia looked up at him with tears in her eyes, searching his for what, she did not know. "How old are they?"

"Shelby and Kaela are both nine."

One hand flew to her mouth. "Twins?"

"No, sweetheart. They're half-sisters."

A jolt passed through her body. "They're the same age but half-sisters, and if you and I have only known each other for nine years, something isn't adding up."

This time Sean reached out and took a hold of her free hand and Georgia let him. He was the only connection she had to reality and he was her life line.

"Kaela is your birth daughter. Your first husband, Colin Charles is her father. You left him because he had an affair. Both you and his mistress were pregnant at the same time. The girls were born two weeks apart."

She held on tight to his hand in case he tried to let go. "How did I ... we end up with both of them?"

"When the girls were five, your ex-husband died of a heart attack. Six months later, Julie, Shelby's mother, died from a brain tumour ..."

"That's Julie?" Georgia was stunned

Sean leaned forward. "You remember her?"

"Umm, not really. When I first woke up the nurse was giving me hydromorphone. I told her Julie was on the same drug. But I couldn't remember who she was."

Sean beamed. "This is all very positive. You're remembering a few things. It's just a matter of time."

"I hope so. So tell me more about Julie."

"You and she had become friends. You were there for her during the end of her illness and promised to adopt Shelby. Ten months later, you and I married and I adopted the girls."

Georgia let out a deep sigh. "Do you have a picture of them?"

"I do". Sean stood and pulled his wallet from his back pocket. He gave her a picture that showed all four of them together.

Georgia stared at the picture, awestruck. "They're beautiful. They do look like twins though and must take after their father with that blond hair and blue eyes."

Sean laughed. "Yes and yes. And they love you to pieces."

She smiled and held up the picture. "Can I hold onto this for awhile?"

"Of course."

She leaned the picture on the over-bed table against a vase of flowers from Sean where she could view it whenever she wanted.

She faced Sean again. "Where are the girls right now?"

"At your maternal grandmother's home in Gibsons. We have a home down the block from hers. We haven't told them anything except that we extended our trip to L.A. for a couple of days."

Where was Gibsons? There was so much she wanted to say and ask Sean but before she got started two people entered the room. An older gentleman and woman approached the bed. Georgia looked to Sean for direction.

He stood and embraced the woman. "Hi, Mom." Then he reached out and shook hands with the man. "You made it. Long trip."

The man nodded and placed a hand on Sean's shoulder. "It was that."

My parents.

The frail woman who reached out to her had a kind face. Georgia let her place her arms around her and hold her close. Her mother kissed her on the cheek and backed away so her father could hug her as well. "Hi Ginger Cake." His voice was husky with emotion.

Georgia could only assume that he was calling her fondly by a nickname. She squeezed him back and smiled at him. It was all very strange to have these people showing her affection when she felt so disassociated from them. But she intuitively understood that they needed to reach out to her and show their love and support as any parent would do.

As they gathered chairs to sit by her bedside, she wrapped her arms across her chest and held on tight, bracing herself for that look of hurt and confusion when they realized that she truly didn't know them or anything about her past. It was a look she knew she'd see over and over again until her memory returned.

Chapter 19

Wednesday

Georgia closed her eyes and tried to focus on the image that just flashed so fleetingly in her mind. *Night time, poor visibility and raining. A black pick-up truck beside her car moving into her lane, forcing her onto the soft, muddy shoulder. Her car sliding and losing control.* She opened her eyes and sighed. *That's it. Nothing more. Is that what happened? Did someone drive me off the road? But how did I end up in the river?*

"Good morning. How are you feeling?"

Sean entered her room and sat on the edge of the bed. He took a hold of her hand and squeezed it. This was the extent of their touching the past few days. She'd come to find it comforting but felt glad he hadn't tried to kiss her. A handsome man and easy to look at, she mused that under any other circumstances she was sure she'd be attracted to him and flattered by his attention. But it was all too weird to think they'd been intimate for years but he was a stranger.

"Headaches are lessening. They've cut back my meds." She paused, then added: " I think I just had a memory recall ... "

A knock on her door interrupted her. A man and woman stood by her door carrying flowers, looking a little apprehensive. The man spoke in a quiet tone. "May we come in?"

Sean stood, looking as perplexed as Georgia. He leaned down to her and whispered: "Hold onto that thought." He turned back to the couple. "Were you looking for my wife, Georgia Charles-Dixon?"

"Yes, sir. My name is Dylan Ortega. This is my wife, Camila. I'm the person who found your wife."

Sean sprang forward and shook the man's hand. "Of course. Please come in. I'm Sean, Georgia's husband." He smiled at Camila and led them into the room. "It's such a pleasure to meet you. What can I say? There's no words to express my gratitude."

Dylan looked uncomfortable. "I'm just glad I was there at the right time."

"You saved my wife's life and I'll always be grateful."

Dylan moved closer to the bed. "We brought you these. I'm happy to see you're awake at last."

"Thank you so much. I heard you were hospitalized for hypothermia. How are you feeling?" Georgia asked.

Sean reached out and took the flowers. "I'll see if I can find another vase for these." He left the room.

Dylan shrugged at Georgia. "That's all behind me. I hope it's okay that we came to visit you."

"Are you kidding? If you hadn't, we would have searched for you. If it wasn't for you, I'd be fish food in the Gulf of Mexico by now." Georgia smiled at Camila. "You must be very proud of your husband."

Sean returned triumphant and placed the flowers on the side table.

Camila moved forward shyly. "Yes, we're all so proud of him. He did a brave thing."

Georgia looked at Dylan. "He's my hero. Whatever were you doing out there on such an ugly night? And however did you see me out in that river?"

An embarrassed look crossed Dylan's face and he glanced at Camila. She moved beside him and took his hand, smiled and nodded at him encouragingly.

"Camila and I had a nasty argument and I left the house to drive off my anger. I soon realized that it was stupid to be out there but

I wasn't ready to go home. I went to a lookout in a park beside the water. There's a place where the river joins the lake. I was focused on that very spot and could tell there was something strange about it. There you were caught in a whirlpool. It was either pure coincidence or fate that I happened to be there at that precise moment."

Georgia's eyes teared up and she shuddered. "Whatever it was, you gave me back to my family." To lighten the moment, she added: "But for the life of me, I haven't a clue who any of them are at the present time. And I'm glad you guys had a bad disagreement." It was a feeble attempt at black humour and they all laughed—sort of, but it kept her from crying. Georgia clipped her laugh into a snort which triggered another Déjà Vu.

She looked at Sean. "Do I always snort when I laugh?"

Sean gave her a broad smile. "Yes."

This time they all laughed.

Dylan shifted from one foot to the other. "So you really don't remember anything?"

"Nothing. A few flashes here and there, which the doctors say are encouraging."

"Well, we don't want to intrude. We just wanted to pay our respects and wish you a healthy recovery. Including the return of your memory."

Sean searched his coat and pulled out pen and paper. "Georgia and I would never consider your visits intrusive. Please, give me your phone number and address. We really would like to keep in touch."

"Of course."

As they exchanged information, two more people appeared at the door. They seemed surprised to see Dylan and Camila. The Ortega's said their good-byes. Sean shook Dylan's hand once more, thanking him again and again.

Georgia smiled at Camila. "Thank you so much for the beautiful flowers. We'll talk soon." She glanced at the new visitors, once again without recognition. She sighed.

Dylan nodded at the men in the doorway as he and Camila took their leave. "Detectives."

They nodded back and one spoke. "Mr. Ortega. Have a good day."

So they're detectives. Guess I wouldn't have known who they were even with my memory intact.

The detectives shook Sean's hand. "Good morning, Sean," one said.

They turned to Georgia. "I'm Detective Brown and this is Detective Calloway. We're with the Port Arthur Police Department. It's good to see you awake."

"Hello," Georgia said.

"We're working your case. We understand that you have no memory of what happened to you. However, we wanted to introduce ourselves and let you know that we will do all that we can to figure out what happened to you," Detective Brown said.

Detective Calloway picked up the conversation. "We spoke with Dr. Edwards this morning. He says you've had a few memory flashbacks. We were wondering if anything else has surfaced that you could tell us about."

Georgia stared from one to the other. "I did have an incident this morning before all my visitors arrived."

"Can you tell us about it?" Detective Calloway asked.

"Sure, it wasn't much. It was dark, raining and I was driving. A black pick-up came up beside me. Then he moved into my lane, forcing me to drive onto the shoulder. That's all I remember."

The two detectives exchanged glances and Calloway wrote into a small notebook. "That's a lot at this point," he said.

Georgia hit the button on her bed and brought her headboard up higher into a sitting position. "What more can you do, Detectives?"

"We know you had a white rental car that is missing. We're searching for that. We also have officers checking out restaurants and gas stations along your route to establish a time frame from when you detoured off the highway to when you arrived here at the hospital. Whatever happened to you took place on that stretch of road," Detective Brown said.

Calloway spoke next. "We're trying to narrow it down between Bridge City and here. There's a series of bridges and waterways along the river running parallel with the highway. You couldn't have been in the water too long so it's logical that you may have gone off the road into the water through that stretch."

Georgia shuddered at the thought of being in the cold water at this time of year. She pulled the blanket up over her arms.

Sean moved closer to the bed and touched her arm. "Are you all right?"

"I'm fine." She gave him a semblance of a smile.

"You're a very lucky woman to have survived those waters at this time of year," Detective Calloway said.

"Yes, I am. Thanks to Dylan Ortega," Georgia mused.

The detectives gave each another look that Georgia noticed.

"We'll leave you now. If you recall anything else that can help us, Sean has our card. Meanwhile, we'll keep you posted on our investigation. Good day."

After they left, Georgia turned to Sean. "Did you see that look they exchanged when I mentioned Dylan Ortega?"

"I did. I wonder if they think he was more involved than he's said."

She knitted her eyebrows. "Hmm ... he seems like such a nice man. I got good vibes from him."

"I did too. But don't forget that they are law enforcement. They're trained to look at anyone as a suspect, especially someone who's the only one they're aware of to have contact with you around the time of your accident. We just have to let them do their job, hon."

"You're right, of course. But my gut tells me he's straight up."

Chapter 20

Thursday

Dr. Edwards sat at the head of the conference table. His medical team took up the chairs to his left, Georgia sat in her wheelchair with her parents and husband on the right side of the table.

He looked at Georgia and smiled. "I've just had a meeting with my team. All test results are in. The MRI we did a couple of days ago was normal. Same results as the CT scan we did on Sunday. Your blood gasses are normal. X-rays normal. Your physiotherapy is progressing well. Your headaches are the main concern. But they have improved somewhat and we've been able to cut back on your meds. We all concur that you may have to deal with your headaches for awhile and they can be handled with prescription drugs. Based on the test results and the fact that you've had some memory resurgence, we feel that your memory should return in the near future. Good news right?"

"Absolutely. So where do we go from here?" Georgia asked.

"We feel that you might do better from now on if you were back home with your friends and family around you. It may help bring the memories back sooner. I spoke with your family doctor this morning and he recommended a leading Neurologist to take over your care. I then contacted the Neurologist, Dr. Cara Townsend at Vancouver General Hospital and she's agreed to take on your case. However, because of the long distance involved, we'd like to keep you here until at least Monday and get you a little stronger."

"Can she travel commercially?" Sean asked.

"We'd recommend the use of a Commercial Medical Transport Airline. They can provide a medical escort who will take care of all the paperwork for you when you reach Canada. And they provide a paramedic to make sure she's comfortable and stable during the trip."

Georgia's father cleared his throat. "What about all of us? Can we travel on the plane with her?"

"Absolutely. We recommend it."

"Will I go directly home or into the hospital there?" Georgia asked.

"Dr. Townsend wants you in the hospital for a couple of days. Your medical escort will make all the arrangements to have you transported by ambulance from the airport. I'll be forwarding all our records with you, but I'm sure your new doctor will want to do her own tests and check you out before she discharges you home."

"Can you recommend a medical transport airline?" Sean asked.

"Yes. Aero Medical Transport Company. We've used them on other occasions and have been very satisfied with their services. We took the liberty of contacting them. Here's a list of their services and the costs involved for your trip." Dr. Edwards handed him the sheet. "Any more questions?"

Georgia exchanged looks with her family and they all shook their heads no.

"If you wish, we can make the arrangements with Aero and you'll be good to go." Dr Edwards said.

Sean studied the sheet of costs. "Please, go ahead. I want the best for my wife and the cost isn't a factor."

"All right. Georgia, we'll continue with your physio for the next four days and make the necessary arrangements for your discharge on Monday. I won't be here on the weekend but I'll stop in tomorrow to see you." Dr. Edwards stood and gathered his notes. "One more thing. I contacted the detectives handling your case to let them know you'll be discharged on Monday. They said they would pop in on the weekend to update you and say goodbye."

"Thank you, Doctor." she said. She looked at the other medical team members. "And I want to thank all of you for looking after me. I can't say enough about this hospital and the staff. I'll always be grateful for your professional and caring support."

Chapter 21

Friday

Detective Calloway punched the button labelled Line 1 on his desk phone. "Calloway here."

"Detective, this is Officer Stone. I'm at the Do Stop Cafe in Bridge City. There's a waitress here who says Georgia Charles-Dixon was here last Friday night. She came in for coffee and left shortly after that."

"Good job, Officer. We'll be there in twenty." Calloway grabbed his jacket and headed to the washroom where his partner had headed a few minutes earlier. He pushed the door open. "You done in there? We've got some travelling to do."

A voice yelled out from within. "On my way."

Detective Brown emerged a minute later. "What's up?"

"Did you wash your hands?"

"Piss off. Your OCD is getting worse, Calloway."

Detective Calloway slapped him on the shoulder. "Just teasing ya, big guy. We're on our way to Bridge City. There's a waitress there says she saw Georgia last Friday night."

Twenty minutes later they entered the Do Stop Cafe. There were two waitresses working the floor. The place wasn't packed but they were busy. They found a quiet table in the corner. Officer Stone joined them and pointed out the waitress. She came right over when she saw them.

"Ya all must be the detectives from Port Arthur. Would you like a cup of coffee?" she asked.

"Yes, please." Detective Calloway said. The others nodded.

She returned with a pot and filled their cups. She took the pot back and spoke to the other waitress, nodding towards their table. A moment later, she joined them. "I'm Cassie Turner," she said.

Introductions were made around the table.

Calloway pulled a picture out of his file and showed it to her. "Is this the woman you saw here Friday night?"

"That's her, hon. Pretty little thing. The officer here wouldn't give me any information about her. Is she all right?"

Calloway ignored her question for the moment. "Can you tell us what time she arrived here Friday evening?"

"About eight. I know 'cause we're usually open until ten but there was no one here except my nephew and his girlfriend. We were thinkin' of closin' early 'cause of the storm."

"Did you talk to her at all?"

"A little. She was from Canada and she'd been visiting Lake Charles for the day. I remember tellin' her she shouldn't be out drivin' in that storm and she said she was almost to Houston so she'd continue 'cause she had a flight to catch in the mornin'."

"Did anyone else come in after her?" Detective Brown asked.

"One man came in a few minutes after she did."

"Can you describe him for us?" Detective Brown asked.

"About five feet nine inches, dark hair"

"And did you talk with him at all?" Brown asked.

"No. He was eatin' a muffin and I didn't want to disturb him. I decided to close up once they were done, so I was cleanin' up behind the counter."

"Do you know which direction he was travelling and what he was driving?"

"No and no." Her face clouded over. "Hey, is she all right? You never told me. Did that man hurt her?"

"A couple more questions and we'll answer yours if we can, okay?" Calloway said.

She nodded and waited.

"What time did Georgia leave?" Calloway asked.

"About 8:15 p.m. And the man left right after."

Calloway searched through his folder and pulled out another picture. "Is this the man that was in here?"

Cassie furrowed her brow. "He looks familiar. I've seen him in here before. Similar looks to the other man, but that's not him."

"Are you sure? Take another look."

"Nope. Not him."

Calloway sighed and put the picture of Dylan Ortega back in the folder. "In answer to your question. Mrs. Charles-Dixon did have an accident and went off the highway into the river, she ..."

She gasped and cut him off. "Oh no ... is she okay."

"She's in the hospital in Port Arthur and she's doing well. They're releasing her on Monday."

"I had a bad feelin' that night, poor little thing. Do you think that man had anything to do with it?"

"At the moment there's no evidence that anyone else was involved. These are routine questions to establish who saw her that night and establish a time frame." Calloway added.

"Well, I'm just glad that she's okay. If you see that sweet thing before she goes home, tell her I wish her all the best."

A few minutes later, they were heading back to Port Arthur. Detective Brown was driving. "So now we have a search area of approximately four miles, assuming logically that she went into the river on this side of the Neches. That narrows it down," he said. "And since we don't know if the other patron was heading east or west, maybe she went off the road on her own and Ortega *is* a hero."

"Don't forget, Georgia's memory recall of a black truck forcing her off the road. And Ortega has a black truck," Calloway said.

"She might be confused. She does have a head injury. And she didn't recall being forced into the water by the other vehicle."

Calloway stared out the passenger window as they followed the waterway east. "True. The waitress did remember seeing Ortega at the cafe before. Do you think she may have recognized him but didn't want to get involved? We're talking small town here. People tend to protect their own."

"I didn't get that impression. Ortega left home at ten minutes to eight. Georgia arrived at eight. The unidentified man arrived a few minutes later. I don't think Ortega had enough time to drive to the cafe and arrive when the stranger did."

"You're probably right there. But he could have headed towards Bridge City and turned around when he realized it was a bad idea being on the roads," Calloway said.

"Where's your mind going on this? Why are you so hell-bent on not believing Ortega's story?"

Calloway stared at his partner's profile. "I'm not. I'm just trying to cover all the bases is all. If Georgia passed him heading east and he was heading west, he could have turned around and ended up behind her. He admitted he was full of anger and not paying attention to the road."

"All right. But if he hydroplaned, it was an accident. Why change the story?"

"Because he was scared. If she died he could be charged with vehicular homicide and driving with undue care and attention."

Brown nodded in agreement. "Okay, in his story he comes out a hero but in Georgia's memory recall he forced her off the road and perhaps into the water."

"It's one scenario. But we need proof. Our next step is to get personnel searching along the water's edge for anything to indicate a car went off into the water. We also need a diver. We'd best get back to the office. It's Friday afternoon and we need to get a frog man on board before they disappear for the weekend."

" I think we should start with Rainbow Bridge over the Neches River and work back towards Bridge City. Assuming at this point, Ortega pulled her out of the lake as he said, the further she's away from it the less likely she would have survived," Brown said.

"All right, that's our plan."

As the car sped towards Port Arthur, Calloway stared down into the dark water and watched the strong current pulling the churning water towards Lake Sabine. *You're a lucky woman, Miss Georgia. A very lucky woman.*

Luck was on their side. After returning to the office and calling in a diver, two officers called in saying they'd found something at Rainbow Bridge. The two detectives found themselves standing on the shoulder of the road in a light rain. One of the officers approached them.

"Over here, guys." He led them over to a big rock. There were chips and cracks in it from a recent blunt force impact. Within the cracks he could see white paint. Using a small knife, Calloway dug out some of the paint chips and put them in a baggie. He watched his partner lean down and pick up an object in the mud with gloved hands. The detective held it up for him to examine. It was a broken piece of a car mirror, one edge encased with white plastic. Calloway opened a plastic bag and Brown dropped it in.

"Looks like you were right, Brown," Calloway said He looked at the bridge span and cement abutment in front of them. "If this is where she went into the water, she couldn't have been any closer to Rainbow Bridge."

The other officer spoke. "It appears like she flipped sideways over this rock and went into the water to the right. The diver went down a couple of minutes before you got here. All we can do now is wait."

Calloway pulled his collar up to keep the rain from dripping down his back. "If she'd of gone straight forward over the abutment, instead of to the right, the car would have been caught up in the current and possibly ended up in the lake. We might never find it." He motioned to his right. "Let's hope it's down there."

It wasn't a long wait. The diver's head popped up and he gave them a thumbs up. A cheer sounded out and high fives amongst the small group standing on the shore. The diver emerged out of the water and handed two items to the detectives. One was a plasticised envelope with the registration of the vehicle, confirming it was a rental. The second was a leather purse. Detective Brown opened the water-filled satchel and retrieved a wallet. He opened it, pumped his fist into the air and yelled: "Yes." He flashed the open wallet around the group, showing the driver's license of one Georgia Charles-Dixon.

"Good work everyone," Calloway said. He turned to one of the officers. "Can you call in for a crane truck and a flat deck tow truck?" While they waited, he took pictures of the purse and contents, and the damaged rock.

A few minutes later, the officer relayed the message that the trucks were on their way. They moved their vehicles back along the highway to make room. Calloway sent the officers out to set up roadblocks and close one lane of the highway. The diver worked with the crane truck driver and an hour later the car was ready to be pulled up from the depths of the river. The highway and bridge were closed completely for safety reasons. It was evening by the time the car was out of the water, loaded on the flat-deck, and normality returned to the highway.

Detective Calloway thanked everyone involved. "A great day's work and thank you to everyone here for a job well done."

Chapter 22

On Saturday, the detectives found Georgia in the common room with her parents, Sean and Dr. Edwards who'd been called in on an emergency earlier that morning. Sean introduced them to his in-laws and pulled two chairs into their circle.

Detective Calloway took the lead. "We have some good news for you, Miss Georgia. We found your car late yesterday. You went off the road beside the Rainbow Bridge over the Neches River."

Her mother gasped and Georgia reached for Sean's hand.

"In lieu of your memory recall of being forced off the road, we're holding the contents of the car as evidence, but I think we can return this." Calloway retrieved her wallet from his pocket and handed it to her. It appears your ID and credit cards are intact and we've taken pictures of all the contents."

"Thank you so much. It would be a nightmare to replace everything," Georgia said.

"We understand you're going home on Monday. That's great news." Calloway looked to Dr. Edwards for confirmation.

"Yes, she's ready to go home and recuperate with her family. We've arranged for a medical transport plane to take her back home to Canada," Dr. Edwards said.

"Wonderful news. We spoke to a waitress at the Do Stop Cafe in Bridge City. Apparently you stopped for coffee there. She remembers when you left so we have a definite time frame leading up to your accidents. She sends her best wishes in your recovery."

Georgia smiled. "How very nice of her." Her face clouded over. "Of course, I don't remember her or even stopping there."

"Well, Miss Georgia, we just wanted to update you on the news and say goodbye. We have your contact information and will continue to work the case and stay in touch with you. You or Sean can call anytime if you have any questions about our progress here. Should you have any memory recall regarding the accident or your full memory returns, please let us know."

Dr. Edwards spoke up first. "I have no doubt her memory will return, but be aware that sometimes everything returns except the accident itself. The trauma to the brain sometimes prevents recall of the actual incident that caused it."

"We understand, Doctor," Calloway said. The two detectives stood and shook hands with everyone present.

As they were leaving the room, Georgia stopped them. "Can I ask you something? Do you think Dylan Ortega has anything to do with my accident?"

"We have no proof of that. He is on our radar as he's the only one we know of who had contact with you on that stretch of road. And that makes him a person of interest," Calloway said.

"I see. Thank you for everything, Detectives."

Both men nodded and Calloway said: "Our pleasure indeed, Miss Georgia."

Detective Scott Calloway sat back in his chair and studied Dylan Ortega. The man's expression was blank. "We called you back in to go over your statement once more, Mr. Ortega."

Dylan nodded.

"We've been looking at the time-line. We know the approximate time you say you were travelling on the highway and the approximate time Miss Georgia went into the water by the Rainbow Bridge." Calloway leaned forward towards Dylan. "You told us that you never saw anyone on the road that night. I want you to think back and answer the question again. Did you see anyone on the road—and did you pass anyone?"

Calloway noticed a slight jerk of Ortega's head and his eyes grew larger. "Uh … I did pass a car before I turned off onto Old Ferry Road."

Calloway leaned in closer. "But your statement says you didn't see anyone. Why did you omit that information?"

Dylan looked flustered. "I didn't omit it, you …"

Calloway cut him off, raising his voice. "But you never mentioned it previously. Why not?"

"Because you specifically asked me if I saw anyone driving west from Bridge City and I didn't. You never asked if I saw anyone else heading east."

"Tell us about the car you passed."

"I hadn't been on the road more than ten minutes and drove around a curve. She was travelling really slow in a small car. I knew I was driving a little too fast for the road conditions and didn't want to spike the brakes. So I pulled out into the opposite lane to pass her."

"How do you know the driver was a female?" Detective Brown asked.

"Because when I got into the other lane and looked over, I could see she was a woman."

"Describe her, race, age, etc." Brown said.

"She was white, looked to be in her seventies, grey hair."

Calloway tapped his fingers on the table. "And you saw all that as you were passing her?"

"My truck hit a puddle and I hydroplaned towards her car. I glanced over and she was staring at me full-faced. Her hands were clinging to that steering wheel and the look of fear on her face shook me. I'll never forget it." Dylan paused and stared at the table.

"Continue. What happened next?" Calloway asked.

"I managed to pull out of the skid and passed her safely. She pulled over to the side of the road for a moment. I realized I needed to slow down and I tapped my brakes and brought my speed to an acceptable level."

"Can you give us any details about the car?"

"No, just that it was small. That's all I remember," Dylan said.

Calloway stood and stretched his legs, put his hands on the table and looked directly into Dylan's eyes. "What I don't understand, Mr. Ortega, is if it was such a profound experience that you'll never forget the look on that woman's face, why you conveniently forgot it in your statement."

Dylan's face turned red and his anger level rose. "It wasn't significant to the questions you asked me at the time and I never thought about it until now."

"Everything is significant in an investigation, sir. Everything," Calloway retorted.

"You interviewed me in my hospital bed the morning after the incident. I was recovering from hypothermia and still in a state of shock about the whole thing. Passing that woman had nothing to do with Mrs. Charles-Dixon's accident. I didn't think of it at the time."

Calloway sat down again and fell silent.

Detective Brown was writing notes. He put his pen down and looked at Dylan. "You said the woman you passed pulled over and stopped. How do you know she was okay?"

"Because it was a straight stretch of road and once I'd slowed down I looked in my rear view mirror. She'd pulled back out onto the highway and was travelling behind me. She was still driving extremely slow. Too slow to be on the highway because even at my safe driving speed, her lights were falling further and further back."

"And then you hit Old Ferry Road and turned off the highway?" Brown asked.

"That's right. I never saw her again."

Calloway stood and started to pace back and forth across the room. "Dylan, here's another scenario. Here me out. Forget the old woman you say you passed for the moment. You're driving down the highway at way too fast a speed, thinking about the fight you had with your wife. You don't turn off at Old Ferry Road, but keep going east towards Bridge City. Meanwhile, Miss Georgia is heading west towards you. You may or may not see her pass you because of your state of mind..."

"Didn't happen," Dylan snapped.

The detective put his finger up. "Bear with me. You realize you shouldn't be out on the highway in the current weather, so you turn around and head west towards Port Arthur. You come across Miss Georgia, pull out to pass her, hydroplane towards her car. She goes off the road and into the water. You stop and pull her out of the water. Take her to the hospital and fabricate a story to protect yourself."

"That's ridiculous."

"Why? Calloway leaned against the wall and folded his arms across his chest.

"Because I had no way of knowing she'd wake up with amnesia. She could have woken up and refuted my story. It makes no sense for me to lie."

"Well, sir, you had a lot of stress going on in your life. You knew when we interviewed you that she was still in a coma and had flat-lined at least once. Maybe you panicked, bought yourself some time. If that's what happened, Dylan, tell us. It was an accident. The fact that you stopped and pulled her out of the water will be in your favour."

Calloway could see the veins moving in Ortega's forehead. He knew the man was ready to explode, but he didn't. He kept his cool.

"Detective, at some point Mrs. Charles-Dixon *will* regain her memory and she'll tell you what happened. And it won't have anything to do with me."

"The point is, she has remembered a couple of moments about the accident. They involve a black pick-up that pulled out and pushed her off the road. And since you are the only person we can connect to Miss Georgia that evening, that makes you a person of interest, sir."

"I may be a person of interest, but I'm not that person."

"Let's go back to your version of events. If another black pick-up forced our victim off the road, according to our time calculations, the vehicle should have passed you coming from the east a few minutes later. But … you saw no one. So you see, that is a dilemma for us," Detective Calloway said.

"Then I would say that he passed by after I turned off onto Old Ferry Road and that's why I didn't see him. You need to find the woman I passed heading west. If she was still on the highway, the vehicle would have passed her," Dylan said.

"Thank you, Mr. Ortega for telling us how to do our job," Calloway said.

His sarcasm wasn't lost on Dylan. "Anytime, detective."

Brown stood and headed to the door. "We'll amend your statement to include this new information, Mr. Ortega. We'll have it back for signature shortly and you can go."

Detective Calloway followed his partner out the door.

While they waited for the revised paperwork, Calloway grabbed them both a coffee. They waited in an office and watched Dylan on a remote screen.

"So what do you think, Scott?" Brown asked.

Calloway sighed. "He's right about her waking up and pointing the finger at him. But he may have panicked and made up the story because she was unconscious the whole time he drove to the hospital."

"And it was easy to perpetuate the lie the longer she was in a coma. But I'm not buying it. The timing works with his version. Our scenario really stretches the time-line to the point that either our calculations are wrong or he's telling the truth."

"Or he and his wife could be lying about the time he left home and the waitress could be out on her estimate of when Miss Georgia left the cafe."

A clerk brought the updated statement in and handed it to Jarrod. He flipped the papers back and forth. "So what's our next move."

"We'll put out a press release requesting the publics' help from anyone who may have been on the road that night between Port Arthur
and Bridge City. If Ortega's telling the truth, maybe we can find the
old lady he claims he passed." Scott stood, drained his paper coffee cup
and threw it across the room into the waste basket. "Bull's eye! First,
let's go get Mr. Ortega's John Henry and send him on his way."

PART TWO

*"One day I just woke up
and realized that I
can't touch yesterday.
So why the heck was I
letting it touch me?"*

Steve Maraboli

Chapter 23

Gibsons, British Columbia

Georgia placed her head back on the headrest and closed her eyes. Sean manoeuvred his way through ferry traffic and started up the hill that would take them into Gibsons and home. They'd stayed in the car on the forty minute ferry ride from West Vancouver to Langdale Terminal on the Sunshine Coast. She wasn't ready to sit on the passenger deck where people might recognize her and stop to talk. Besides, her headaches may have reduced somewhat but they were still intense. She was tired. It had been a long few days.

They'd flown from Port Arthur, Texas to Vancouver, British Columbia after she'd been discharged. The two days she spent in the Vancouver General Hospital were filled with tests and no rest. They'd been very thorough and in the end, Dr. Townsend, who Georgia trusted and come to like, concurred with her Texas medical team. *Go home and your memory will return.*

She felt Sean squeeze her hand. "Almost there, sweetheart,"

Her eyes popped open. Her heart began to pound and she started to shake.

Sean glanced at her. "What's wrong? Why are you trembling" He spoke in a soft, soothing tone.

"I'm scared to death," she whispered. She took deep gulps of air to calm herself.

He pulled over to the side of the road, undid his seatbelt and turned to face her. "Talk to me. Tell me what you're thinking?"

"I guess it's because I'm facing the reality of my situation here. In Texas, home was a long way away. The hospital became my safe zone. I mean according to you we're frequent users of that beautiful ferry trip across Howe Sound and yet it means nothing to me. And now I'm about to see the home we've shared for three years and I know I won't recognize anything."

Sean slid his arm around her shoulder and she laid her head on his shoulder. This was the most intimate they'd been since her accident but she trusted him. He was her life line for her past life and her present one.

"Listen to me. I can only guess how difficult this must be for you. But we have to be patient and give you time to heal."

"You mean I have to be patient. You've been wonderful and so supportive."

"And why wouldn't I be? You're a wonderful person, trust me. You've been a great mother and a very loving wife to me. You mean the world to me."

"You've shown me that the past ten days. I'm lucky to have you in my corner. I know that. What I'm afraid of most is the girls. You're an adult and understand my condition. But they're children. They'll feel like they've lost their mother. I don't know if I can handle the pain in their eyes when they realize I don't remember them."

"I get that. The thing is, you may not remember them, but you still have the same compassion and gentleness you always did. I've seen it. And once they get over the initial shock, I know you will help them emotionally with this. You're still you."

She lifted her head and mustered a smile for him. "Thank you. I needed to hear that. Let's go home."

Sean brought the few belongings they'd accumulated in Houston and Port Arthur into the house. He'd returned to Houston and checked out of the hotel, bringing Georgia's things with him and bought some new clothes for Georgia to travel home in. Their friend and agent,

Trent Matheson was in L.A. on business and Sean made arrangements with the hotel to close out his room account and give his belongings to Trent.

Georgia wandered around the ground level of the house, admiring the old country kitchen and the wide oak plank flooring throughout. Sean led her upstairs and showed her the bedrooms. He showed her the girls' room that they shared, one that was turned into an office, and a guest room.

"This is the master bedroom with an ensuite." He placed their bags on the bed.

Georgia stared at the king-sized bed. It was a large room. There were two bay windows on either side of the bed with padded window seats and pillows. The wall at the end of the bed had an oval rug in front of an electric fireplace, with two armchairs facing each other on either side. The walls were an almond colour. The bedding, curtains and accessories were in muted tones of green, burgundy, and beige. *A lovely room, warm and cozy.*

Sean cleared his throat. "Listen, I'll sleep in the guest bedroom and you can have this one," he said.

She looked at Sean. "Is that what you want?"

A quirky smile slightly lifted the corners of his mouth and his right eye twitched. "Well, no. But I thought you might want to settle in and adjust to your surroundings for awhile."

She searched his face. *Naturally, any husband would want to sleep next to his wife, especially after what they'd been through. But he's still a stranger, albeit a very nice one and so sensitive to my feelings.* "Thank you."

Their awkward moment was interrupted by the ringing of the door-bell.

"I bet that's Grams and the girls. They probably saw us drive by her house," he said.

Georgia stiffened. "Oh my God, I forgot you said she lives right down the street."

"And seeing that look of fear on your face, is why I didn't point it out to you." Sean moved closer and took her hands in his. "Breathe. Come on, sweetheart. Let's go meet your daughters."

She stood back from the door in the hallway as Sean opened it. Two exuberant girls squealed from the stoop. "Poppy." They threw themselves at him together, each wrapping their arms around his waist. Sean laughed and hugged them tight. While they were preoccupied, a spry, elderly woman side-stepped them and walked over to her with her arms out. "Hello, sweetheart." Georgia stepped into her arms, knowing it was expected.

"You must be happy to be home," her grandmother said. "I mean ... I guess you don't remember it as home, but it must be good to get away from hospitals and planes."

Poor woman, she's not quite sure what to say or not to say. Georgia threw her a smile. "It is good to get away from doctors and tests. Thank you for caring for the girls."

The woman flipped a hand in the air. "They're such good girls and no bother. You know I ... " The woman bit her lip, looking embarrassed and finished in a whisper, "... love having them."

"It's okay, Grams." Georgia used the name Sean had called her grandmother to make her feel more comfortable. "It's going to take us all some time to adjust to my current condition."

She turned back to Sean and the girls. The girls were holding hands, staring at her in silence. *Oh my God.* Two things struck her at once. First, how much they looked alike. *Which one was which? What had Sean told her? Shelby, her adoptive daughter has a thinner, straighter nose and is a little taller than her half-sister. Kaela's nose is like mine, shorter and wider.*

The second thing she noted was the look of utter fear on their faces. *They're scared to death, poor little darlings.* Instinctively, she fell onto her knees and put her arms out to them. She smiled her biggest smile yet to hide her own nervousness. "Where's my hugs?"

Kaela ran to her first. "Oh, mommy, we were so scared."

Shelby was silent and held back for a few seconds and then charged right in.

They clung to her and Georgia let them. She didn't recognize the girls anymore than anyone else in her life, but even though she felt a disassociation with them, instinctively, she felt a bond. *A mother's instinct or just a natural sense of compassion most would feel towards a child?* It really didn't matter at this point, and she relaxed into the moment. It wasn't as bad as she'd expected. *At least I didn't wake up hating kids.*

The girls let go and Georgia leaned back. She touched Shelby's face and ran her other hand over Kaela's hair. "My beautiful girls." She took it all in, finding it hard to believe they were hers.

"Mommy, is it true you don't know who we are?" Kaela asked.

Georgia looked from one child to the other. She knew she must choose her words carefully. "I know you're my daughters. The head injury from the accident is still healing and when it does, the doctors are confident my memories will come back."

Tears formed in Kaela's eyes. "You don't remember anything?"

"No, sweetheart. Meanwhile, we can spend lots of time together and you can both tell me about all the fun things we've done. Okay?"

Kaela wiped at her eyes, and nodded in response.

Georgia looked at her other daughter. Shelby still silent, looked so sad. "Would you like to help me try to remember too?"

The Crisis Worker in Port Arthur had told her learning about her past may not trigger the memories but she wanted the girls to feel connected to her and feel they were helping.

Shelby ignored her question and asked one of her own. "Do you still love us?" Her eyes were filled with such sadness, Georgia was overwhelmed. The question cut through her heart like a knife. *The psychiatrist also said not to lie to the girls; be upfront. How could I not say I love them? It would crush them. And how can I not love them? They're mine.*

Georgia pulled the girls to her and hugged them tight. For the first time since the accident, she let her guard down and let her tears flow. "Of course I love you."

Shelby and Kaela cried with her.

Chapter 24

"I feel like a bad person," Georgia said.

Sean smiled. "Don't be so hard on yourself. People who care about you aren't sure what to do. They know you don't know who they are. But on the other hand, they feel it would be rude to ignore you and not show their support. They all want you to know they're here for you."

"I know and I'm certainly grateful for their concern. But I've only been home three days and every time the phone rings, I cringe. It's so hard to know what to say to them."

"If they've taken the time to call, let them take the lead. It's their dime."

They were sitting in the living room.

"I guess I'm a little on edge because my mother is staying down the street at Gram's. She'll be here soon."

She studied Sean across the room. *How can I tell him it's the look in their eyes or the disappointment in their voices because I don't know them that upsets me? If I tell him, he'll realize I feel that way about him too. Oh they try to cover it, but I'm too observant. It's like all my senses are fine tuned to compensate for my lack of memory.* "When my parents were in Texas, you carried most of the conversation. You made it easy for me. Once you leave for your appointment today, I'll be alone with her."

This time, Sean laughed aloud and Georgia was taken back. "I'm sorry. I didn't mean to trivialize your concern. It's just that you and your mother have always so close and it's hard for me to imagine you being afraid to be alone with her. She'll know what to say to you to put you at ease."

"I know I'm being silly. It's just that she acts like I have an illness and if she makes me some chicken soup, I'll be better."

Sean stared at her in silence. "And if it makes her feel helpful, is that such a bad thing? Besides, what do we know about the healing properties of chicken soup?"

Georgia knew he was going for the humour to distract her, but what she'd said a moment ago sent chills up her spine. She stared at Sean with big eyes and her mouth hanging open.

"Georgia?"

She shook her head and sat back. "I ... I think I had a déjà vu. Who's Marian?"

Sean became excited. "She's your best friend. The one I told you about that lives in Whitehorse in the Yukon Territories." He proceeded cautiously. "Do you remember her?"

Georgia felt stunned. She pursed her lips. "I remember *something*. I said those same words to her once about my mom. Her response was similar to yours."

"Do you remember anything else?"

As hard as she tried, nothing more came to mind. "No." Disappointment filled her to the core.

"But this is a good sign, isn't it? Maybe your memory's starting to return."

Georgia brightened up. "You're right. This is good."

They both smiled, each quietly absorbing what this moment could mean.

"You know, this gives you an insight into your mother's coping skills. You've recalled a situation in the past where she exhibited the same form of behavior. It's who she is."

Georgia thought about her children. "Do you suppose that all mothers act this way towards their children? I mean, if you can't fix what's wrong with them, the tendency would be to nurture them, regardless of their age."

"Exactly, sweetheart. It comes from her heart, a place of love. Let her give it. All you have to do is accept it."

"Wow. You're a pretty smart guy, you know that?" Georgia felt better. The look in Sean's eyes as he gave her a wide smile wasn't one of disappointment or expectation. It was a look of love. She'd seen it before, only then it made her uncomfortable. However, this time it warmed her. She truly felt his love.

The doorbell rang. She knew it was her mother and watching Sean head to the door, her feeling of anxiety disappeared.

Georgia sat beside her mother on the couch. As they sipped their tea, her mother turned the pages of one of the many albums of family photographs she'd brought with her.

"Who is that?" Georgia asked.

Her mother laughed. It was a picture of a boy hanging upside down in a tree, covered with mud. "That is Kris. Your brother."

"Aw, the air force guy."

"He called the other day. He apologizes for not calling you yet. He's been busy since his Syrian deployment. He said to give you his love and he'll call soon."

"Is he in danger where he is? I've read about the situation in the middle east and it's very frightening," Georgia asked.

"There's always a danger element with these things. But Canada's role changed about three months ago when our new government was formed. Kris isn't involved with bombing attacks any more. They're doing refuelling, food, and training missions."

Georgia saw her mother's pain as she talked about her son. *It's not just me she's worried about.* She placed an arm around her mother's shoulders. "He'll be fine."

"His deployment ends in a couple of months and he'll be home for a spell." Her mother sighed. "Oh look … here's one of you when you broke your arm."

"How old was I."

"Five. You were very brave when they put you to sleep. You'd broken it in two places and they had to reset it."

Georgia chuckled. "Sounds like you had your hands full with my brother and I."

"Oh you both had your moments but you were good kids."

They spent another hour looking at the pictures. Her mother identified all the people in the albums and the occasions surrounding them all. Some of the stories were funny and they shared many a laugh. But since Georgia couldn't remember any of them, she felt disconnected. This made her feel lost. Her mother on the other hand, seemed relaxed and truly enjoyed telling her about their family.

When they were done, her mother looked at her with expectation. "So have you had any memories return?"

As much as Georgia knew it would hurt her, she sadly answered. "No." She couldn't tell her about her déjà vu experience earlier in case her mother asked for more details. It would be too difficult to explain because it was after all about her mother.

"You will, sweetheart. You need more rest and healing time."

Georgia frowned and rubbed her forehead. "I think I need to lie down for awhile, Mom. My headache's returned."

"I'll go see what Grams is up to and let you have a nap. I don't want to wear you out. We've had a lovely chat, haven't we?"

Georgia walked her to the door. Her mother wrapped her arms around her and Georgia returned her hug. She was getting good at giving people what they needed. She went upstairs and lay on her bed. It wasn't that she didn't care about these people because she did.

I just don't know anything about them. Deceitful. That's how I feel. I can't help it. I'm in such a lonely space.

She rolled onto her side and pulled a comforter up to her chin.

Will it always be like this? Me—on the outside looking in?

Chapter 25

ICE Headquarters (Immigration and Customs Enforcement), Buffalo, New York

Agent Douglas West pulled his collar up and held his hands over his frozen ears. He lowered his head and pushed forward against the fierce wind. *Great time to come off vacation.* He and his wife had returned two days previous from a two week holiday in the Bahamas. Feeling chilled to the bone was in sharp contrast to the hot, sun-filled days that had left a deep tan on his winter white skin. The roads were empty, save for vehicles abandoned by inept drivers and those involved in accidents that awaited tow trucks. All were buried in the snow drifts from the massive blizzard that hit their city yesterday. Even sand trucks had their hands full this morning as the temperatures had dropped overnight and the weather system was now an ice storm. Power outages were a given and soon the electric company vehicles would join the city trucks on even worse streets. The city was in a virtual shut down. *Smart people stayed home today.*

His team were in the middle of an important investigation. When his boss called him in to a meeting, he'd walked the six blocks from his condo to their field office on Delaware Street. He was an HSI agent (Homeland Security Investigations) targeting human smuggling and trafficking offenders at the US/Canada border. They worked with immigration and other government agencies.

They'd been working on a particular smuggling ring that took women and children back and forth across the border. Human trafficking is one of the most heinous crimes because they are usually underage victims, from all over the globe, who are forced into labour servitude and the sex trade industry against their will. They often don't speak English, have no paperwork and are controlled by fear and physical violence.

Agent West entered the building and made his way to their offices. He joined his colleagues in the conference room. His boss, Special Agent-in-Charge, Harry Riggs nodded his head. "Looking good, West. Must have hated returning to this weather."

"You could say that again. Coming home to the cold was bad enough. But this ice storm really slapped me in the face." They all laughed and threw comments his way.

"Poor baby. Sit down and I'll fill you in on what we working peons accomplished while you were playing in the sandbox." Special Agent Riggs passed some papers around the table. "Two weeks ago, DEA Agents (Drug Enforcement Administration) arrested a guy by the name of Timothy Dietz for drug smuggling into Canada. They were working with Border Patrol." Riggs pointed at another agent. "Alan, here, thought he looked familiar. He searched through our portfolio on the trafficking ring and guess what he found. Dietz also worked for the smuggling ring as a driver and transported human cargo back and forth across the border. We've been working with DEA and their perp, and knowing he faced a lot of down time in prison, he rolled over not only on his drug connections, but on our smuggling ring leaders. They're all incarcerated awaiting trial."

"Wow, I didn't think you could handle things with my being gone. Maybe I should go back to the Bahamas for a little more fun in the sun. It would be a sacrifice but someone's gotta do it," Agent West said.

His colleagues hooted and shouted word bombs while showering him with pens, paper clips and any other small items they could find on the table.

"Huh, fat chance, West," Riggs said with a grin. "Our work isn't over on this case. We now know who the top guy is of this trafficking group, it's Aylmer Teslin. However, we don't have any evidence to take him down. Dietz mentioned another name to us who has never been on our radar, Daniel Barton. Apparently, he runs his own human smuggling show. No priors. A clean record. He lives alone on Lamica Lake near Malone. Keeps to himself. According to Dietz, Teslin has tried to recruit him before, but Daniel Barton prefers to work alone. Dietz figures Teslin will approach him again, now his crew is busted."

"So what's Plan A?" Agent West asked.

"Barton, our subject of interest, was out of town last week. While he was gone we planted a bug on his phone and in his house, along with some hidden cameras. If Teslin does come calling we'll be listening. If not, we might catch ourselves another perp. Meanwhile, Dietz is in a safe house. He'll go into the Witness Protection Program."

Special Agent Riggs stood and faced a map behind him. He took a pointer and tapped the map."This is Barton's place. It's quite remote which gives us a treed advantage. This area is behind his house. This is an empty cabin on a property listed in an estate sale. We've acquired access to it. The story is a family bought the property on a time-share. We're all set up with surveillance equipment. Luckily, the access road into the cabin comes off a different road than Barton's. We have one team of two agents on shift this week."

Riggs turned and crossed his arms across his chest and looked directly at Agent West. A huge grin spread across his face. "We're pulling them out and we want you on point, West."

His colleagues laughed. One yelled out: "Wear your woollies, Doug." And another: "Don't forget your scarf and mittens."

"Okay, okay. Settle down," Riggs said. "You're on reprieve for now, West. The roads are too dangerous to drive in this ice storm. We're talking a five hour trip. The team that's there right now is pulling double duty until you can get there. Agent Morse, you're partnering with Doug. Your cover story—buddies on a ski vacation. Titus Mountain

Ski Hill is seven miles south of Malone. Take the unmarked four-by. You're there indefinitely."

Agent West smiled at Barry Morse who gave him a thumbs up.

Special Agent Riggs gathered his papers. 'Since we're here, we might as well get some paperwork done. If the power goes down, even though we have generator back-up, we'll probably call it a day."

His charges groaned.

No sooner had they all settled at their desk and powered up their computers, the power went. A big cheer went up around the office. In a matter of seconds the back-up power came on.

Riggs came out of his office. "Okay, ladies and gents, everybody gets to go home. West, Morse ... pack your things when you get home and be ready for the call. Everyone stay safe."

Chapter 26

Gibsons, British Columbia

Georgia watched through the picture window as Sean walked the girls to school. She hadn't been out of the house since they'd returned home two weeks previously. She wasn't ready to deal with the teachers and parents with their inquisitive looks, pitying stares, or questions she had no answers to. It was hard enough dealing with close friends and relatives.

It had been a month since her accident and her memory still hadn't returned. The headaches were still with her and she'd had no memory recalls since the hospital. She felt discouraged. *Is my memory ever going to come back?*

Anxiety took over and she tried to calm her nerves. Georgia sat down. She stared out the picture window to the park across the street and focused on her breathing. It seemed like a losing battle. The feeling of hyperventilating crept up on her and just before it took hold, a voice spoke behind her.

"Deep breaths will help you, my child."

Georgia spun around to see the native spirit called Nonnock sitting at the kitchen counter.

Her soft voice repeated a chant. "In and out, deep breaths and hold, slowly release through the mouth, in and out …"

Georgia focused on her iridescent grey eyes and concentrated on her words. Soon the anxiety passed. "Thank you." She joined Nonnock at the counter and sat opposite her on a stool.

"You're welcome. I'm happy to see you home and becoming stronger," she said.

"You say I know you but my memory hasn't come back. It's so frustrating."

"I know, child. You're fighting a huge battle."

"The hardest thing is sorting out what I do know and what I don't in the world at large. Like I know who the politicians are and their purpose, and professions like teachers and on and on. But I don't understand any kind of sports and I'm scared to death to drive a car. It's so bizarre."

"You must be patient and give your physical body time to heal. Meanwhile you're doing the right things."

Georgia sighed. "I spend many hours watching the news on television and relearning about life through movies. Sean taught me how to use the computer to look up definitions of things I hear about on the television but don't understand."

"That's good. You have a very loving husband who cares so much for you. You should be feeling grateful for his support."

Georgia's eyes filled with tears. "Truly I am. I know what love is but I'm not sure I feel it. I have compassion and warm feelings towards Sean, my daughters, and family members but the connection is still not there. Sometimes I feel like I'm floating out of body in the corner of the room looking down on these wonderful people who love me and wonder if they really belong in my life."

"You're still the same person inside. Don't give up on yourself."

"I'm afraid Sean will give up on me. He's still sleeping in the guest bedroom and I know he needs more from me. I have no concept about intimacy except what I've read about. I know what sex is but feel like a virgin. I'm not sure I'd know what to do."

"Child, Sean loves and respects you. By nature, he's a very patient man. How do feel when he holds your hand or hugs you?"

"At first, I felt anxious. Now I enjoy it. We cuddle sometimes in the evenings watching television. I feel safe. But that isn't love is it?"

Nonnock stood and stared past Georgia out of the window. "No. Maybe you need to talk to Sean about your feelings."

"He might think I don't love him anymore and he'll be hurt." Georgia frowned. "I understand what love is and obviously I loved him once. Do I love him now? I'm so confused."

"Talk to him. Let him in and he won't feel left out. You will know when you are ready to invite him back into your bed. Relax and time will take care of the rest. I see Sean is returning home so I must leave."

Georgia turned and watched Sean heading up the walkway to the front door. "Every morning I wake up with hope that today will be the day my memory returns. And every day is a disappointment."

"Do you remember in the hospital when I told you that this would be the hardest thing you'd ever face?"

"Yes."

"You must find your inner strength."

Georgia gave Nonnock a long stare. "I'm not sure I know how to do that."

"Return to the place of your rebirth."

"And where is that?"

A grey mist formed around Nonnock and when it dissipated, the spirit was gone. A voice echoed around the room. "Sean knows this place and he knows of me. Ask him, child."

The front door opened and closed. Georgia walked to the counter and picked up the coffee pot. She poured one cup and when Sean joined her she held it up and nodded towards the pot. "Want one?"

"Yes, please. It's a beautiful day out there but a bit nippy."

She took them to the counter and pulled out a stool. She studied Sean's face. "Do you know who Nonnock is?

Sean stared across from her with raised eyebrows. "I do. Do you remember her?"

"No. She visited me once in the hospital and then again this morning. She says she's a native spirit. A Tahltan elder. And that she's known me a long time." Georgia paused. "So is she real?"

"Yes. She's for real."

Georgia relaxed her shoulders. "I was beginning to think I was going loony tunes. What's our connection?"

Sean let out a whistle and ran his hand through his hair. "I've stayed away from explaining some areas of the past because so much has happened in your life. Nonnock is one of those complications. Your current experience is overwhelming enough; dealing with the girls, me, and family members. I was holding off until you were comfortable with all of us first."

"Okay. But if this spirit is going to keep popping up, I'd like to know who she is."

"Of course and so you should. I just don't know where to begin," Sean said.

Georgia reached out and touched his hand. "Start at the beginning." She watched the twitching of his right eye.

"I'll give you the facts first, straight up. The details can come later." He brought his hands up and rubbed his face. "Some of this you already know, so bear with me. Eleven years ago, your first husband, Colin, had an affair with his legal assistant, Julie. She got pregnant and he left you for her. Four months later, you went to the Yukon to visit your best friend, Marion for four weeks. You discovered you were five months pregnant as well. The day before you were to come home to Vancouver, you were kidnapped by bank robbers in Whitehorse..."

Her eyebrows shot up. "What? Please go on."

"They travelled into northwestern British Columbia into Tahltan First Nations territory. You managed to escape and disappeared into the wilderness. You found a cabin and spent the winter lost and alone."

"I did?" Georgia's head spun. "How could I possibly survive?"

"The cabin was well-stocked with food and you managed to salvage some meat from a caribou downed by wolves." Sean smiled. "If you could see the expression on your face right now."

"Me? You're kidding right?"

"No, I'm not. Physically, you did what you needed to do to survive. But you did suffer mentally and emotionally. Especially since you were pregnant and scared to death of childbirth all alone in the middle of nowhere. That's when Nonnock joined you. You had many talks with her about her life and yours. She was there for you."

"And how did I get out of there?"

"That's where I came in. It was my cabin. I arrived in the spring and a helicopter flew us all out. You were an overnight celebrity. A heroine to women everywhere. You wrote a book about your experience and a movie was filmed using the original cabin."

Georgia was speechless. Sean sat holding her hand while she digested this newfound information. "Is that why you've been fielding calls the past two weeks from the media?" Sean nodded. "I wondered why they were so interested in a car accident so far away."

"I was hoping you'd be too absorbed with what was happening inside the house and dealing with your headaches to notice."

"I might have lost my memory but not my hearing or eyesight."

"The media was around in Texas too, but we were able to protect you from them in the hospital."

Georgia reached for the lap top sitting on the counter and powered it up. Once online, she typed in her name. Her eyes popped and her chin dropped open. "Omigod ... I'm everywhere." She swallowed hard. "I have a zillion questions. Should I be reading all this?"

Sean laughed. 'Well, you can't always believe what you read on the Internet, hon. Hang on." He left the room and returned with a book in his hand. "Here. I think it's time you read this. Your story, written in your own words. It's the most accurate you're going to find."

Georgia took the book and stared at it. "And a movie, too?"

"And another book. But that can wait until you've read this one."

"You told me in the hospital in Port Arthur that I had written two books, I forgot to ask what they were about." A determined look crossed her face and she pushed her shoulders back. "You know, I really appreciate that you have been so protective and supportive. But I'm ready to take it all on now. I want to know everything."

Sean beamed. "That's the Georgia I know."

She could see the admiration in his eyes and that made her feel that much stronger. *Grab the moment, girlie. Hmm ... girlie?* She ignored the strange sounding word and spoke out before she lost her courage.

"I've been thinking ..." she faltered. She thought about her conversation with Nonnock.

"About?"

"I think ... I ... maybe it's time you moved back into the master bedroom. I mean if you want to." Georgia held her breath as she waited for his answer.

He didn't keep her waiting. His expression softened and he spoke in barely a whisper. "Of course I want to, but only if you're comfortable with it."

Georgia reached out and took his hands. "I am."

Sean smiled. "I've missed reaching out and feeling you beside me."

Her confidence faltered a little. He looked so happy and she wasn't sure how she'd react if he wanted something more than cuddling from her. *What if I'm a disappointment to him?*

As if he could read her mind, Sean squeezed her hands back. "I want you to know that I won't push you into anything intimate until I know you're ready. Okay?"

She relaxed and marvelled once again at his sensitivity. "You seem so in-tune with my thoughts and emotions."

"That's because I know you so well; your quirky mannerisms, your body language, and your expressive eyes. You're still my Georgia. The person you are is still in there somewhere and I'm waiting right here for you." Sean leaned across the counter and brushed her lips gently with his, kissed her nose and sat back.

Georgia reached for the laptop and typed in define quirky. "Quirky, characterized by peculiar or unexpected, strange, not normal." She looked at Sean with one eyebrow raised. "That doesn't sound very flattering."

Sean laughed. "By that definition maybe. I'd define your quirkiness as unconventional but so cool. And very appealing."

She laughed which turned into a snort. "Nice save."

"There you go." Sean pointed at her. "Your laugh that turns into a snort is quirky and one of the things I so love about you."

Chapter 27

The door to the girl's bedroom was closed. Georgia placed the heavy laundry basket on the floor and reached up to knock on the door before turning the handle to open it. Her hand stopped mid-air. One of the girls was crying and the other was talking to her. Georgia froze and listened by the door.

"Shelby, Mommy still loves us. She just can't remember the past stuff," Kaela said.

"But it's not the same."

"Sure it is. We're her daughters, she'll always love us. Here blow your nose."

Georgia heard Shelby blow. "She'll love you 'cause you're her blood daughter. All she's had of me is the past three years. If she can't remember me, she might not love me the same."

Listening to the pain in her daughter's voice broke Georgia's heart. She wanted to burst into the room and take Shelby into her arms and comfort her. But she held back. It was a private moment between the sisters and Georgia wanted to hear more.

Kaela spoke again. "If that were true, she wouldn't love me any more than you 'cause she doesn't remember giving birth to me or anything else.

"Darcy Brooks told me she should have died in that accident 'cause she's useless as a mom if she doesn't know who we are."

Georgia seethed inside. *Darcy, you son of a bitch.*

"Darcy Brooks is a bully and a stupid butthead." Kaela said. That made Shelby giggle and Georgia smiled. "You don't believe him do you, Shelby?"

"Of course not. It's just that I told Mommy on the phone the day she went away that I got an 'A' on my school project and she said she was proud of me. When I brought it home today, she didn't remember it or that we worked on it together. It's weird. And it makes me sad."

"Me too. I've shown her pictures of trips we took and I know Poppy showed her their wedding album. Nothing we've done has helped her."

"I heard Mommy and Poppy talking. They're worried she can't remember yet." Shelby said.

"I'm not giving up hope that her memory will come back. You shouldn't either."

"I won't." Shelby didn't sound too confident but the tears had stopped.

Kaela sounded so determined and strong. Georgia was happy she was there to support her sister. Another talk was in order with the girls, but she didn't want them to know that she'd been eavesdropping. She picked up the laundry basket and moved down the hall to her bedroom.

She lay on the bed and curled into a fetal position. Her talk that morning with Sean had lifted her up and hearing her daughters' struggle with her memory loss brought her back down. It was always the same. Highs and lows. Frustration was always the norm. A new word haunted her and jolted Georgia's psyche; depression. She wouldn't put a voice to the word; as if keeping it in her thinking she could ignore it and push it away.

Her eyes rested on the bedside table and the book she'd written about her winter lost and alone in the wilderness. She hadn't opened it since Sean gave it to her earlier that day. She picked it up and studied the cover of *Winter's Captive*. It was beautifully done with a picture of Georgia standing in a snowstorm by the cabin. She ran her hand over the picture, taking in all the details. She turned it over and read the back cover.

This is a true story of one woman's incredible survival against all odds in the Canadian northern wilderness, and her ensuing emotional and spiritual journey towards empowerment.

She got up and settled in a chair beside the electric fireplace.

Sean poked his head in the door. "The girls want to know if we can order in pizza for dinner. What do you say?"

"Sounds good. Umm ... what do we usually get?

"Shelby and I like Hawaiian. You and Kaela love pepperoni, green peppers, onions, and black olives. I'll order one of each." Sean looked at the book in her hands. "I'll call you when dinner is served."

"Okay." Georgia opened the book to Chapter 1. *This is me, my story. My very essence is in these pages. Okay girlie, let's find out who you are.*

Georgia took a deep breath and started to read.

A while later, she heard the doorbell. *Probably the pizza.* Reluctantly, she put the book down. It was fascinating reading about her life, especially since she'd written the words herself. She wished she could sit and read it all the way to the end but she knew she must join the others for pizza. She washed up for dinner and joined them down in the kitchen.

"Mmm ... so good," Georgia reached for a second piece.

"We always eat the leftovers cold for breakfast, Mommy," Kaela said.

Shelby nodded, her mouth full.

"Really?" Georgia said.

Shelby looked at Georgia shyly. "We can, can't we? Eat the leftovers in the morning?"

Georgia wondered if other kid's moms let them eat cold pizza for breakfast on a school morning. *Was it the best thing to let them eat for breakfast? Who cares?* She acknowledged the necessity that she and the girls do the same things they'd always done, regardless of what anyone else might think. The expectant look on Kaela's face and the blank expression on Shelby's face spoke volumes to her. Georgia knew that this singular tradition held a lot of importance to her daughters. She gave them a huge smile. "Absolutely."

The girls fist pumped and shouted. "Yay!"

They all laughed and Georgia ended hers with a snort.

Sean poked her arm. "Quirky."

That night Georgia exited the en suite into the master bedroom. Sean was already settled in bed, propped up and reading a book. *Our first night sharing the bed.* She felt awkward but was determined not to show it. She settled in the chair by the fireplace and opened her book to the bookmark she'd placed in it.

Sean was watching her which made her feel a little uneasy. *Maybe he expects me to climb in beside him.* Finally, she returned his stare. "What?"

"Oh, nothing. I was thinking about our conversation this morning when I said you're still the same Georgia somewhere inside. You never read in bed because you always fall asleep after a couple of pages. And here you are, settled in the same chair you always sit in at night to read. How'd you know to do that? It's interesting."

Georgia relaxed and shrugged her shoulders. "Maybe you're right and some things haven't changed about me. They're happening naturally." She settled back into the chair. "I'm really enjoying this book. It's like reading someone's diary ... except it's my life. I don't want to put it down."

"It must seem strange, reading things about yourself. I hope it helps." Sean put his book down and turned out his bedside lamp. "Don't stay up all night, you need your rest. Good night."

Hours later, after reading a section about Sean and the role he played in finding her at the cabin, she glanced at the clock—three o'clock. *Wow, where did the time go?* She watched Sean sleeping. She'd learned a lot about this stranger who was her husband from the book she'd written. Her own words were telling her that he was a good man, one the girls adored, and one she should be grateful for having in her life. She studied his face and smiled. *A very handsome man to boot and he doesn't snore ...*

The clock radio alarm startled Georgia awake. Sean reached out and turned it off. He sat up and looked at her still in the chair by the fireplace. His face turned to stone. He got up and disappeared into the en suite. She busied herself with the making of the bed and waited for him to come out. When he did, he left the bedroom without acknowledging her.

While she took a shower, Georgia pondered why Sean seemed so distant this morning. These past weeks she'd observed him enough to know that he usually woke up in good humour and ready to chat. She still hadn't figured it out, when she'd dressed and woken up the girls.

When she went down to the kitchen, Sean was nowhere to be found. The counter was set with plates and the boxes of pizza and the coffee pot had completed its cycle. She poured herself a cup and waited for the girls to join her.

"Where's Poppy?" Kaela asked.

"I think he went for a walk. It's a beautiful morning." Georgia said. They ate their cold leftovers and Georgia sent the girls upstairs to brush their teeth and gather their things for school. She packed their lunch kits.

Sean returned in time to walk to the girls to school. When he returned he grabbed a couple of pieces of pizza and a mug of coffee and disappeared once again. Georgia cleaned up the kitchen. *Something's wrong.* She refilled her coffee cup and went in search of her husband. She found him in his office on his computer.

"Are you angry with me?"

Sean glanced at her and returned to his computer. "No." Silence filled the room.

"Something's wrong, Sean. Talk to me."

He slammed his lap top lid down. "I should be saying that to you."

Georgia felt puzzled. "You *are* angry. I don't understand."

"I'm not angry. I'm ... frustrated. It was your idea to invite me back into our bedroom, not mine. Then you spend the night sleeping in the arm chair. I get that you may not be ready for us, but don't play with my feelings. I'd rather sleep in separate bedrooms then be made to feel like an idiot."

Georgia recoiled. This wasn't a Sean that she knew. "I never intended to sleep in the chair. I ... "

"Maybe not, but you did. I've tried to be so gentle and patient these past weeks. It's not all about you, Georgia. This is just as hard on me too." Sean got up and pushed past her. He grabbed his car keys off the hall table. "You pushed me away and it hurts."

"I didn't mean to hurt you. I ... "

"Well you did and it tells me that you still don't trust me." He left the house and Georgia waited in the office doorway to hear the engine start and for Sean to drive away. When he did, she burst into tears and ran upstairs. She flung herself on the bed and let the tears flow. All the fears and frustrations poured out of her. When she was spent, Georgia fell asleep.

She woke up an hour later and washed her face. Settling into her chair, she picked up her book to finish it. Georgia couldn't concentrate. She found herself rereading sentences and finally put the book down. *Perhaps Sean is right. I invited him back because Nonnock told me to think about it. Maybe I rushed into it too fast. But why?* Georgia looked at the book. She did want to get back to it last night. *But did I use it to avoid getting into bed with Sean? Not consciously.*

Georgia thought about Sean's words that it wasn't all about her. Her face reddened. She knew how hard it must be for those around her. *We're all victims in this situation, not just me. I have been a little self-absorbed. Understandable, but no excuse.*

The front door opened and closed. Georgia listened to the sound of Sean's footsteps moving around downstairs and eventually on the stairs. She stared at the open doorway to the hall, waiting for him to appear.

When he did, her heart sunk. They stared at each other in silence. Sean looked broken. "I'm sorry," he whispered.

Georgia stood and ran into his arms. "No, I'm sorry." They clung to each other in silence.

Chapter 28

Malone, New York

Agent Doug West stood and stretched his cramped legs, shook out his arms, and twisted his neck around. He'd been monitoring the video screens for a couple of hours. Their surveillance equipment was set up in one of the bedrooms in case someone came knocking on their door. They'd been watching the Barton property for weeks. It had been quiet. Barton hadn't left his residence except to cut wood in the backyard for the woodstove, shovel the driveway, and the odd trip to town for groceries. No phone calls of interest were recorded either.

The cameras inside the house showed him watching movies, playing video games, or sitting on the computer. *The man sure knows how to amuse himself. Me—I'd go stir crazy.*

The door opened to the cottage and his partner came in with a large bag of wood pellets. "Sure glad we have a pellet stove in here. It's a lot easier than chopping wood," Agent Barry Morse said.

West moved to the doorway which opened into the living room. "And you can control the heat with the pellets better than logs. But from what I can see of our person of interest's lifestyle, he needs the exercise from chopping wood. So far, his daily routine is pretty boring to me."

Morse opened the bag and poured some pellets into the hopper that fed the stove. "I don't know. Pretty peaceful here. No nagging wife or noisy kids. He might be on to a good thing. How about I take over for a bit while you make us some fresh coffee."

"Sure." West moved into the open kitchen/living room area. He set the pot up. "Think I'll get some fresh air while it drips."

He grabbed his parka and scarf and stepped out into the crisp, cold air. The untouched snow shone like diamonds where the sunlight reflected off of it. *It is beautiful here. Certainly a great vacation spot for weekends.*

The door to the cottage flew open. "He's on the move. Meet you in the garage," Barry yelled. He slammed the door shut and was gone.

Doug ran to the side door of the garage. As he entered, Barry was coming through the opposite door from the house. Doug took the driver's seat and hit the remote to open the garage door. Barry turned on the GPS tracker on the dash and tuned into Barton's vehicle. Doug started to back out of the garage. Barry threw his arm out.

"Wait. He's heading this way."

The two men stared at the screen.

"Holy shit, he's turned up our road. Better pull in and close the garage door."

Doug did exactly that and they watched the red marker move closer to their address. It stopped at the end of their driveway. They jumped out of the vehicle and ran back into the house. Through the living room window, they watched their person of interest get out and stare at the For Sale sign with the SOLD sticker on it at the end of the driveway. Barton turned to stare at the house. Doug gave the man a wave and headed to the door.

"I'd best be neighbourly and introduce myself. You stay here."

Barry walked over to the bedroom door and closed it.

When Doug walked onto the outer deck, Barton walked towards him. "Hi there. Can I help you?"

"I've been seeing your lights through the trees at night for weeks and wondered who might be at the cottage. It's been empty since old man Bridges died."

Doug extended his hand to the man. "My name is Douglas Prior. My family bought the place."

Barton shook hands. "Dan Barton. I live behind you on the other side of the trees. Just wanted to make sure there weren't any squatters here. Not many people live this way year round."

"Good to know someone looks out for the absentee owners."

"So you're living up here permanently?" Barton asked.

"Me and my buddy have been up on holidays for the skiing Not sure how long we'll stay. Last week my brother and his wife were up. We're a big family and we're time-sharing, so you're going to see different people up at different times."

Barry poked his head out the door. "Coffee's ready."

"That's Barry Coldwell. Barry this is Dan Barton, a neighbour."

The two men acknowledged each other. "Would you like to join us for a coffee, Dan? Barry asked.

"Uh ... no thanks. I'm off to run some errands around Malone. Enjoy your stay, guys."

"Nice to meet you, Dan. You're welcome to pop by anytime," Doug said.

Doug watched their case walk to his car. The man turned into their driveway and backed into the road to head in the same direction he'd come from. Doug gave him a wave and headed back to the cabin. He found Barry back in the bedroom following the tracking device on the monitor.

"Now what? We can't exactly follow him now can we? He thinks we're having coffee," Doug said.

"We'll have to use the tracking info. He's heading into Malone."

"I don't think he was being neighbourly. He was checking us out." Doug went into the kitchen and brought back two cups of coffee.

"Thanks. He's stopped, I'm switching to satellite." Barry zoomed in. "He's in the post office."

They spent the next hour following Barton around Malone on his errands and tracked him back home again.

Barry got up and headed to the kitchen. "Whatcha' want for lunch?"

"We've Chinese left from last night."

"Okay. I'll throw it all together in a stir fry."

Doug sat down and put the headphones on. He watched their charge put his groceries away and make himself something to eat. "Everybody's hungry. Our friend is making his lunch too."

He picked up a fiction book on the desk. A murder thriller. *My favourite genre* While glancing up at the screens every few minutes, he started to read.

The phone rang in the Barton home. Doug threw the book down and watched the man head to the phone.

He flipped the speaker on and pulled the headphones off. He turned up the volume so Barry could hear. Doug shouted: "Showtime."

Barton picked up the receiver. "Hello?"

"Dan, Peter here."

"Peter. How's biz?"

"Hopping. How's the ice fishing up your way?"

"Couldn't be better."

"I'd like to bring up a party on Friday. Can you handle it?"

"You bet. How many in the party?"

"Two. Usual package deal?" Peter asked.

"Yup."

"Be there about eight."

"See you then." Barton hung up.

Barry had joined him in the bedroom.

"Okay. I think we're in business," Doug said. He flipped the speaker off. "No niceties there. For two friends that call was short and curt wouldn't you say?"

Barry nodded. "Definitely sounded cryptic. Lunch is ready."

"I'll be there in a minute. Just checking to see if that number was traceable."

It was Friday night. Barry and Doug watched a vehicle drive into Barton's driveway and park. Three men emerged and went into the house. The time was right on eight o'clock. Barry enhanced the monitor picture to bring up the license number of the car and saved a picture. He then picked up the phone which was a secure line and asked dispatch to run a trace on the number.

Doug's attention was drawn to another monitor covering the living room. Two Asian men were invited to sit down and wait. Barton lead the other man into the kitchen.

A voice came through Doug's earpiece. "You getting this, West?" It was from one of the surveillance vehicles down the road from Barton's residence."

"Got it, Ryan. Two Asians. And probably Barton's man, Peter."

"You're right on time, Peter," Dan Barton said.

"It was an easy trip. The roads were good." The man called Peter handed Dan an envelope. Barton opened it and pulled out some large bills. He counted them, placed the money back in the envelope and put it in his jeans pocket.

"There's plenty more of that coming. Business is active right now."

Barton nodded. "Want a coffee before you leave?"

"No. I have to get back to New York. I'll stop down the road for some dinner. I'll be in touch."

Barton walked him to the door. Peter glanced at the two men. "This gentleman will see you to your destination. You're in good hands." He and Barton shook hands and Peter was gone.

Barry spoke to the surveillance team. "Heads up, Ryan. Your person of interest is on his way out." He held up a notepad. "Names Peter Vaser, 1128 Weston Rd, Muttontown, New York. It's out on Long Island."

"Got him. We're right behind him."

Barton sat down with the two Asian men. "We'll leave in an hour. When we get to our destination, you'll wait there for a few hours. I'll hand you over to the party who'll take you across. No questions. No conversation at all. The less I know about you the better it is for you. The less you know about any of us, the better for everyone. Understand?"

The Asians looked at each other and nodded.

Dan smiled. "Good. Now come with me. I'll show you to a room where you can relax until it's time to leave." He led them to a spare bedroom with a queen sized bed, an armchair and an en suite. "You can freshen up in there if you wish. I'll bring you some coffee and snacks."

Barton returned with a tray and put it on a small round table by the armchair. "I'll come for you when it's time."

One of the men lay down on the bed. The other sat in the armchair sipping coffee. They spoke quietly to each other in their native tongue."

"Showtime in an hour, boys," Doug said to the other surveillance car left at Barton's.

Doug and Barry prepped their gear and clothes. They would be joining the surveillance team once they set out for the border.

Chapter 29

Vancouver General Hospital, British Columbia

Georgia joined Sean in her neuropsychologist's reception room. She'd undergone two hours of cognitive testing and her head was pounding.

"How did it go?" Sean asked.

"I haven't a clue. The first hour was taken up with answering questions and being told to remember five things I'd be asked to repeat at the end of the test. I remembered three. The rest of the time I looked at pictures and identified them. Grade one stuff."

"What kind of images?"

"Animals, numbers, trees and rocks. Simple things like that. It was humiliating when I couldn't identify some of them. I feel stupid."

Sean reached out and squeezed her hand. "You're an accident victim, not stupid."

She gave him a weak smile.

Five minutes later they were led into Dr. Angela Toews office. The doctor went over the test results. "Our main concern is that your cognitive abilities are slow to return. All our diagnostic tests are normal. The second concern is that your memory should have returned by now. This rules out Retrograde Amnesia as we know it."

Georgia sat stoically opposite Dr. Toews. *What was she saying?* "If my amnesia isn't from a physical cause, then what's causing it?"

"It's possible that your amnesia source is psychogenic; a Dissocia-tive Amnesia."

Georgia was puzzled. "And what causes that?"

"Mostly, repressed emotional trauma from psychological distress. I'd like to have a psychiatrist assess you."

Sean leaned forward in his seat beside her. "I'm sorry but I don't be-lieve that. Georgia is the strongest person I know. She's been through a lot in the past and is a strong fighter."

"And it's because of her past that I believe we should pursue this. This current trauma may have been the straw that broke the camel's back so to speak and Georgia is blocking it mentally. At the very least, an assessment can rule it out," Dr. Scott said.

"Can you recommend someone?" Georgia asked.

"I can do better than that. I'd reached this conclusion prior to your appointment. We needed the cognitive reports to confirm it. I set up an appointment with Dr. Gayle Wassin at the Medical Hospital at the University of British Columbia." Dr. Toews looked at her watch. "If you're agreeable, she's available in an hour to see you."

Georgia looked at Sean. He took her hand and squeezed it. "I think we should do everything we can to try to figure out what's happening." She turned back to Dr. Toews. "I'll be there."

"Good. I'll give her a call and let her know you're on your way. Here's a map of UBC. The hospital and wing are marked in yellow. Good luck, Georgia."

An hour later, Georgia and Sean sat in front of a small, grey-haired woman, with warm, smiling eyes. "I'm so glad to meet you, Georgia. I have a copy of your medical records and am well-versed with your medical history. What I'd like to do is spend some time talking about the things that happened in your past. I realize you can't concur events since you don't remember them. However, Sean, anything you can confirm would be appreciated. Shall we get started?"

They spent the next hour going over what the doctor knew about her previous kidnapping, her winter lost at the cabin, childbirth all alone, and then five years later her ordeal with the stalker. Sean told her about Julie's death and their adoption of Shelby, Kaela's half-sister. The doctor asked Sean about Georgia's childhood and if he knew of any childhood trauma she may have endured. He knew of none. She also asked him about their marriage and the days leading up to their trip to the United States.

Dr. Wassin spent some time talking to Georgia about her time since she woke up in the hospital. How she was coping with her memory loss, her children, and her marriage.

"Most of what Sean discussed with you the past hour I already knew. Some of it, I didn't. It's very strange when I learn something I didn't know about myself."

"Are you experiencing any depression?" she asked.

"Sometimes. My headaches are getting better, which is promising. I try to stay positive. I feel depressed when one of the kids is upset because I can only tell them things will get better; and I don't know if they will. But after Dr. Toews diagnosis today, I know when I get home, I'll feel depressed. Mostly, I'm frustrated."

"Okay. So you're having high's and low's."

"I guess so."

"I have to say after spending the past two hours talking with you, I really don't think you're suffering from Dissociative Amnesia. I'm ruling it out. However, we can keep seeing each other to discuss your depression and I can give you some meds to help with that."

Georgia saw no point in continuing the visits to Dr. Wassin. She thought of Nonnock, whom she would never talk to Dr. Wassin about. They might think she was delusional. But her native spirit was her confident. She knew that from reading the first book about her life. She didn't like anti-depressant medications either. "I think I'll try to handle it on my own for now, Doctor. I have a strong family base around me and I don't want to take pills unless it's absolutely necessary. I'm already on pain meds for the headaches."

"Alright. I'll give you my card. You can call if you decide otherwise. If I did prescribe some meds, you'd come off your current prescription and I'd give you one combo pill for both pain and depression."

Dr. Wassin handed her a card. "Hang on a second." The doctor opened her drawer and shuffled through some papers. She found a pamphlet and gave it to Georgia. "This is from the British Columbia Brain Injury Association. They have support groups all over the province. I do believe they have one on the Sunshine Coast in Sechelt. You might feel more comfortable in a group setting with other brain injury patients. You may be the only one with amnesia symptoms but the common denominator for all of you is depression and dealing with day to day family life." Dr. Wassin picked up a prescription pad and wrote on it. "This is a referral to the group. You're free to call them if you so wish."

"Thank you for your time, Dr. Toews. And for the information."

Georgia stood and the doctor shook hands with her and Sean.

"Good luck to you."

Back in their car, they headed towards the north shore and the Sea to Sky Highway to catch the ferry back to Gibsons.

Sean glanced at her. "You must be exhausted. It was a long day."

"I am and it certainly was. At least we know I'm not psychogenic," Georgia said.

Sean noted the sarcasm in her voice. "It's one more thing they've ruled out. We'll go back to your neurologist and start again. Something is going on and we're not going to stop until we figure it out. Your doctors may not have all the answers for us yet but they're taking good care of you. They keep trying new things. Sooner or later the puzzle will be solved."

Georgia sighed. "I wish I could be as patient as you."

"That part's easy 'cause baby, you're worth it. Have I ever told you that I won the lotto the day I met you?"

Georgia laughed and her spirits lifted. "According to my book, the first time I set eyes on you, with your mud-caked face, and your clothes dripping mud and snow on the cabin floor, you scared the wits out of me. I guess I can't claim the same."

"Liar."

"What?" Georgia couldn't believe he'd called her a liar.

" It was a mere hour later that you pretended to be reading while you were lusting after my naked body standing in a tub of hot water behind you."

Georgia blushed. "I was not lusting."

"What would you call it?"

"Curiosity … maybe?"

Sean laughed. "Same thing." All the stress in his face was gone. He looked handsome and boyish; his eyes lit up with laughter.

She giggled, enjoying this light-hearted moment with him—one of the few they'd had over the past few months. Her face warmed for a second time as her mind wandered and wondered at the prospect of what his naked body *did* look like.

Chapter 30

Sean stood and reached for his jacket on the chair. "Time to pick the girls up from school."

"How about I come with you?"

He looked surprised. "Of course, if you're ready."

Georgia jumped out of her chair and headed to the hall closet before she changed her mind. "Just need to get my coat."

"I meant ready to face everyone at the school."

"It's been six weeks. The girls need me to get more involved in their lives. It's time."

He gave her a big smile. "Okay. Let's go."

They walked down the street holding hands. The school was a mere block away. To Georgia's thinking, they reached it all too fast. Other mothers were standing in groups talking as they moved onto the school grounds. Sean lead them to a group that Georgia assumed she always hung with. The women didn't try to hide their surprise at seeing her but they appeared to be genuinely happy she'd joined them. They all knew she didn't recognize them but made no reference to her memory loss.

The bell rang and the doors to the school flew open and kids rushed out, heading in all directions. One of the women turned to Georgia. "It's good to see you looking so well. I'm Carole, Jenny's mom."

Jenny had been one of the girls that had visited the house to play with the girls in the past couple of weeks. Georgia smiled. "Hi Carole.

Jenny is such a sweet girl. She's welcome any time." Her nerves settled down as they chatted like two moms.

A few minutes later, Shelby and Kaela came out the door, followed by a boy who reached out and pulled on the back of Shelby's hoody. *Darcy Brooks, I'll bet.* Shelby gave him a dirty look and pulled away from him. The boy laughed and was about to reach out and grab her jacket for a second time. Seconds before he did, he glanced up and Georgia locked eyes with him. She raised one eyebrow and stared him down. He backed away from the girls and joined some other boys. Sean and the girls called her one eyebrow stare her Dana Scully impression from the television show, X Files. *It isn't really an impression but one of my quirky characteristics that Sean says he loves so much.* She smiled, which soon turned to a laugh when the girls saw her standing with Poppy.

Both girls yelled: "Mommy." They ran to her and threw their arms around her. Georgia was so glad she'd come. She knew most of the adults and other students were watching her but she shrugged it off. They headed home with each girl on either side of her holding her hand. *This is a good moment.*

That evening, Georgia was tucking the girls into bed. After kissing Kaela goodnight, she sat on Shelby's bed. "Who was that boy that pulled your hoody today?"

Her daughter's face clouded over. "Darcy Brooks," she said angrily.

"Hmm... I thought as much."

"Why is he so mean?" Shelby asked.

"Whatever's going on with Darcy Brooks has everything to do with him and nothing to do with you girls. Behavior like his usually comes from insecurities and it's an attention getting device. It might stem from something that's happening at home with his family."

Kaela sat up in her bed. "We have things happening with our family but we don't have bad behaviors."

"That's right." Shelby said, defiantly. "A bad thing happened to you, Mommy but we don't take it out on the kids at school."

"I'm happy to hear that." Georgia studied her girls. "People act out in different ways. Darcy Books is acting out his way for reasons we may never know. But, I can tell you this. When he does or says something to you that you don't like, he's doing it to get a reaction from you. Once he gets that reaction he feels empowered and he's happy for awhile."

"He's not happy for long then, 'cause he keeps doing it," Shelby said.

"That's right. May I make a suggestion? Next time he does or says something that upsets you, don't give him power over you."

"How do we do that?" Shelby asked.

"By ignoring what he does. Say something nice to him and walk away. Try it a few times. When he's not getting a reaction from you, he won't have power over you and he won't be happy. He'll be confused for awhile and keep trying, but eventually he'll stop and find someone else to bully. I hate that he bullies anyone but he'll leave you alone."

"You're so smart, Mommy. Do you know this because it happened to you?" Kaela asked.

Georgia thought about how to answer the question. She realized that as long as she presented herself to the girls as a victim, they'd have trouble accepting the truth about her memory loss. Instead of tensing up at the question, she laughed. "Well, I don't know because I don't remember. But it probably did because bullying has been around for a long time." She smiled at her girls. "In a nutshell, if you can't change a situation, you can still change the way you react to it. And in Darcy Brooks case, that means not reacting at all. Okay?"

Shelby and Kaela made a pact with each other that they would try hard not to react to the bully.

Georgia reached down a kissed Shelby goodnight. "Love you, sweetheart."

Her daughter kissed her back. "Don't worry, Mommy. Your memory will come back. Love you."

Georgia joined Sean in the living room. She looked at him with a smile on her lips and tears in her eyes.

"What's wrong?" he asked.

Her smile grew wider. "I just had a very loving, heart-to-heart mommy moment with the girls and it really didn't matter if I had my memory or not."

Two weeks later they were back at the Vancouver General Hospital. Georgia's neurologist, Dr. Townsend opened Georgia's file sitting on the desk in front of her. "I've read the reports from your neuropsychologist and the psychiatrist at UBC. Give me a moment to check something."

Georgia and Sean waited while the doctor went through her medical records.

"Did anyone ever mention a SPECT scan to either of you?" Dr. Townsend asked.

"Not to me," Sean said.

"Nor me. What is it?" Georgia asked.

"It's like a more advanced MRI that measures the amount of blood flowing through the brain. It shows us irregularities in the flow. It's a nuclear imaging test that uses gamma rays. SPECT stands for Single-Photon Emission Computed Tomography. We see images in 3-D which gives us a better idea of what might be going on," Dr. Townsend said.

"How is the test administered?" Georgia asked.

"The technician injects a radioactive dye into your arm, waits for half an hour for the dye to reach your brain and takes pictures with the camera."

"Why wasn't this test performed earlier?" Georgia asked.

"Initially, you were diagnosed with Retrograde Amnesia. The standard MRI's were normal and we were all so sure that your memory would return within a couple of weeks." Dr. Townsend stood. "Give me a minute, I'm going to make a call and ask that an emergency scan be done as soon as possible."

They waited in her office for another fifteen minutes. Dr. Wassin returned with a big smile. "I called in some favours and we got lucky." She handed them a card with the date and time.

The third week in April, found them once again sitting in Dr. Townsend's office. Georgia had no expectations that this test would tell them something the other tests hadn't.

The neurologist joined them. "I have the results of your SPECT scan and we found something irregular."

Georgia's eyebrows shot up. She sat up straighter and leaned towards the doctor expectantly.

"There's a significant decrease in blood flow to the temporal lobes of your brain which I believe was caused by a traumatic event. We know you hit your head during the accident. Every other area of the brain has normal blood circulation."

"So this is what's causing my memory loss?"

"Long-term memories are stored in the temporal lobes. The scan indicates that the neural connector or thread that travels from the brain to the temporal lobes has been severed. A portion of the thread is missing. So yes, this would definitely be the cause of your memory loss. It is a form of retrograde amnesia that is very rare."

Georgia let out the breath she'd been holding in. "Can you fix it?"

"Unfortunately, there is no surgical procedure to fix the problem. It may heal on its own– or maybe it won't."

"If it does heal, how long will it take.?" Sean asked.

"We have no way of knowing. It could be weeks, months or up to a couple of years. Beyond that, there's a good chance it will never heal itself." She turned to Georgia. "If your memories do return, they'll start from your earliest ones and work their way up to your latest memories. And if the missing thread replicates itself, the longer it takes to heal, the less memories you may get back. They could return up to a certain age and stop. I'm afraid we have no set answers for you."

"Wow," Georgia said. "At least we know what it is and what we're dealing with. And there's still that hope that my memories will return."

"There is always that hope but I don't want you to waste the next two years hanging onto that hope. You have a lot to live for. If the worst case scenario happens, you have a husband, two daughters, and family members that love you and are there for you. You can create new family memories as you've been doing for the past nine weeks. I suggest you build your life around that. Move forward, my dear and enjoy your life."

Once again, Sean and Georgia found themselves driving back to catch the ferry home to Gibsons. Seam left her to her own thoughts until they were sitting in the line-up waiting to board.

"You've been quiet. Are you alright?"

"Yes. In fact, I'm relieved that we finally have the answer to my problem. At least, the tests are done with and no more doctor visits for awhile."

"What do you think we should tell the girls?" Sean asked.

Georgia stared at the water churning around the Queen of Cowichan as the vessel made her way into the dock. "We should tell them what the test found. I don't want to mislead them."

"Do we need to tell them your memory may not return at all?"

"That could buy us some time to rebuild our strength as a family unit and allow them to feel secure about the fact that I'm still their mother."

"True."

"But as the doctor said, we have to start living life as though it may not return. If we have to tell them later that my memory's not going to return, they might feel we mislead them. If they were to ask me if we knew this already, I don't think I could lie."

A thought popped into her head like a thunderbolt. She turned to stare at Sean's profile, trying to gauge his feelings. She reached over and touched Sean's arm. "How about you? How do you feel about the test results and what it may mean to us?" She caught the twitching of his right eye and swallowed hard. Since their confrontation weeks back, Sean had quietly moved back into the guest bedroom. He wouldn't discuss it, telling her when the time was right they'd both know it. *But that was before we knew what we know today. Maybe he'll find it all too difficult and the effort too much to handle.*

Sean placed his hand over hers. His fingers rubbed her wedding ring. He turned and stared deep into her eyes. "You and I have been through a lot. More than a lot of couples. These rings we're wearing represent all of the good and the bad. I'm not willing to lose all that we had, even if that means starting a new life together. I'm in this for the long haul, one day at a time."

Georgia searched his eyes for doubt. She'd seen the flicker of disappointment when Dr. Townsend had presented her diagnosis. All she saw now was love.

"Are we good?" he asked.

She nodded and gave him a semblance of a smile.

"We'll tell the girls everything…together," he said.

The relief she'd felt over finally knowing what was wrong faded as the reality of what they still had to face surfaced. An actuality still filled with uncertainty.

Her attention was drawn back to the sound of the cars departing from the ferry and she watched the vehicles disembark without really seeing them.

All this pain and upset over a minute piece of missing thread.

Chapter 31

Dan Barton knocked on the bedroom door and opened it. "Time to go."

The Asian men followed him through the house and out the front door to his black pick- up. He headed north on Highway 37 to Fort Covington. Twenty minutes later, they drove onto the St. Regis Mohawk Reservation and continued along Highway 37 to the west until they reached St. Regis Road. Dan took a right, driving deep into indigenous territory. A Mohawk Tribal Police vehicle passed them going in the opposite direction. Dan drove the speed limit and was grateful for his tinted windows. Ten minutes later they reached the cabin he always used to house his clients. It belonged to his partner's family. It was well-hidden from view and the neighbours never questioned it's occasional use. Most people minded their own business.

He led them inside. "No lights, I'm afraid." He walked over to a stove and stoked it. His partner had been by and warmed up the place. "Stay inside until I return."

Dan drove to his partner's home and honked the horn. Henry Reed climbed into the passenger side of the vehicle.

"Henry. Kids have been put to bed. How's it going?"

"Things are getting tight, you know? Have been since 9/11 happened. Now we have cameras posted at all roads in and out of Mohawk territory on both sides of the Canada/US border. More tribal police out patrolling. We don't even get to cross the bridge with a wave anymore. Sometimes it takes two hours to go back and forth. Hard on all our kids cause we don't have a high school on this side of the reserve. They have to bus over that bridge daily."

"It's not like you to be this jumpy, my friend. We've been careful, kept small and to ourselves. So far, we've been off the radar."

Henry wiggled in his seat. "Ya, well you don't know that while you were away there was a big bust. Teslin's crew got arrested. Almost everyone went down but him."

Barton let out a whistle. "This is bad news. But we both know Teslin got greedy. Too many people worked for him and knew about his operation."

His partner was silent for a moment. "I heard he's gonna start courting you again."

"No doubt." Barton sighed.

"There will be a lot of business floating around—that equates to a lot of money."

"We've done all right. You know I don't go for human trafficking, especially women and children. Our business has always been human smuggling with those who choose to migrate back and forth," Barton said.

"I know. But I for one could use the extra money we could bring our way."

"If you'd of stayed out of the casino and put it away like I did, you'd be doing well by now. I've been thinking lately that it might be time for me to retire."

Henry shifted towards him. "Really? Why?"

"For all the things we just talked about here. I have enough put away. Things are only going to get tighter with law enforcement. The Tribal Police don't like the reputation smuggling and trafficking have given the Mohawk people. They're working closely with agencies on both sides of the border. How would your wife and kids feel if you get caught and go to jail?"

"That's got me nervous all right. Look...if Teslin does come to see you, will you at least consider it for the rest of this season? We only work when the river's frozen, because there are too many cross-border agencies on the water the rest of the year. We've got a little time left. We could make a lot of money in a short period of time."

Barton put his head back on the headrest and closed his eyes. "And that could be when we get caught. You know if we're caught for smuggling we're looking at a maximum sentence of fourteen years. But trafficking in the sex trade industry could pack a sentence of twenty-five years. And if you get a hard-nosed judge, more. Are you prepared for that?"

"I hear ya. But we're talking a couple of months work here. Like you said, we've been careful. We could get away with it, buddy."

Dan sat up straight and gripped the steering wheel. "You know it's not only about getting caught. Trafficking of women and kids in the sex trade industry is over my line."

"Me too, but Teslin will get them across with or without you and me. And if not him, someone else."

"Maybe that justification works for you, but not for me. I'll tell you what, if Teslin does contact me and I decide to say no, I'll pass your name on to him. It's your choice if you choose to work with him. If you do then our dealings will end right there. I'll be retired. Deal?"

"I don't want to see our partnership end but if those are your terms—deal," Henry said.

"Teslin may end up being your only employer. I can't guarantee my New York City contacts will want to continue the arrangement if I drop out, especially if Teslin is in the picture."

"Well, it buys me some time until I figure some things out. Thanks, Dan."

"For what? Sending you to the devil? I'd suggest you strongly consider getting out of this business too when the season is over. Stay out of that casino and find other work."

"I'll think about it."

Barton turned the key and started up the engine. "I'll meet you back at the cabin."

Henry got out of the pick-up and walked back into his house.

Back at the cabin, Dan waited to hear Henry's SUV outside. "On the road again, boys." He led his clients outside. Henry exited his vehicle and approached the men. He looked the two border jumpers up and down, nodded towards the SUV for them to follow him. Once they were settled in the back seat, he turned to his partner. Barton handed him an envelope of cash money which Henry pocketed. The two men shook hands. Henry gave his partner a quick hug and got into the driver's seat.

Dan leaned on the open car door. "Take care, friend. Safe travels." He shut the door and watched Henry drive away. He returned to the cabin, broke up the coals in the stove to let the fire go out, locked up and drove off the property.

He marvelled at how light-hearted he felt. "Retired," he said, aloud. It was a bit of a shocker that he actually had done it. It wasn't his intention to take his thoughts on the subject seriously until the end of his smuggling season. But feeling pushed by Henry's revelations that night made it an easy one. He knew exactly where he would go. Staying in New York state was not an option. Once the break was made, he knew he needed to put distance between himself and those he'd done business with. He left St. Regis and found his way along Highway 37, contemplating a life of fishing, better weather, and a sense of peacefulness. Dan laughed. Becoming a law-abiding citizen might be a little boring, but he savoured the idea of it. Perhaps it was his age, not that far from sixty. *Maybe I'll find a girlfriend.* Living alone had always been his choice. He'd always been a loner and when he got involved in illegal practices, it was safer. He'd dated girls over the years but never allowed himself to get close. He smiled. *A little companionship could be nice. And the benefits could be enjoyed during the long hours of retirement.* Another laugh escaped his lips and he turned up his favourite CD and sang along.

He turned off of Highway 37 and headed towards his house. Dan turned into the driveway and parked. As he walked towards the front door, a number of vehicles pulled into his yard and stopped in a row, their headlights lighting up the front yard. Barton spun around and was blinded by the bright lights. His hands flew up to his brows to shield his vision.

Car doors flew open and men jumped out with guns drawn; all yelling at the same time.

"Freeze, FBI."

"Police, don't move."

"Down on the ground."

"On the ground, now."

"Hands behind your head."

The moment moved slowly, as if in slow motion. Barton lay on the ground on his stomach, his hands behind his head. One officer had a knee in his back, another a hand holding his head down, while yet another pulled his hands down and handcuffed them behind his back.

Reality sunk in. "Fuck," Barton whispered.

Chapter 32

Shelby and Kaela stared at Georgia in silence. They never interrupted her once as she told them about her condition and the prognosis. When she finished, as usual, Kaela spoke first.

"So if your thread regrows, your memory will return?"

"That's right."

"How much does it need to grow?" Kaela asked.

"It's minute, very tiny."

Shelby looked at her with big sad eyes. "So we may never get you back? You promised me you'd never leave but you did."

"Oh sweetheart, you've not lost me. I'm still here and I'm not going anywhere."

"But it's not the same."

Georgia's heart went out to her daughters. She reached out and took their hands. "Since I've been home, I remember everything you've said and all the things we've done together. We're building new memories. And you both have done such a great job in filling me in on our past memories. Maybe my memory won't come back, maybe it will only partially, but I won't forget all the things you've told me about our lives together or the ones we have now."

Shelby's eyes filled with tears. "Will you still want us as your daughters if you never remember us from before?"

"Oh, Shelby, of course I will. We belong together. Nothing will separate us. And think of all the wonderful things I'll get to experience with you both in the future. Graduation, boyfriends ... " The girls giggled at that. "... college, careers, weddings, maybe grandkids. We have a lot to look forward to."

Kaela perked up. "Well ... a tiny little piece of thread shouldn't be so hard to grow. You're strong, Mommy. You can do it."

Georgia smiled.

Shelby grasped at Kaela's positive strength. "I'm not giving up hope, Mommy. You'll get better," Shelby said.

"I hope so. But your father and I wanted you both to know that it's not a certainty and we must keep rebuilding our lives together regardless of what happens."

She gave each girl a hug. "I'm so proud of you girls. You've shown so much strength throughout this. I love you both very much." She sent the girls upstairs to get ready for bed. "We'll be up in a minute to tuck you in."

Georgia looked at Sean and took a couple of deep breathes. "That wasn't as bad as I thought it would be."

He gave her a wink. "Remember, one day at a time."

The beginning of May brought warm days and the scent of flowers. Georgia hadn't experienced any more memory recalls and she started to read the second book she'd written. As the story unravelled about her ex-husband's second wife, Julie, and their daughter, Shelby, the complications of Georgia's past life shocked her. The relationship she developed with Julie up until her death surprised her. And reading of Shelby's loss of both of her parents filled her with guilt. The child had suffered so much. *No wonder she feels abandoned by my not remembering her.*

As she read about the insecurities she'd felt about her relationship with Sean, she experienced guilt yet again. She had the utmost respect for this man who never gave up on her. He had a quiet strength she wasn't aware of with her memory loss and that explained his determination to stand by her side. A warm fondness towards Sean was growing within her. *Am I falling in love with my husband?*

And there was Kaela. Her natural daughter, struggling to find her own place in everyone's lives. She gained an insight into her daughter's character as she read about her love for Sean. And once she'd embraced her half-sister, a fierce sense of loyalty and protective love had emerged.

Then there was her stalker. That story terrified her. *How did I ever cope all those months?* An impulse to skip to the end of the book and find out what had happened engulfed her. In the end, Georgia decided it was important to read the story—her story—in sequence.

That night, Sean went to bed early to read. Georgia stayed downstairs to finish some chores and fold laundry. She finally retired for the night, heading to the ensuite to prep for bed. She stared at her image in the mirror of the en suite and made a decision. With the bed turned down, she left the room and headed to the guest room. The door was partially open. She knocked on the door and poked her head in the opening.

Sean put his book down. "Hi."

Georgia walked into the room and over to the bed. She held her hand out. "It's time for you to return to our room."

Sean never said a word. He climbed out of bed, turned the bedside lamp off, and let Georgia lead him to the master bedroom. They got into bed on their usual sides, meeting in the middle. Sean put his arms around her and she snuggled against his shoulder. "One day at a time," he said.

"Can I ask you something?"

"Of course," Sean said.

"When Nonnock visited me back in March, she said I should go back to the place where it all began. I'd forgotten about that dealing with everything else on our plate. She said you'd know where that is."

"I'm sure she means up north at the cabin."

"Reading my books, I think so too. The girls are almost finished for the year. What if we take them out of school and go up there? We could home school them for the little bit of work left."

Sean pulled his arm back and they turned to face each other. 'I suppose we could. Are you sure you want to be that far away from your doctors?

"There's really nothing left for them to do is there?"

"How about your headaches?"

"They're manageable now with my meds. I've even cut back on the dosage."

"Okay. One more question. Why now when we could wait until next month when the girls are done?"

"You know I'm fighting depression. I'm on a roller coaster. I'm trying to stay strong and handle it on my own. Another month of this and I'm sure I'll slip over the edge. That means more meds."

Sean stroked her hair. "There's nothing wrong with taking pills if you need them. I'm concerned if you think a geographical cure is the answer. I don't think it will be."

"It's not about that. In my first book, I wrote that I was reborn at the cabin, that I'd found the essence of my soul there. And when I left the cabin, a small part of my essence remained. Something in my gut tells me it's important to listen to Nonnock and go back to the cabin."

He leaned forward and kissed the tip of her nose. "She's a wise spirit and elder of the Tahltan people. We'll go."

They spent the next couple of days prepping to go and running errands. Georgia felt a new sense of peace and couldn't wait for them to leave at week's end.

Sean was in a meeting at the school with the principal, making arrangements for the girls to leave school. Georgia had just taken a load of laundry upstairs to fold when the phone rang. She ran to her bedroom to answer it.

"Hello."

"Hi. Is this Georgia Charles-Dixon?"

"Yes. How can I help you?"

"This is Doctor Sam Swartz. I'm with the UBC Medical Centre. Do you have a moment to talk?" he asked.

Georgia sat on the bed. "I do."

"May I call you Georgia?"

"Certainly, Doctor."

"Dr. Townsend spoke to me about your case. As part of our medical centre here at the university, we have a number of research laboratories for various brain disorders. We run clinical trials on various conditions. One of our trials involves traumatic brain injury. You are unique to us because you are the only amnesia patient we have at the moment. But your condition makes you a candidate to be a part of the clinical research for Neuroplasticity."

She shifted on the bed for more comfort. "And what exactly is that?"

"It's the brain's ability to form new neural connections, Neuroplasticity allows the neurons to compensate for injury and adjust their activities in response to new situations. In your case you have a damaged neuron thread that may or may not heal itself. With neurplasticity, undamaged neuron pathways can grow new threads and connect to other undamaged pathways which can take over the function of the damaged thread."

Excited at what she was hearing, Georgia sat up straighter. "So what does the clinical trial involve?"

"In order for Neuroplasticity to work, the brain needs stimulation and repetitiveness. We create a software package of brain stimulating exercises to the needs of each patient. You would work on the computer with these exercises repetitively for so many hours a day, every day. It's non-invasive and only requires your dedication to do the exercises. Your package would be modified to your specific condition for memory stimulation to include auditory and visual exercises."

"Wow. It sounds like something I should participate in. My problem is that we're leaving to go to our cabin up north in a matter of days."

"How long will you be gone for?"

"That's the crux of the problem. We're going indefinitely."

"Do you have a laptop?"

"Yes."

The front door opened and closed. Sean had returned from his meeting. He called her name and started up the stairs.

"If it's possible to delay your trip for a few days we may have a solution for you."

"It's possible we could do that. What do you have in mind?"

Sean entered the bedroom and Georgia held up her finger and pointed to the phone.

"If you could come in on Monday next week. I can show you the lab setting and what the program looks like. If you still want to participate, we'll sign you up. You can leave your laptop. It'll take us a couple of days to put your package together and load it into your computer. We'll give your some training and away you go. We can check in with you once a week or you can call anytime if you have any questions."

"Why don't I save us some time here. I would love to come in Monday and see your facility but I've already decided to participate. Would it be possible for you to have the software ready for Monday? I could come back for training when it's loaded but that could save us a few days next week."

"That's wonderful. Welcome aboard. We'll have the paperwork ready for you to sign on Monday. If all goes well, you can come in on Tuesday morning for training. Meanwhile, give me your email address and I'll send you more information about neuroplasticity and the program."

When Georgia hung up the phone, Sean was leaning against the doorjamb. He gave her a quizzical look. "What was that all about?"

"They want me to participate in a brain injury clinical trial at UBC Medical Centre. It's non-invasive, all done by computer and I can do it up at the cabin." She explained how the program works.

"It sounds like a positive step."

"I think it will give me a focus too. It could help me with my depression I think."

"I think you're right. Let's go downstairs. I'll make us a cup of tea and tell you about my meeting at the school," Sean said.

Ten minutes later, they were sipping tea on the patio.

"Mrs. Springer was very supportive. Since they only have about three weeks of real work left, she'll get their teachers to print off some exercises for them to complete under our guidance. She said the girls were both doing well and were moving on to the next grade at an above average level. And as we know, the month of June is review and field trips. She'll send the work home with the girls on Friday."

Georgia laughed. "Wait until we tell them tonight. They'll be thrilled. Now we were planning to leave Saturday. We could still leave Gibsons and go to the condo in Vancouver for a few days until UBC is finished with me and my training."

"Sure. That way you get to visit with your parents before we leave for the cabin."

"Everything's working out well. I really feel we're doing the right thing. I can't wait to see the cabin. It feels like a good fit to me."

"For me too."

Chapter 33

Cabin, northwestern British Columbia

Georgia left the door open to the cabin to let out the stale air. It was too early in the season to worry about bugs. But soon, Sean would reinstall the screen doors. They'd flown to Terrace and on to Dease Lake where they picked up their jeep stored at their friend, Tom's house. The drive in had been easy. Unseasonably, warm temperatures brought spring break-up on the roads early. With the snow all gone, the meadow showed signs of new shoots and the bushes were popping their leaves.

She wandered through the cabin, checking out each room to get a feel for the place. She wouldn't let the disappointment of not remembering a place that had played such a crucial role in her life pull her down. A fresh breeze blew through the open doors as Georgia unpacked groceries. She went upstairs to the loft and unpacked their clothes. It was a huge loft with an office set up at one end and a king-sized bed that faced east, affording them a beautiful view of the Cassiar Mountains through the floor to ceiling windows of the living room below. The loft took up the space of half of the cabin with a railing across it for safety. She walked to the railing and looked down at the living room below. The living room was the original cabin where she'd spent her winter lost and alone eight years previously. The addition Sean had built onto it was beautifully done. All wood floors and log walls to match the old cabin. There were sliding wall sections on both sides of the loft that could be pulled across the front of the railing for privacy. She stared out the huge windows at the snow-capped peaks of the Cassiars. *I may not remember it here, but somehow I know I've come home.*

Sean was out back in the shed, doing maintenance on the generator before starting it up. A few minutes later, the lights came on. She returned to the kitchen and made a pot of coffee; calling out to Sean to join her for a cup.

"In a bit, sweetheart," he said. "Just setting up the radio-telephone and satellite television signal."

Cell service to this remote area of British Columbia was non-existent. It was imperative to have the radio-telephone in case of emergencies. Their closest neighbour was a twenty minute drive away at the new mine site.

Georgia checked on the girls who were spread out on the floor in their bedroom playing a board game. "All unpacked?"

"Yes, Mommy," Kaela answered. Shelby joined her with a: "Yup."

She gave them a smile and a thumbs up. "Awesome."

Georgia took her coffee out to the porch and sat in one of the Cape Cod style chairs that Sean had made. There were two chairs joined with a wooden table top in-between, perfect for drinks and snacks. On the other end of the porch was a matching set. The peace and tranquility soothed her soul. She put her head back and closed her eyes. Her hearing intensified and she listened to the activity around her that the naked eye hadn't shown her—the rustling leaves in the breeze, birds chirping in the trees, the spring run-off in the stream lapping against rocks and the wooden bridge supports that lead to another meadow. Scurrying noises in the grass; probably field mice. A buzzing sound caught her attention and her eyes popped open. A bumble bee flew around the porch before it disappeared around the corner of the cabin. Georgia smiled. Insects were coming to life after all.

Sean joined her on the porch. "You look relaxed."

"I was thinking about how some people think it's boring out here. I just sat with my eyes closed and heard so much of what they are missing. Mother nature is teaming with life. What the eyes don't show you, the ears tell you. All you have to do is listen."

"Wow, that's profound. You've talked many times about this place over the years, but you've never stated it quite like that." Sean gave her a long stare.

"What?"

He smiled. "We're still like-minded."

"Even though I don't remember the house and area, I feel so at home here. I belong."

Sean reached out and squeezed her arm. "Then, we made the right decision in coming."

Georgia warmed at his touch and smiled. "Yes, I think so too."

They sat in silence, enjoying their coffee and the quiet solitude until a cry broke through their muse. "Kraa, Kraa." A black raven flew into the meadow and headed to the porch. It landed on the railing and stared at them.

"Do you think it's Grampa Feathers?" Georgia asked.

"Absolutely. He's the only raven we've seen around here in years and that's his favourite perch. Hi Gramps."

Georgia recalled all the things she'd written about the bird in her books. She hadn't finished reading the second book as yet. She'd brought it with her to finish. She studied the bird. His black feathers shone with an iridescent green. "He's beautiful."

The raven flew from the railing and settled on the arm of Georgia's chair. Feathers had been her constant companion during her winter at the cabin alone. He was there the day she gave birth to Kaela. And he came to protect her daughters when the stalker had kidnapped them and he helped the girls escape into the wilderness. It was then, they discovered he was the spirit of Sean's grandfather, a Tahltan elder who'd passed on many years previously. Of course, Georgia didn't remember any of this. She'd read it in her books. She cocked her head sideways like the raven and stared into his black eyes. *So what do you think, Feathers? Will you help me rediscover my essence here, black bird?*

The raven moved his head from side to side, a low gurgling croak barely audible escaped from the back of his throat.

Sean leaned towards the open cabin door. "Girls—Grampa Feathers is here."

Shelby and Kaela joined them on porch. The raven looked at the girls. Shelby laughed. "He's winking at us."

"He is too," Kaela said.

The black bird turned to Georgia and with one last stare, he flew into the meadow. With twists and turns and soaring heights, he dove back down to the meadow. Georgia jumped out of her chair and ran into the meadow. She ran around the perimeter and Feathers followed her, somersaulting in the air above her head. Sean and the girls were clapping and cheering them on. When the raven flew off into the forest, she turned and walked back to the porch. The girls were giggling and Sean looked the happiest she'd seen him since she woke up in the hospital in Texas with no idea who she was.

"I can't believe I could do that without bringing on a headache," she said.

"That's because you've returned home and you're relaxed." He held out his arms and Georgia stepped into them. She laid her head on his shoulder. *Home.*

They all turned in early that night. It had been a long day. Georgia and Sean laid in the bed facing each other. "Still happy we came?" he asked.

"You bet." She leaned forward and kissed him, short but firmly on the lips. It surprised them both. This was the first time she'd initiated anything more than a hand hold or hug. Something awakened in Sean. He moved closer and returned the kiss. All his pent up passion exploded with that kiss. Georgia found herself responding and their kisses became longer and more frantic. Sean moved one hand to her breasts and stroked them, paying attention to her nipples between his fingers. She rolled onto her back and Sean's hand moved down her body to find her sweet spot. When he did, she cried out—not with frenzied passion but in a frantic panic. She pushed him away.

The silence between them was deafening.

"It's too soon. It's okay," Sean said. But his tone was flat, his voice filled with disappointment. He rolled away from her and pulled up the comforter up over his shoulders.

She looked over at his back which now seemed like an impenetrable wall. *Why'd I do that?* She felt confused and the more she tried to figure it out, the more her head began to pound.

Eventually, she rolled over to her side of the bed, feeling the weight that hung heavy between them as they fell asleep—back-to-back.

Chapter 34

ICE Headquarters), Buffalo, New York

The ICE agents entered the interrogation room and flashed their badges. "Special Agent Douglas West, Immigration and Customs Enforcement and my partner, Special Agent Barry Morse," West said.

Dan Barton leaned back in his chair and folded his arms across his chest. "The neighbours," he said. His sarcasm was duly noted. "So what's this all about?"

West smiled. "Come on Dan. You know why you're here,"

Barton shrugged. "Afraid not. You take me down on my own property, haul me in here and leave me waiting for hours. And no one's told me why."

"Would you like to tell us about your activities tonight?" West asked.

"I got bored. I went for a long drive. That's it."

"What route did you take?" Morse asked.

"I went north on 37 as far as I could and then I came back."

West leaned across the table. "And what about your two friends, Dan?"

Barton's face was stoic. He stared the agent down. "What friends?"

West knew Barton was playing cat and mouse with them. "The two Asians you took onto the St. Regis Reserve. They didn't come back with you."

"Don't know what you're talking about. I was alone."

It was time to lay their cards on the table.

"Okay Dan. The game's over. We've been watching you for weeks. Here's what we know. Your New York connection brought you two Asian men tonight. You drove them to the Mohawk Reservation and turned them over to your native partner. He took them across the border into Canada."

"If that were true, you'd of arrested us all on the spot. All you law enforcement agencies are in cahoots with the St. Regis Tribal Police. Why would you let me leave and drive home? Makes no sense."

West tapped his pen on the table. "Oh, but it does. Let me tell you the why of it. We want you to work undercover for us."

Barton laughed. "I'm nobody's snitch. So you either charge me with something or let me go home. Either way, I've got nothing more to say."

"So be it. You certainly aren't going home, my friend. Maybe not for another twenty-five years." West said. He stood and gathered his papers.

Barton sat up straight and pointed at him. "That's for human trafficking. I've never crossed that line. If you think you have any evidence to charge me it could only be for human smuggling and that carries a sentence up to fourteen years."

West smiled. "You know the law, Dan."

Dan Barton pursed his lips. He knew he'd said too much.

"And we do have plenty of evidence. You see, a number of weeks back, when you were out of town, we paid your home a visit. Your house is full of hidden audio/video equipment. Your phone is tapped. Your car has a tracking device on it. We were there tonight at St. Regis with, as you said, collaborating agencies—Ice, Tribal Police, FBI, and local police enforcement."

Barton sunk back into his chair; a look of defeat on his face.

"Can we get you anything, while we prepare your charges?" West asked.

Barton glared at him and said nothing.

West turned to his partner. "While we're at it, we'd best draw up arrest warrants for Peter Vaser and Henry Reed. We'll put the word out to pick them up." He turned back to Barton whose face had paled. "Too bad. We really weren't interested in you or your partners. You only came on our radar recently. We're after bigger fish." The two agents headed to the door.

"Wait," Barton said.

The two agents turned around, set their paperwork back on the table, and sat down. Agent West folded his hands on the table and stared at Dan.

"Are you telling me that you haven't picked up anyone else? Just me?" Dan asked.

'That's right. The Canadians picked up the Asians on the other side, but your contacts don't know we've got you or them." West said.

Barton stared at his hands and took a deep breath. "If I work with you, what's in it for me?"

"We're after one man. Get us that man, testify in court for us, and we'll put you in the FBI's Witness Protection Program."

"And what about Vaser and Reed?"

"Vaser and Reed will be left alone in regards to this case. They won't be charged with tonight's activity." West said.

"If I do this, I might need my partner's help. What then?"

Agent West learned across the table. "Let me make it clear. He'll get immunity from prosecution but only while you're working for us on this case. If down the road, he and Vaser continue what they're doing under different circumstances and we arrest them, they'll face the consequences. Fair enough?"

Barton nodded affirmatively. "So who is the man you want me to take down for you?"

"Teslin—Aylmer Teslin," West said.

A smile starting slowly at the corners of Dan Barton's mouth, grew into a broad beam. "I just might enjoy this gig. I hate Aylmer Teslin and what he represents. I'd love to see him brought to his knees."

The two agents exchanged a glance.

"Is there anything personal in this, Dan? We can't have you compromise our case if you attack this as a personal vendetta." Agent West asked.

"Nope. My relationship with Teslin is non-existent. He admires and respects my operation. On a number of occasions he's tried to recruit me. The problem is I detest his operation. Women and children trafficked across the line against their will is not how I want to make my money."

"And that's why we feel you're the best man to work with us on this," Agent Morse said. "But hear me on this. Maybe you don't deal with the sex trade industry, running women and children, or drugs, but what you do is still illegal and jeopardizes the security of our country. How do you know you aren't transporting terrorists?"

"Because I scan my clients carefully. If I don't like their looks, I won't carry them. And t if they don't pass the scrutiny of my partner, he has the right to refuse transfer from me to him."

"Well your holier than thou attitude is commendable to a point, sir. But people don't sneak across the border to go have tea with their mothers. What you do is still against the law," Morse said.

West added. "One more thing. We can't let you keep any money exchanges with Teslin. You'll have to turn all monies over to us. We'll pay you as an informant and cover monies you might need to pay out to Reed. But if things go the way we hope, you won't get as far as the reserve and your partner. The takedown will happen before then."

"All right. There's one other issue. Under witness protection, I know where I want to go. I have the say in that, not the FBI."

"I'll have to run that past them. It can't be anywhere anyone knows you under your old name, no family connections, etc."

"I have no family. I changed my name years ago, so no one knows what my birth name was. The few friends I have are here in Malone or on the Mohawk Reservation. Put it all in writing and I'll sign it, but only after my lawyer approves it."

Agent West pushed a blank sheet of paper towards Dan. "Write down the relocation site you'd like to move to. We'll take care of it," West said.

The agents stood once again and gathered their papers.

"I'd sure like a sandwich and a black coffee while I'm waiting," Barton said.

"You've got it," West said.

Outside the room, the agents pumped air and fist bumped. Agent West mouthed the word, "Yes."

Malone, New York

Dan Barton poured a shot of whiskey into each of the two glasses on the counter. He headed into the living room. As he handed his guest one, he glanced out of the window. Two henchmen leaned against his guest's car, smoking cigarettes. *Don't they know smoking is dangerous to their health?*

"Whatcha staring at?" Aylmer Teslin asked.

"Your guys. I don't understand why anyone who can read would smoke."

Teslin laughed. "Those two probably can't read. Their talents lie in other areas, if you know what I mean."

Dan sat down opposite his visitor. "So what can I do for you today?"

"You were away awhile back. Don't know if you knew my team got nabbed by the authorities. A driver turned snitch on me. Wasn't even trucking for me. It was his own stint. The coward turned in my crew for immunity. Fortunately, they had nothing on me."

"Ya, I heard. You got lucky there."

"I've been laying low for a few months. Took my girlfriend to Mexico for some fun in the sun. But I need to get back to business now."

"And what's that got to do with me?"

"I have a proposition for you. Let's become partners. The big bucks are in the services I offer."

Dan shifted back into his seat. "I figured you'd be back to see me when you lost your crew. We've been down this road before, Teslin. I like my set-up. It's small and I've managed to stay under the radar."

Teslin leaned forward. He shook his head. "I have a lot of respect for you, Dan. We could do well together."

"You certainly don't need a partner. You've cornered most of the market over the years. And why me? There are others out there."

"Because you're the only one I trust. You're right in that you've flown under the radar. That's because you're discreet and so is your team. My business needs you."

Dan studied the man sitting before him. It was time to reel him in. "I'll let you in on a little secret. After the feds busted your guys, I did some real soul searching. I have a nice little nest egg. I'm thinking it's time for me to retire."

Teslin choked on his whiskey. "Retire? Retire? People like you and me don't retire. What'll you do with yourself?"

"What I always do when I'm not transporting goods. Fishing. I'll just do more of it."

Teslin sat back and studied Dan. "I'll tell you what. Give me three months work. You'll be far too busy working to fish. But you'll be making a shit load of dough. If I like your team, I'll take them on and you can follow your dreams."

"I could get caught with a few months work, especially if I'm out there on a regular basis. If I retire now, it's done. I don't know if it's worth the risk." Dan stood and reached for Teslin's glass. "Another one?"

The man handed his glass to Dan. "Sure. That's good whiskey. What is it?

"Single malt scotch, Glenfiddoch. Only stuff I'll drink."

Dan poured them another drink and returned to the living room. He stood staring out the window. Finally, he turned back to Teslin.

"If I'm going to take a chance on this, it has to be worth my time and the risk. So … partners, fifty-fifty split, and I'll give you six months.

"Really? Why six months?"

"Because six months will add to my retirement fund quite nicely. Anything less won't cut it. And one more thing. I only deal with you, no go-betweens."

Teslin stared hard at him. "I don't know about that Dan. I'm sitting here because I've never put myself on the front lines. It's a rule I've never broken."

"And I'm standing here because I've never dealt with a middle man. The more people involved, the more likely it is to get caught."

Dan knew he was taking a chance challenging Teslin, but if he didn't work directly with him, ICE wouldn't get what they wanted. "Partners work together and that way they can protect each other. If you need me and my team like you say, you'll have to break your rule."

They stared at each other in silence. Dan decided to say nothing more. He'd outwait the man. He concentrated on sipping his whiskey.

Teslin stood, clinked his glass against Dan's. "Only for you, friend. Here's to partners."

Dan smiled. "To partners."

The two men downed their drinks and shook hands. Dan walked Aylmer to the door.

"I'll be in touch soon. Get your team on the ready," Aylmer said.

Dan watched the three men climb in the black Escalade and drive away. He shut the door and turned to where he knew a hidden camera was recording and gave it a thumbs up.

Chapter 35

Cabin, northwestern British Columbia

Georgia slept late the next morning, waking to the smell of coffee and bacon. She slipped into a pair of jeans and a t-shirt and padded down the stairs in bare feet and into the bathroom. Voices from the kitchen carried through the walls. She smiled. The girls were talking up a storm and all she heard from Sean was the odd, 'Mmm …' or 'Uh-huh …'.

When she joined them, the girls ran and gave her a hug. Sean was at the stove making pancakes. He spoke to her over his shoulder. "Your coffee's on the table."

"Sit down, Mommy," Kaela said. "Me and Shelby are helping Poppy make breakfast."

She sat down and sipped her coffee. "Mmm … this is good."

The girls bustled around setting the table and soon they were all sitting together enjoying Sean's efforts. Georgia was grateful for the girls banter. They were both in great moods and had no idea how there humour and antics were covering for the fact that she and Sean hadn't spoken a word to each other, let alone looked at each other. At least not at the same time. There were moments when she felt his gaze upon her and she stole glances his way when he wasn't looking.

After breakfast, as Georgia cleaned up the kitchen, Sean spoke to the girls. "You have schoolwork to do and I have wood to chop. I'll see you all later." The girls groaned. Georgia turned from the sink to see

Sean disappearing down the hall to the back door. "No complaining, girls. Remember our deal when we took you out of school early. While you two sit at the table and do your work, I'll set up the laptop in the office and work on my exercises for UBC. Okay?"

"Okay," the girls chorused.

After lunch, Sean decided they should hike down to his favourite fishing hole. He was pleasant enough but still hadn't looked at her. She felt frustrated because she didn't know how to open up the dialogue with him about last night. And if she did, she had no idea what to say to him about it.

"I think I'll stay here and finish reading my second book. I have a slight headache from concentrating on my exercises all morning."

Sean finally looked at her but his face was blank. *Maybe he thinks I don't want to be near him. Maybe I don't.*

"You do that. Come on, girls. Let's go to the shed and dig out the tackle and rods."

Georgia escaped to the loft and lay on the bed. She rested her eyes for a bit, hoping to fall asleep. When that didn't happen, she sat up and picked up her book. The next few hours took her through to the final hours with the stalker who'd kidnapped her. *I killed him. Wow. Where did that come from.* She couldn't believe she was capable of killing a man. *He was a bastard for sure, but still.* Georgia stared at her hands. They began to shake. *I held a gun in my hands and shot a man to death. How could I not carry the guilt of that.* She threw the book across the room, ashamed of what the woman she no long knew had done. She stared out the windows at the Cassiars, lost in thought, unaware that Nonnock had joined her.

"Hello, child."

Georgia gasped in surprise. "Uh ..." She turned to see the native spirit sitting on the opposite site of the bed. "You startled me."

"I'm sorry. It's good you returned to your beginnings here. But you are in a bad way today. Tell me what's troubling you."

Georgia sighed. "A lot of things."

"Why did you toss your book."

"I killed a man, Nonnock. I can't even believe I'm saying those words."

"If you hadn't, he would have killed you. Child, you must finish reading the book. Instead of judging the person you have no memory of, you need to find out more about who your stalker was and what he was capable of. Then you'll understand."

"And what kind of mother sends her kids into the wilderness to fend for themselves?" Georgia shook her head in disbelief.

Nonnock reached across the bed and grabbed her arm firmly. "Georgia ... did you hear what I said?" The Elder's sharp words cut through Georgia's wall of confusion.

"Yes, finish the book."

"It's all there for you to understand."

Nonnock released her arm. "Now what else is upsetting you?"

Georgia frowned. "I just realized that if my memories start to return, I'll relive the pain of all the bad things that happened to me in the past."

"Do you remember reading in your first book, about how your fear of the unknown kept you mentally paralyzed?"

Georgia nodded.

"This is the same thing, child. If the bad memories return, you know they are in the past. You overcame them and survived. You are a survivor and always will be."

Georgia weighed her words. "That Georgia was a very brave and strong woman. What if I can't live up to her?"

Nonnock laughed a sound like the tinkling of glasses. "Silly, girl. You *are* that Georgia. You just don't remember her."

This made Georgia smile. "It's easy to forget I'm her. So often I feel I'm on the outside of my body looking in. I feel my sense of self is lost more than my memory. Everything I gained as a person and a woman is gone. I want to get back in and connect my body and soul once more."

"I understand. But know that fundamentally your soul is still there. Your battle is a tough one but you must not give up. If you lose this war within yourself, you'll never be happy."

"I worry about the girls. But they're so much more resilient than we adults. They seem to be finding their way through all of this. Some days it's like role reversal. They're the adults and I'm the child. And Sean ... what's there to say. He's wonderful and so patient." She paused. "I disappointed him last night. It seems I'm always hurting him."

"I'm sure that's not your intention. He knows that."

Georgia wasn't entirely comfortable talking to Nonnock about intimacy. But she learned from her books that Nonnock had always been her mentor and was a very wise woman. *God knows I could use a woman to talk to.* She took a deep breath and plunged into the issue. "Sean and I have been sharing a bed for a number of weeks now ...never intimately. I started something with him last night and he responded passionately. Then I panicked and shut it down. It hurt him and I feel terrible."

"Do you know why you reacted in that manner/"

Georgia snorted. "I've been asking myself that all day."

"Any conclusions/"

"Oh, Nonnock ... I still have procedural memory and know how to do a lot of things. But ... " Georgia trailed off.

"What are you trying to say?"

"That I'm thirty-eight years old and once he started to make love to me, other than kissing, which I've seen on television over the past few months, I didn't know how to respond ..." Once Georgia started talking, she couldn't stop. "...I mean he knew what he was doing—boy, did he know what he was doing. But I didn't know what to do in return...to him. My knowledge of sex is something I lost in the accident. I felt like a virgin and lost my nerve."

"I get it. But, my dear, you and Sean go back a lot of years. You must get over thinking of him as a stranger and tell him what you're feeling. Sean is a good man. He can help you."

"You're probably right," Georgia said. But she didn't sound too confident. "I guess I'm afraid I won't please him anymore and he'll be disappointed."

"As I said Sean can help you. He remembers what your lovemaking was like. He'll teach you—but first you have to tell him."

Georgia picked at a thread in the comforter and it reminded her of the missing thread in her head. She looked up at Nonnock. "What if my brain doesn't heal and my memory never returns? That's not something I have control over."

Nonnock rose and walked around the bottom of the bed. She sat on the edge beside her and took placed in hand in Georgia's.

"If that happens, you will build new memories. The future is yours to mold however you choose child. There's a mythologist and writer. His name is Joseph Campbell. He once wrote these words:

We must let go of the life we planned so as to accept the one that is waiting for us."

"Wise words; easy to say, not so easy to live. I'm afraid if my memory doesn't return, Sean will fall out of love with me because I'll never be the Georgia he fell n love with. If he can't handle the disappointment of that, we're doomed."

"Sean is fighting his own inner battles. But he's proven to you he's trying and wants to continue to try. Again, it goes back to fearing the unknown. Maybe your relationship won't survive your memory loss if it's permanent. But if it breaks down, wouldn't you rather know that you both tried your best, rather than sealing its failure by isolating yourself out of fear?"

Georgia gave Nonnock a grim smile. "I've got a lot of issues and you've given me lots to think about."

"It's time for me to leave. We've discussed a lot today. My final words—finish reading the book. The answers are all in there." With that, Nonnock was gone in a swirl of mist.

Georgia watched the white haze dissipate ending her vision of Nonnock. One word resonated in her mind. *Fear. Funny. I thought I'd dealt with that one years ago. Now here it is haunting me once again. One thing's apparent. if I let this phobia get a grip on me, I'll lose Sean for sure.*

Chapter 36

It was now the second week in June. The girls had finished their exercises and Sean had driven them into Dease Lake that morning to mail their final schoolwork to their teachers back home. Georgia wasn't expecting them for a few more hours. She stayed behind, dedicating her mornings to her study program for the Medical Centre at UBC. The exercises were repetitive and some days it was hard to keep her focus. But she knew if the program helped her, the benefits were life-changing. She vowed to keep at them.

Finished with her work for the day, she settled on the bed to finish the last chapters of her book. Georgia hadn't picked it up since her visit with Nonnock. She hadn't felt ready until now. Every time she finished another chapter, she relived the pain of her situation—then and now. Emotions were high and the tension still hung in the air since the night she'd pushed Sean away. Georgia had tried to talk to him. She was willing to bring her wall down but Sean built his taller and thicker. He wouldn't let her in. One excuse led to another. We'll talk later, he'd say, or there's nothing to talk about, or she wasn't ready, or leave it, I don't want to discuss it. Frustration levels rose and they were at an impasse.

Georgia picked up the book and began reading from where she'd killed her stalker. Tears ran down her cheeks when Sean found the girls at the waterfall. But as she read further, it was her conversation with Sean when they were reunited that chilled her the bone.

"I killed him, Sean"

"The man kidnapped you and your kids and he beat you. If the only way for you to escape him was to shoot him, then he deserved to die."

"But I had the gun. I could have fired a warning shot or wounded him when he charged me."

"If you hadn't shot him, he may have overpowered you. Look at yourself, Georgia. You're badly injured. There's no guarantees a warning shot or an injury would have stopped him."

Sean changed his approach. "There was a briefcase on the seat beside you in the car. Do you know what was in it?"

"No, I didn't open it."

"When you went into the ditch it must have fallen on the floor and flipped open. There were pictures of women, Georgia. Lots of women, beaten and dead. Dates, maps marked with X's, including his wife's, to indicate their burial locations. Journals with details of the last twenty years of his life. I read some of it while we waited for the Medi-vac. He was a demented murderer and a serial killer."

"I was so lucky."

"Georgia, for twenty years that man terrorized, and murdered women and held them under mental and physical slavery. Don't let him hold you under mental slavery after he's dead."

"What did you say?"

"What?"

"When I passed out in the ditch, I had a vision. Nonnock said to me, 'Don't lock your mind into mental slavery'."

"Then, I guess you needed to hear it again, my love."

A shudder ran down her spine. Her hands started to shake first, moving through her body to the tips of her toes, causing her to drop the book. *This is what Nonnock wanted me to read.* Georgia retrieved the book and continued on to the last chapter dedicated to her wedding to Sean here at the cabin. The preparations for the ceremony as she contemplated her vows with Sean captivated her. Georgia giggled at the cuteness of the girls in their dual roles of ring bearers and flower girls. She was profoundly moved when she read Sean's vows to her and laughed loudly at his humour.

"Georgia, I take you to be my wife, my friend, my partner, my love, and embrace the responsibility of being a father to your children. From the first moment I saw you, I knew you were the one for me. Your beauty, heart, and mind inspire me. I promise to be honest and faithful–and as the only man in a household with three females, I promise to put the toilet seat down."

Then came the part where Sean spoke to each of the girls. First he took hold of Kaela's hand.

"The first time I saw you, you were this tiny little bundle of joy. You opened my heart and taught me a different kind of love. I promise to be there for you, to guide you, and protect you." Sean opened his hand to reveal a white gold amulet on a white gold chain. He placed the pendant around her neck. *"I give you this amulet engraved with the wolf. Like the wolf, you're strong and intelligent, and have proven yourself as a great protector. The wolf represents family and togetherness. Welcome to my family."*

Georgia was overwhelmed with emotion. She continued reading as he turned to Shelby.

"My dear, sweet Shelby, I thought I was blessed to gain one daughter, and now I have two. You're the quiet one–thank God." Another laugh echoed through the trees. Sean looked over at Kaela and gave her a wink. He placed the second pendant around her neck. *"You're a deep thinker and an old soul. I promise to be there for you, to guide you, and protect you. I give you this amulet engraved with the hummingbird, not only because you love this bird, but because when you see a hummingbird during a time of pain or sorrow, a healing will soon follow. This bird also represents love and joy. Welcome to our family."* Sean raised both of Shelby's hands and kissed each one."

Georgia used the sleeve of her sweatshirt to wipe the tears streaming down her face. The insights both books gave her into the personality and character of her husband and children were invaluable. The second book took her through the loss her natural child, Kaela suffered from the demise of her father. She also reconnected with the extreme pain Shelby internalized with the deaths of both her parents.

And then there was Sean. Georgia searched back in the book to the vow she'd made to Sean.

"Sean, I take you to be my husband, my friend, my partner, my love, and the father of my children. You've shown me the power of a love that is honest and supportive. Trusting in what we know and what is yet to come, whether in success or failure, I give you my love unconditionally."

It was the words 'in success or failure' and 'give you my love unconditionally' that sliced right through her. She'd trusted her instincts back then. Sean was a compassionate and supportive man. Georgia needed to trust her instincts a second time. *How many amnesiacs get to experience first-hand, written in their own words, the journey they all travelled to this point in their lives. So I don't remember. Does it really matter? These books are my memories. Nonnock's right. All the answers are right here.*

Georgia took a shower and changed into clean clothes. It was as though she'd washed away her fears and insecurities.

Chapter 37

Port Arthur, Texas

After four months of chasing dead-end leads that left the detectives totally frustrated, something happened that day that started the wheels rolling to move the Charles-Dixon case forward.

That morning, Calloway joined his partner Detective Jarrod Brown in the interrogation room. An elderly lady with white hair sat at the table with Brown. "Sorry, got delayed in the D.A.'s office."

"This is Mrs. Agnes Collier from Houston," Brown said.

Calloway nodded to the woman and sat down. "I'm Detective Scott Calloway."

"Miss Agnes came to see us regarding the night of the Charles-Dixon accident. All I have so far is her contact information. Miss Agnes why don't you tell us why you're here," Brown said.

"I was travelling Highway 73 that night, on my way to New Orleans to stay with my daughter. Her husband fell ill and she needed help with her two small children. I only returned home a week ago. That's why I never saw the newspaper article asking anyone on the road that night to please contact your office. Yesterday, I was going through my mail when I starting reading the old newspapers—and there it was."

"And did you see anything that night that you think we should know about?" Calloway asked.

"It was an awful night and I shouldn't have been on the road at all. I had just left Port Arthur proper heading east, when a black pick-up came up behind me at a fast speed. Way too fast for the road conditions I might add."

"Do you remember what time it was?" Brown asked.

"It was ten minutes after eight that night. I remember because I was thinking I needed a break and looked at the dash clock. I decided instead to continue on to Bridge City and find a motel for the night and drive on to New Orleans in the morning. It was then that I noticed the truck behind me." She paused, lost in thought.

"Please continue, Miss Agnes," Calloway said.

"Well, he never even slowed down. He pulled into the oncoming lane and passed me at full speed. But his wheels hit a puddle and he hydroplaned sideways towards me. Scared the wits out of me. At the last minute, he pulled out of the skid and pulled ahead of me, moving back in front of my car. It shook me up and I pulled over to the side of the road."

"Did you get a look at the driver?" Brown asked.

"No, he had dark windows. Besides I was hanging on to the steering wheel for dear life, thinking out what to do to avoid him hitting me."

"And what did the truck do?" Callow asked.

"It must of scared him too because he slowed down and continued on at a reasonable speed. I pulled back onto the road and followed him. He was a ways ahead of me but I could see his tail lights."

Brown asked the next question. "And did you follow him all the way to Bridge City?"

"No. Only for about five minutes I think and he turned right onto a side road. When I passed the road and glanced down it, I could see his tail lights in the distance."

The detectives exchanged glances. Calloway knew they were both thinking the same thing. Miss Agnes had just corroborated Dylan Ortega's story. She was his alibi. "Did you see anyone else on the road that night?"

"Not going in my direction. But a few moments later another dark pick-up came towards me heading west."

"This next question is very important. So please think about it carefully before you answer. Did that vehicle pass you this side of the Rainbow Bridge or on the other side?" Detective Calloway asked.

"Oh definitely this side. It was just past the road the other vehicle turned up. I remember thinking that all three of us were crazy to be out there in that storm. I was very nervous."

"And you saw no one else on the road that night?" Calloway asked.

"Not until I reached Bridge City. I pulled into a motel. I was going to check in and walk over to the cafe across from it but the open sign shut off. Four people came out, climbed into two vehicles and drove off."

Calloway asked another question. "Do you remember the name of the cafe?"

"The Do Stop Cafe. I've been to it a number of times over the years."

"And what time was this?" Detective Brown asked.

"Around eight-thirty."

Another glance was shared between the two men. Miss Agnes had confirmed the testimony of Cassie Turner, the waitress at the cafe as well, thus establishing without a doubt the time-line for Miss Georgia's accident.

"We want to thank you for taking time to come here and give us your statement. You're a good citizen," Brown said.

"I hope it helps y'all."

"It absolutely has. Now, if you could wait for the statement to be typed out, we'll get you to sign it and send you on your way," Calloway said.

Calloway finished his updated report on the case. He called the D.A. to let him know Ortega was off the person of interest list and headed to the Mayor's office.

A couple of hours later, he and Detective Brown were knocking on Dylan Ortega's front door.

Camilla answered the door and stiffened when she saw the two men.

"Good afternoon, Mrs. Ortega. Is your husband at home? We'd like a few words with him," Calloway said.

Camilla stood to the side and gestured them into the hallway. She led them into the living room without a word. "Please, sit. I'll get my husband."

She and Dylan returned a moment later.

Calloway smiled at the couple who were ill at ease. "We felt we owed you a visit in person, sir, rather than call you on the telephone with an update on the Charles-Dixon case. A witness has come forward who backed your story the night of the accident. The woman you passed east of Port Charles was away in New Orleans and recently returned. She's provided us with a statement. You're no longer a person of interest in the case."

Camilla threw her shoulders back and held her head high. "He should never have been a suspect in the first place ... "

Dylan put his arm around her shoulders. "It's all right Camilla; the detectives were only doing their job. We knew this day would come." He turned to the law enforcement officers. "Thank you for letting us know. Have you fund the other driver that passed Miss Georgia that night?"

"Not yet. As you know these things take time. On a happier note, I'm pleased to tell you that I had a meeting in the Mayor's office today. The city of Port Arthur wishes to honour you as a hometown hero. The Mayor is setting up a ceremony in the latter part of July. She'll be sending you a letter soon with all the details."

Camilla's demeanor changed. She clapped her hands. "Oh Dylan. Do you hear that? My husband to be honoured. How wonderful."

"I don't know what to say. It's not necessary."

Detective Calloway stood. "The city thinks so. And I'm sure Miss Georgia will too. Believe me, it's going to be a grand affair with press and dignitaries. You deserve this, Mr. Ortega. And to be sure, we'll be there, along with the Chief of Police and many other officials." He extended his hand to Dylan. "I want to apologize to you for any pain we caused you or your family and I want to thank you for your patience in allowing us to do our job. We'll see you in July."

Dylan shook hands with the two detectives and the men took their leave.

Chapter 38

Cabin, Northwestern British Columbia

Sean watched Georgia move around the cabin. She appeared happier than he'd seen her since the accident. She smiled more, her face less strained. At thirty-eight, she was a beautiful woman with the body and skin of a woman in her twenties. However, it had always been her inner beauty and strength that he'd loved and been proud of.

But he felt he was failing her. Yes, he'd been patient and supportive. But every time Georgia relaxed and reached out to him, he'd rushed her. Guilt filled his psyche, for pushing her into an intimacy she wasn't ready for. He'd let his needs push her away again. The only answer, as he saw it, was to keep his distance.

Georgia turned and caught him staring at her. She gave him a big smile, the one that always had a big effect on him. His whole body warmed. Warming bells went off. He nodded to her and turned away.

"Sean?" she said, softly.

He steeled his body and turned back to her. "Yes?"

"We need to talk. The girls are busy in their room for awhile."

Sean scanned her face and gauged her mood. Her eyes held a plea. She looked so vulnerable. *No, no, no. This will take us back to where I'll screw up again.*

"I have some things that need doing in the shed. Later." He turned on his heel and left the cabin.

He didn't go to the shed. The noise of running water pulled him along a path through the trees out back and onto the bank of the stream. He sat down and stared into the water, completely lost in thought.

"Kraa, Kraa."

He looked up to see Feathers on the other side of the stream sitting on a branch. The raven flew across to his side and the bird turned grey and became an intangible mist, which grew larger and larger until a the form of a Tahltan elder walked out of the vapour. He came and sat down beside Sean. "You look good, grandson."

This was the first time, Sean had seen Feathers take form as his grandfather and he reached out to touch the man sitting beside him. "Gramps," he whispered. He had no other words.

His grandfather smiled at him. "It warms me to see that you kept the cabin and what you've done with it. You're the only one in our family who appreciated it and shared with me all that it meant as a Tahltan."

Sean smiled. "We had some fun times here when I was a child. It's a part of who I am. I thank you for that. There aren't any words to explain to you what you gave me then and what you've given me as a spirit protector to my children."

"Words aren't necessary. I knew of your thanks on your wedding day, right here at the cabin. You wore my buckskin vest and gave your daughters amulets representing Tahltan beliefs."

Together they watched a trout jump high out in the air, flapping hard in the water on its side to rid itself of lice. "Nice one," Sean said. "I should have brought my fishing rod."

Gramps smiled. "One of things we shared all those years ago. You loved to fish."

"Still do." Sean looked back at his grandfather. "When did you return to the cabin? The years I came here to write, I never saw you."

"Oh my boy, I never left Tahltan territory. I was always around. But it wasn't until Georgia arrived here many moons ago, so lost and so scared, that I felt the need to stay at the cabin. But she had Nonnock, so

I stayed as a companion to her. And when your daughters were alone in the wilderness, I became their protector."

"And we're so grateful you did."

"And you, grandson, so wisely figured out who I was."

Sean studied his grandfathers face. "Why did you come today?"

"Because you needed me. Georgia and your daughters are now my peoples too. You were right to bring her back to the beginnings of your family, but you're struggling. I wish to help."

A frown creased Sean's forehead. "I'm a fool."

"How so?"

"I have never seen myself as strong as Georgia. Watching her struggle tears me apart. And when she turns to me for strength, my expectations are too high and I end up pushing her away."

"A united family builds strength and love. You're a family because of your unity in the past. But your family circle was broken with Georgia's memory loss so it's hard to see to the future."

"Gramps, all I want is to love her and protect her. I frightened her when I pushed my male needs on her. Today, I could see she was comfortable with me again and at ease. My fear isn't just that I'll push her away again, but that I won't please her."

"You mean intimately, between a man and a woman?"

Sean shifted uncomfortably. "That's one aspect of it, yes. But if she doesn't remember our past, maybe she'll never love me again in that way. I'm afraid of losing her." Sean sighed. "See how selfish I'm being? Worrying about my feelings?"

"Your family has experienced a terrible upset. It affects each and every one of you as individuals. Of course, you'll think about your own pain. The only way to help Georgia's pain, is to examine your own. If she loved you once, she'll love you again." His grandfather reached out and patted his shoulder. "You're a good man, Sean. Listen to your instincts."

"My instinct is telling me to keep a distance, give her some space."

"That's not your instinct. That's your bruised ego. Maybe she's not ready to accept you as a lover, but she wasn't ready at the beginning to accept you into her bed. But she has now. The two of you have always had communication and communion. You mustn't close the door of communication between you or your communion will suffer. Talking will strengthen your bond. Sean, be honest with her about how you feel and encourage her to be honest back."

His grandfather stood and a grey mist surrounded him. "The past is the past, whether she remembers it or not. You both must rebuild a future together. That's where your eyes must look, to the future or you'll lose that too."

Sean watched his grandfather disappear and the grey cloud shrink and turn black. A black bird emerged from the black form and flew away. He stared into the white frothy water moving downstream and contemplated his grandfather's words. *Yes, I've been pushing her away. But it was because I didn't want to get carried away with my emotions and scare her off again. Good God, I sound like a schoolboy who can't control his urges. How pathetic.*

But it wasn't really about the sex, it was about wanting to feel the closeness they shared. Sean sat by the water for another hour examining his feelings and what he perceived were Georgia's. His grandfather was right. She'd been trying to talk to him for days. Before he could be honest with Georgia, he had to be honest with himself.

As Sean approached the cabin, he could hear squeals of delight coming from inside. He slipped in the back door. Georgia was leaning against the kitchen counter. Her facial expression was one of complete surprise. Her eyes were huge and her hands crossed over her mouth. The girls were jumping up and down in front of her.

"What's going on?"

Georgia shifted her eyes to him, totally speechless.

Kaela spoke first. "Poppy ..." she screamed.

Shelby yelled over her sister. "Mommy's getting her memory back."

His eyebrows shot up and he looked at Georgia. "Really?"

"Well ... some of it. Only childhood stuff," she said, looking shocked. Then she came to life. "Ask me something, anything about my childhood."

"Uh ... tell us about when you broke your arm," Sean threw out there.

"No, no. Something that I didn't write about in my books. Something the kids wouldn't know about and I couldn't have read somewhere."

Sean thought quickly. "What's the name of the preschool you attended."

"Cookies 'n' Milk Preschool in Lynn Valley. Another question." Georgia was so excited.

"What was your kindergarten teacher's name?"

"Mrs. Quinn, she was so pretty ... tall, long brown hair, big blue eyes. I loved her. Another one."

Sean faltered. "I can't think."

"Okay, then I'll tell you. My grade seven teacher was Mr. Frank. He was mean to girls and always tried to embarrass us." Georgia's voice had reached a fever pitch. Once she started talking she couldn't stop. "I couldn't wait to go to high school. Lindsay Place High School. We called it Banjo High 'cause it was shaped like a banjo." She paused for a breathe. "We wore uniforms to school—grey skirts, white blouses and navy blue blazers, and the boys grey trousers. On the last day of high school before exams started, we wore our uniforms for the last time. The girls cut their skirts into shreds and the boys their pants. All the younger kids in school were so envious as we paraded around the halls in our rags. It was a tradition we were allowed to get away with."

Sean and the girls spent several minutes throwing questions at her. Georgia answered them all. She started to laugh and they followed suit. They danced around the kitchen and came together in a family group hug. They wordlessly held each other in a tight circle until Shelby's quiet voice broke their silence.

"Mommy, when will you remember us?"

Before Georgia could answer, they were interrupted by the sound of a helicopter.

Chapter 39

The *whap whap* of the helicopter blades reached a fever pitch and the big bird landed in the meadow on the other side of the gazebo. Sean, Georgia and the girls waited on the porch, while their friend, Tom, turned off the motor and the blades came to a stop.

"Good to see you, friend," Sean said. He and Tom exchanged a man hug. "What brings you our way today?"

"The wife and kids are away for a few days in Prince George so I thought I'd fly in and see you all."

"Join us for a coffee?" Georgia asked.

"You bet" Tom followed them up onto the porch, while the girls played in the gazebo.

Georgia went inside to set up a tray of cups and a snack. She could hear the sound of laughter coming from the porch and smiled. It was good to hear Sean bantering with his old friend. Things had been warmer between her and Sean during the day but he still wasn't opening up to her. At night, he'd read until she was asleep. Once in a while, she'd catch him staring at her and she always responded with a big smile. The decision was made to back off and not force him into talking if he wasn't ready. And he appeared more relaxed. Rebuilding their relationship would take time and all she could do was assure Sean in other ways that she was there and not going anywhere.

She joined the men on the porch. The girls were giggling at something per usual as they picked wildflowers in the field and Georgia sat quietly, listening to the men banter about the latest news from town. Her eyes fell to the northeast. The Cassiar Mountains stood tall, almost snow free on their tops. A peacefulness fell over her and she was truly happy for the first time since the accident.

It was a hot day. The hottest one so far with no breeze to blow away the bugs. Georgia stood. "I'll get the *Deep Woods*."

"I've got a better idea,' Tom said. "How about we fly to the waterfall and have a swim in the pool."

Sean bounced up onto his feet. "Great idea. Girls?" he shouted. "How about a helicopter ride to the falls and a swim?"

The adults laughed at the antics of the girls. They screamed with glee and galloped like horses to the porch. "Yay!" They ran past the adults into the cabin, shoving their flowers into Georgia's arms. "For you, Mommy," Kaela panted. "Could you put them in water?"

"Which suits should we wear?" Shelby shouted. "The pink ones or the green?"

"Whatever, but they have to match," Kaela answered.

They listened to them run across the floor and into their bedroom, bantering with excitement.

"Guess that's a yes," Tom said, grinning from ear to ear.

It was a great flight to the falls and a short hike in from the meadow where they landed. Georgia packed a lunch and a couple of blankets to sit on the bank of the river. These were the falls Grampa Feathers had led the girls to when she'd freed them from her stalker. The falls where they went behind the cascading water and into a cave to sleep at night for protection from the wilderness.

The water was glacier fed and cold. They all screamed as they ran into the water together and dove under the still pool to the side of the falls. One by one they swam through the hole in the rocks and into the hidden cave to sit on the dirt floor enjoying the coolness behind the falls.

"No bugs in here," Georgia said. "Or outside for that matter, too much moisture in the air from the falls."

Kaela and Shelby told them of their time spent by the falls and how they survived on blackberries till Sean found them. They never tired of telling their story and Georgia never tired of hearing it. "I love blackberries, but it's too early in the season," Kaela said.

"Too bad, so sad," Shelby echoed.

Sean stepped into the small pool of water. "Which reminds me of food. Anyone ready for lunch? I'm starving."

They spent the afternoon swimming in the shallow pool and sunning on the bank. *A perfect day*, Georgia thought.

They landed in the meadow early evening. The girls ran ahead and into the cabin, while Georgia and Sean said their goodbyes to Tom.

"Oh... almost forgot. I brought your mail." Tom handed them a pile of envelopes from under one of the seats.

"Thanks, Tom. It was a great day. See you soon," Sean said.

He and Georgia walked to the porch and watched the chopper lift off and head east to Dease Lake.

After a light supper, Georgia sorted the mail into his and hers. They were sitting at the dining table. "Hmm ... I've got two letters from Texas. One from the Port Arthur Police Department and another from the Mayor's office." She opened the one from law enforcement first.

Sean put his mail down and watched her read it.

"It's an update on my case from Detective Calloway. They say Dylan is no longer a person of interest but they still haven't found the man who forced me off the road into the river. The case is still open and they will continue to work on it. My gut instinct was right about Dylan. I'm happy for him and Camilla."

"That's great news, sweetheart," Sean said.

Georgia gave him a warm smile. It was the first endearing word he'd used towards her in weeks.

Sean smiled back and her blood raced. "Open the other one," he coaxed.

"It's an invitation from the Mayor of Port Arthur to attend a ceremony on July 16th to honour Dylan Juan Ortega as a hometown hero. Oh Sean … how wonderful. There's a formal dinner and presentation at the Convention Centre. We've been invited as their guests, all expenses paid by the City of Port Arthur, which includes four plane tickets and a two bedroom suite at the La Quinta Inn and Suites. We hope you and your family will be available to attend this special event. It goes on to say there'll be two hundred guests and dignitaries attending. And they want each of us to make a speech." Georgia stared at Sean. "Wow."

Sean grinned. "I guess we're all going to Texas this summer. Get ready for another hit of over-the-top pubescence. Girls … can you come out here, please?" The girls came running. "I'm afraid we have to go home soon. Guess who's going to Texas in July?"

Shelby and Kaela's faces dropped. Shelby looked at Georgia. "You're not leaving again, are you?" she asked.

"I am, but not alone." She averted her eyes to Sean.

"You're going too, Poppy?" Kaela asked, her voice small.

"I am."

The girls looked at each. "We don't want you guys to go," Kaela said.

Sean feigned a look of surprise. "Really? That's too bad because if Mommy and I don't go, then you girls can't go either."

Silence. Shelby spoke first. "You mean we're all going?"

Sean shrugged. "Only if you girls want to."

"Omigod … we're going to Texas, Shelby." The girls squealed with delight, held hands and jumped up and down.

Georgia laughed as Sean covered his ears with his hands and shook his head.

Shelby suddenly stopped. That pensive stare she was famous for spread across her face. "Why are we going to Texas?"

"Because the man who pulled Mommy out of the lake and saved her life is being honoured as a hero at a big celebration."

"And ..." Georgia added, "... it's a formal dinner so we need to return home and go shopping for new dresses."

"Uhh ..." Kaela said, while Shelby's hands covered her mouth. This set off another dramatic outburst and the girls ran off to their bedroom babbling about clothes and colours.

"Well, it's been quite a day. I think I'll head up to bed and some calm, quiet reading.," Sean said.

"I'll be up in a minute."

Georgia shut off the lights and made sure the girls were settled for the night. She heard Sean pull the sliding wall across the open railings. She climbed the stairs to the loft and stepped into the room.

Sean was sitting up in bed reading. He glanced her way. "Would you close the door?"

She pulled the sliding door across the stair opening. This was the first time they'd closed the loft for privacy since they'd arrived at the cabin. *Hmm ... what's up with that?* As she approached the bed, Sean put his book down.

"Let's talk," he said.

Chapter 40

Malone, New York

Dan Barton studied the three girls he'd shown to his guest bedroom. They couldn't be more than twelve years old. Two of the girls were stoic. They gave the room a once over, curled up together on the bed and appeared to fall asleep. *Probably drugged.* The other one was terrified. She was a tiny little thing, maybe even younger than twelve. Her eyes were laden with tears. She sat in the armchair, pulled her feet up under her and held herself tight with her arms crossed around her abdomen. She stared unblinking at the floor. It tore him apart and he wanted to comfort her, tell her it would be all right. No matter what the agents thought about him and his business, when it came to children and crime, his blood boiled. He knew too well from his childhood what it was like to be bullied and beaten. The female chaperone told him he could leave them now. She was a hard case. Dyed blonde hair with dark roots and too much makeup. Her face was harsh and weathered; her eyes cold and calculating. He had no choice but to leave them alone.

He went to the kitchen and pulled out a bottle of scotch, filled two shot glasses and returned to the living room. He handed one to Aylmer. "To a great partnership, Teslin."

Aylmer raised his glass. "To our first business endeavour and many more."

Dan sat down on the couch, with a glance at his watch. "We'll leave in about twenty minutes."

Yelling came from the bedroom and loud sobbing could be heard, followed by more shouts. Dan heard a loud thump and a bloodcurdling scream. Dan jumped to his feet. "What's going on in there."

'Relax," Teslin said. "Just keeping the girls in line. Sit down."

Everything went quiet and it took every bit of Dan's reserve to sit back down and act like everything was normal. He knew the agents were watching everything on monitors at the house behind his. At least they knew what was happening in the bedroom.

"So's your contact all set?" Teslin asked.

"Yup. I talked to him an hour ago."

"And he knows the contact site once he crosses the border?"

"Not yet. I'll tell him when we transfer the girls over to him."

Aylmer Teslin smiled. "That's what I like about you and your oper-ation. You leave nothing to chance. You're smart."

Dan looked at Teslin's empty glass. "Another?"

"Not me."

"Me neither, I gotta drive." He looked at his watch again.

Teslin pulled an envelope out of his pocket.

Dan eyed the packet and knew it was his share for tonight's job. *This is it. Pay me and let the feds get it on film.*

Aylmer wasn't in a hurry to hand to him, laying it in his lap. "I've got three crossings set up the next couple of weeks." He studied Dan closely.

Dan laughed. "Business is booming already." He tried not to look at the envelope on Aylmer's lap."

"I told you there was lots of money to be made tying in with me. My business is steady and strong."

"I believe you. My teams in this for the long-term, even when I'm ready to opt out."

"Good to hear. And no worries from any of my people the feds nabbed. My lawyer is representing them and they know even if they do some time, they and their families will be well taken care of. I've got their loyalty." A sneer crossed his face. " Not the little snitch of course. He'll be taken care of in due course."

Dan stood. It was time to end this charade. "Time to go."

Aylmer stood and handed him the while envelope. "Your share for tonight's work. Fifty-fifty and lots more to come."

Dan opened the envelope and pulled the money half out of the envelope for the benefit of the hidden camera. *Showtime boys.* He let out a whistle. "You're an honourable man, partner. Just heading for a pee and to lock this away. Be right back." He slapped the envelope against his hand and headed to his bedroom. He took his time opening his safe, locking the money inside. He went into the bathroom, flushed the toilet as if he used it and washed his hands. Federal agents and other policing agencies were scurrying around outside. He wanted to give them time to set-up. Any minute they'd come crashing through the door.

He grabbed a jacket from the bedroom closet and joined Teslin in the living room. "All set." Dan walked to the guest bedroom. *Come on guys. Where are you?* No sooner had the thought come to mind, the door came crashing open and bedlam broke loose.

"Police, on the ground. Now." Agents burst into the room, guns drawn, all yelling at the same time.

Dan dropped onto the floor. Two agents cuffed his hands behind his back. *Déjà Vu.* "Don't move," they yelled at him. He watched from the floor as two agents pulled Teslin down to the ground and held him while a third cuffed him. The other agents burst into the guest bedroom. Dan turned his head and stared into the bedroom. The two girls on the bed were clinging to each other, wide-eyed. The third one lay in a tiny heap on the floor in front of the armchair. Dan's heart skipped a beat.

Three of the agents took down the chaperone. A female agent sat on the bed with the two girls and talked to them quietly, assuring them they were safe. Another agent knelt beside the little one on the floor. He spoke into the microphone he wore around his ear. "We need two ambulances. Three girls." He glanced up at the two on the bed. "Two, awake, ambulatory, drugged. Third, unconscious, weak pulse, fresh needle mark in her arm."

Dan could see the girl had vomited. There was a pool of water on the floor and a strong smell of urine. *Poor little thing.*

The chaperone was complaining loudly to the agents that they were hurting her and her handcuffs were too tight. Dan seethed. *Bitch.* It was a good thing he was handcuffed and on the floor. It would have taken all the agents to pull him off of her otherwise. She was brought out of the bedroom and told to sit on the couch.

One of the agents searched her bag and pulled out a number of drug vials, some full, some empty, and used syringes. He placed them into a plastic bag. A few minutes later, paramedics arrived. The agent held one of the vials up. "This is probably what she gave her. And this syringe is fresh. Still contains a few drops." One of the paramedics wrote down the name on the bottle, while another addressed the child on the floor. The two girls on the bed were being examined by the other two attendants.

Dan turned his face to look back at Teslin. He'd been picked up and was sitting back in the armchair. Agent West stood in front of him with an arrest warrant. "Aylmer Teslin, you're under arrest and charged with the felonious crime of human trafficking. You have the right to remain silent; anything you say can and may be used against you in a court of law; you have the right to have an attorney present before and during questioning; and you have the right if you cannot afford the services of an attorney, to have one appointed, at public expense and without cost to them, to represent you before and during the questioning. Do you understand?"

Teslin was silent.

"Do you understand, sir?"

"Yah, yah," Teslin said.

Agent West turned to two agents. "Get him back to Buffalo. I want him secluded. Agent Schroeder, you and your partner follow them with the two we nabbed outside. Agents Smith and Franklin, you follow with the woman. Agent Cousins, you and your partner go with the ambulances to the hospital and stay with the girls. I'll be following the others back to Buffalo with Barton."

Once the agents bound for Buffalo left, West instructed the officers to bring Barton to the couch.

The paramedics walked the two young girls out to one ambulance. The other two pushed the unconscious child out on a stretcher to the awaiting vehicle.

Alone with Dan, West finally removed his cuffs. "Barton, this is Special Agent Benjamin Samuels with the FBI. He'll be taking you to your new location. Once you're under the Witness Protection Program, Samuels will be your go to guy, the one you contact with any concerns or questions."

Dan nodded to the agent. "Samuels." He rubbed his wrists and watched the ambulances leave through the living room window. "Will the little one be all right?"

"Let's hope so. These girls are the lucky ones. Over three hundred thousand children are trafficked in the United States each year. Their average life span is seven years. They die from attacks, abuse, HIV or other sexually transmitted diseases, drug overdose or suicide."

"Fuck me," Dan said. "That's horrible. What'll happen to these girls now."

"We'll try to find their families. It's dependant on how young they were when abducted. Their names are changed and they can be so traumatized that they don't remember their old names or their families."

"Even if you do find their families, how can they go home after something like this and live normal lives."

"They qualify for a program we call the 'The Three R's', rescue, remove, and reintegration. Hopefully, they can rejoin society and resume their lives.

"I'm glad we got Teslin off the street, but it seems like a losing battle with those numbers."

"We choose to count our victories and celebrate them. There's nothing more satisfying than informing a family we found their child and watch them be reunited." Agent West looked around. "Time for you to say good-bye to this place. Give us that envelope you put in the safe and grab your suitcase."

"Then what?" Dan asked.

"Back to Buffalo to sign a statement and some papers. We're flying back by chopper. We'll be finished and Samuels will have you on your way before the others have finished the drive back. Teslin won't be seeing you again until court."

"Okay. And my things?"

"A truck will be here shortly. Agent Morse is staying here to oversee it. Everything will be packed for you and driven to your new location. They'll be finished and gone in case Teslin gets out on bail."

Dan was shocked. "Wouldn't he be a flight risk?"

"I'm sure the prosecution will argue that. But it always depends on the judge. Some are more lenient than others."

Dan retrieved the money envelope from his safe and turned it over to the agent. He grabbed his computer bag, his cell phone, and a suitcase and rejoined the agent in the living room. He was ready for his new life and glad to be leaving the area. They drove to the Malone-Dufort Airport about four kilometers west of Malone.

As they flew to Buffalo, Dan was lost in thought. He felt bad about not seeing his partner, Henry Reed before he left the state. But the FBI informed him that he couldn't say a word before the take-down, in case something happened and Barton needed to stay undercover. They wouldn't chance Reed knowing anything. They didn't trust him like Dan did. Now he was on his way to a new life. He'd thought of writing Henry a letter but he didn't trust the FBI would give it to him. There was no way, he'd disappear out of state without talking to his friend of twenty years.

He knew what he had to do.

Chapter 41

Finally. Georgia sat on her side of the bed She propped the pillows up and against the headboard. And waited. She'd been wanting this talk for weeks. but now it was here she was apprehensive. *Why am I so nervous. Maybe because he's initiating the conversation. I'm scared of what he might have to say?*

"You'll never guess who I had a chat with a couple of days ago."

Georgia knitted her brows. They'd had no visitors until today. "I don't think I can. Who?"

Sean looked at her with a twinkle in his eye. "My grandfather."

Her mouth dropped open. "You mean, Grampa Feathers?"

"Yup. Only he came to me as himself, not as a raven."

"Omigod. What'd he say?"

"Basically, that we're all victims of your accident. And the one thing we always had was communication. He said we can't commune if we don't talk and the future will be lost to us."

Georgia shifted towards him. "Wise words."

"I'm sorry I shut you out these past weeks. I know you've been wanting to say something. Then you backed away and I was even more scared."

She reached out and touched his arm. "You were scared? Of what?"

Sean looked at her with the expression of a frightened child. "Lots of things."

Her heart went out to him. "I've been frightened too. I am right now."

He took a deep breath and reached out for her hand. "So we've determined we're both scared. That's a start. Let me go first. Whenever you opened up to me, I was so happy that I came on too strong and you'd back away. I've pushed you for intimacy when you weren't ready for it and I'm sorry ..." he paused, searching for his words, "... I don't care about the sex. It was more about feeling close and feeling you might love me again."

"I knew that. I feel awful that I couldn't say the words 'I love you' when you needed to hear them."

"I was a fool to expect it when I was a stranger to you. I was being selfish."

Georgia squeezed his hand. "I finished my second book. It taught me so much about our family and about you—who you are as a person, a husband, and a father. I understand your feelings of loss as well as mine. I'm lucky to have my books as a diary of some of the life we shared before my accident."

"My biggest fear is that you won't fall in love me again and if that happens, I'll lose you."

"Oh Sean, you're still the man I fell in love with once and the books revealed our relationship so deeply." Georgia smiled. "I'm a little embarrassed that I wrote those words for the world to read, but so happy I did, because they gave me an insight to what we once had. I don't want to lose that. And as for me not loving you again, it's too late. I've already fallen back in love with my husband."

He stared deep into her eyes. "Really?"

She nodded affirmatively.

He gave her an impish smile. "Say it. I want to hear the words," he whispered.

Georgia stroked his cheek with her free hand. "I love you, Sean Charles-Dixon, I love you."

He leaned forward and brushed her lips with his and she responded by pressing her mouth hard on his. She parted her lips slightly and his tongue explored hers. It was a long and passionate kiss that said it all. No words were needed. Sean's arms reached out to her and she slipped into them. Then he pulled away. "That's enough. I'm not going to push you until you're ready.

Georgia laughed until she snorted. Suddenly, she felt they'd crossed a barrier and were close again. She could say anything and they'd deal with it.

"And what's so amusing?"

"It's not that I haven't felt ready. I mean I lost my memory not my libido. Once I knew I could trust you and that I felt I could fall in love with you all over again, I was ready. You're very handsome and virile. How could I not be turned on by you?" Now that she'd started the conversation, she'd have to finish it. "I have to tell you something. You know how I've remembered to do some things since the accident but lost the ability to do others? No rhyme or reason to what. Well ... sex is one of the things I have no clue about. If you want to make love to me, you'll be making love to a thirty-eight year old virgin. I'm clueless. I've been so afraid I'll disappoint you and you won't love me anymore."

There I said it. It's out in the open. She shut up and waited.

Sean started to speak but sputtered and stopped. "You mean ... you ... you don't know how?" He stared at Georgia in wonderment. "Wow ... I'm the clueless one. I never thought that was the problem. I was afraid if you didn't love me and we made love, I couldn't satisfy you. And I'd lose you."

"You're still the same person, Sean. If you satisfied me then, I'm sure you can satisfy me now."

The impish grin was back. "You were always such a lusty wench. I mean ... who knew?"

" A lusty wench?"

"Oh yah, baby." Sean pulled her into his arms. "You could never get enough of me."

"You're that good are you?" Georgia giggled.

"Let's find out. A virgin, eh? How lucky can an old man get?"

"Forty-eight isn't old. And physically, I'm not a virgin."

"Zsa Zsa Gabor says all a woman has to do is soak in a hot bath and she's a virgin again."

Georgia feigned a foreign accent and pretended to get out of bed. "So, Darlink, you vant me to take a bath?"

Sean held on tight. "Oh no you don't. You're not leaving here until your homework is done."

For the next while, Sean explored every inch of Georgia's body, showing her all the things he knew she liked. She sighed and cooed under the gentle touch of his fingers and his tongue. She reached a fever pitch and could hardly stand it. Finally, he entered her and took her to realms higher than ever. She arched her body up to his and moved with his motion until they both exploded together and she almost passed out.

She lay next to him in euphoria, totally spent. "Wow. You are good."

"You weren't so bad yourself—for a first-timer."

Georgia smacked his arm. "Weren't so bad? Hey, I'm just getting started."

"I'm happy. I love being your teacher and you're such a fast learner."

She rolled over on top of him and started kissing his face. "Again?"

"Already?"

"But I have so much more to learn and all night to do my lessons. Teach me," she whispered, taking his nipple in her mouth.

Sean let out a gasp. In a raspy voice, Georgia hadn't heard from him before but brought out her desires, he croaked out three words.

"Definitely a wench."

Chapter 42

Gibsons, BC

Georgia and the family returned home the first week of July, pumped for their journey to Texas. They spent the weekend in Vancouver at the condo so Georgia and the girls could shop for new summer dresses for the dinner. The girls both chose a sleeveless, pale pink dress, with a similar satiny sheen top. Shelby's skirt fell in cascading layers of ruffles with a shiny beaded waistband. Kaela's skirt hung in a soft lace overlay with skirt petals layered around the bottom of the skirt and the waistband.

Georgia chose a sleeveless, above the knee black jersey dress, with a turquoise & burgundy native motif following the seam edge of the v-neck and around the hemline. It was chic but semi-formal; perfect for a summer evening. For her feet, she chose a turquoise stiletto, open-toed and for jewellery, turquoise and silver.

Back home in Gibsons, laundry and packing were the order of the day. Sean was folding towels and Georgia was folding clothes for their trip while the girls watched a surfing movie based in Hawaii. It was one of those kids tales of competition, jealousy, friends fall out, and then fall back in.

She listened to the girls banter about Hawaii. "I'd love to go to Hawaii. It's so beautiful," Kaela said.

"Mommy, have you ever been to Hawaii?" Shelby asked. It was an innocent question thrown at her without thought.

Kaela stated to answer for her. "Shelby. How would she know, she ..."

Georgia absentmindedly replied. "Yup. Your father and I went to Hawaii for our honeymoon. We stayed at Grandma Alice's house in Maui. I think he and Julie went there a couple of times too after they were married." As she folded clothes, she was oblivious to the fact that the others were staring at her in silence as she rambled on. "One of the islands, Kona has no soil. It's made up completely of crushed volcanic rock and instead of white sand, the beaches are black. It's much finer than our sand so it feels softer like flour against your skin ..." she giggled, "... we were shocked when it clung to our legs and feet. They looked dirty." She looked at the girls and then at Sean. "What?"

"I don't recall you writing about these things, babe. Do you remember Colin and Julie?" Sean asked softly.

Georgia thought hard on it. Her grin said it all. "Yes, yes.," she whispered. "Colin and I met at the campus library. Later at the law firm, I met Julie at the annual Christmas party." She looked at Shelby. "She was beautiful, your mom. Women envied her."

"Women envy you too, Mommy. You're beautiful," Kaela said.

"Thank you, sweetheart."

Shelby came up to her and gave her a hug. "How much do you remember this time." She looked at Georgia with an expectant look in her eyes.

Georgia smiled down at her. "I think ..." she stared at her daughter pensively, "... that I remember everything up to about twelve years ago. That's over three quarters of my life."

Instead of looking sad this time, Shelby clapped her hands. "You're almost there, Mommy."

Kaela shut off the movie. 'Mommy, this means your thread is still growing."

"I guess it does," Georgia said. "Here, girls. Take these clothes upstairs and put them on the bed in the guest bedroom. They're for our trip. Then come back for these ones. They go in your drawers. Okay/"

Georgia walked over to Sean and he put his arms around her. They hugged in silence for a few minutes. She sighed. "I should have warned them again that my memory may not return completely. But they're so pumped for the trip; I didn't want to bring them down."

"Let them be happy. God knows we need some happy."

She pushed herself back and looked into his face. "How awful for you, though."

"Meaning?"

"Because I remember everything about my first husband now and nothing about you. What if my memory stops right here? Never moves forward to our years together. How does that make you feel?"

"Stop it. We are way beyond this, my love. The way I look at it is this. If you can only remember one of us, let it be Colin. You and I are rebuilding our love. It's fresh, passionate and will only grow deeper. Your memories of Colin show him for what he was. What was it you called him, an Assholian? No envy there."

A slow smile crept across her face. "I see your logic." Georgia leaned forward and gave him a long, loving kiss.

Shelby's voice rang out behind them. "Ewww ... they're at it again." Georgia broke away and turned as two giggling girls disappeared out the room with another pile of laundry.

She and Sean shared a laugh.

"Anyway, there's still hope. It's been almost five months and look at how far you've come. The chances of a full recover are in your favour."

Sean gave her a full smile and a wink and Georgia's knees went weak. She smiled back but pushed away the passionate thoughts he'd stirred up and changed the subject.

"I've got lots to tell them at the Clinical Trial Lab tomorrow.

And it was quite a day. As Georgia and Sean began the repetitive trip back to the ferry that had been a big part of their lives the past months, Georgia prattled on about how the Doctors were pleased with her progress. "They want me to continue with the Clinical Trial. At this point they don't know if the program has helped or if my brain is healing on its own. They can't do another SPECT test until next year. And guess what?"

"What's that, hon?"

"They've asked me if I'd like to be on their Board of Directors and be a spokesperson at conventions and fund raisers. And to talk with families who are dealing with traumatic brain injuries. Isn't that exciting?"

"Wow. That's wonderful news, babe."

"It sounds like a lot of work, but it's only part-time."

"It sounds like you've found what you were looking for. I'm happy for you."

Georgia felt puzzled. "Looking for?"

Sean gave her a glance. "Oh ... of course, you don't remember this yet. When we flew down to L.A. in February, you said you felt done with doing writer's conventions and talking about your books and the past. You wanted to find something else to do part-time." He gave her a warm smile. "I think you've found it."

"I think you're right. I'll still be talking about myself I guess but only since the accident."

They reached the upper levels highway and Georgia stared out the window at the water. "Doesn't it seem strange to you that I've had all this drama in my life. I mean kidnappings, survival, stalkers, accidents and the like? And it's all brought so much attention to me and everyone around me."

"I'm not sure I get your point," Sean said.

"Well, some people live quiet lives, raise their kids, and get old without anything major happening to them. And here I am, with so much drama."

"I see what you're saying. But it's not like you went looking for it. Life happens and yours is what it is. What brought this on?"

"I read an article about my accident online and someone left a comment about how it was time I stopped looking to be in the limelight all the time and put my efforts into raising my family."

Sean laughed. "You never know what motivates people to say the things they do, especially about people they've never met and really don't know. I suggest you stop reading the comment section."

"You're probably right."

"Believe me. You have never been one to look for attention. If anything, you shy away from it. I think it's what you do with it that's important. You're using your life experiences to help others. There's nothing wrong with that."

Departure day arrived. They'd taken the ferry from Gibsons to Vancouver the night before and stayed at the condo. Beside themselves with excitement, the girls had no problem getting up early for the trip to the airport. It was their first trip to the southern states and Georgia made sure they had packed puzzle books and their Android game players to keep them occupied on the long flight.

They chose to take the Canada Line Skytrain from downtown Vancouver to the Vancouver International Airport. A taxi took them from the condo to the Vancouver City Centre station where they checked into an Airport Check-In Kiosk before getting on the train. This saved them from standing in long lines once they reached the airport. The girls had small backpacks. Georgia had a large shoulder purse. And with one suitcase each that met the carry-on dimensions, they were all set.

It was a perfect summer day from Canada to Texas. Perfect flying weather. Their flight was uneventful. Once in awhile, Sean would glance Georgia's way with a quizzical look. He'd say: "Are you all right?" She'd say: "Yes. Couldn't be better."

Finally, Georgia clued in that he was asking her repetitively throughout the trip. "Why do you keep asking me that?"

Sean shrugged. "Oh ... nothing."

Georgia punched his shoulder. "Yes ... something. Give it over."

Sean laughed. "You seem so calm is all; like you're enjoying the flight."

"Why wouldn't I enjoy it. We're starting another unexpected family holiday. You're happy, the girls are happy—so I'm happy."

"And you don't mind flying?"

"I *love* flying."

"*Love* ... you *love* flying." Sean squeezed her hand. "Okay, let's go with that."

"What are you getting at here? You're starting to piss me off."

Sean teased her. "Ooh, don't want to do that. I'm surprised because before your accident you were always a terrible flyer. If there was any turbulence, you'd hang on to me for dear life."

Georgia was surprised to learn this about herself. "Really? That bad?"

"That bad."

"Humph ... maybe something good's come out of my accident. I'm certainly not afraid now."

"It beats nail indents in my arm."

They landed in Houston, caught a connecting flight to Port Arthur, picked up a car rental at the airport and were settled into their suite at the La Quinta Inn by dinnertime. None of them were hungry from sitting all day. They all went swimming in the hotel pool to burn off the girls pent up energy.

They drove around Port Arthur and found their way to Sabine Lake. Georgia stood on the bank and stared out at the water. Sean stood behind her with his hands on her shoulders.

"This is boring," Kaela said to Shelby. She looked up at her parents. "Are we staying here long?"

"No. This is the lake we almost lost your mother in. Mr. Ortega pulled her out of the water and gave her CPR."

"Oh," Kaela said, looking chastised.

"Was it right here, Poppy?" Shelby asked.

"Not this exact spot. Further up the lake."

Georgia turned to Sean. "Why don't you take the girls over to that park for a bit. I'd like a few minutes alone."

"I can do that. Come on girls."

Georgia sat on the bank and removed her sandals. She let her feet dangle in the water. It felt warm. *A lot warmer I bet than the last time I was here.* She took in a deep breath. The smell of flowering shrubs nearby was pleasant but another distinct odour piqued her . She took in more deep breathes. Although this was a lake, it drained into the Gulf of Mexico and all the waters in this basin had the strong smell of saline.

A warm breeze blew across her face and she closed her eyes and cleared her mind, listening for what her inner soul was telling her. *It's strange to be sitting here. What I know about this area and Texas in general is at best, minimal. But these friendly people with their strong southern drawl have impacted my life at a level that will always be with me. A part of me belongs to Texas.*

Squeals of laughter and loud voices broke through her muse. Georgia opened her eyes and smiled. The girls were having fun. She stood and slipped her feet into her sandals and headed to the park.

"Hey. What do you say we find ourselves a Texas native and ask them where the best pizza in town is, eh?"

Chapter 43

Agent West broke into his muse. " Five minutes 'til we land. Tell me something, Barton. You really surprised me back there with the compassion you felt for those girls. It's not usually something people in your line of work have. Why is that?"

Dan stared down the agent. "Some of us are still human. I told you before that I didn't cotton to women and children being exploited and abused. My mother and I suffered at the hands of my father. My mother took me and ran away. She changed our names and I changed mine yet again to protect her from my business. And believe me, if you guys hadn't had me in cuffs, you'd have had to pull me off that bitch for what she did to that young girl. But, then again, back in her day, she was probably a victim herself. As for Teslin, I despise him."

West's look softened. "I hear you. But you'll have to contain your anger in your new life. You can't afford to draw attention to yourself."

Dan smiled. "I don't intend on being around the kind of people that are vexing. Don't worry. My life is all about fishing now."

"Is he still alive/" West asked.

"Who? Oh, my father. Don't know and don't care. After we ran away, we never saw him again."

The helicopter landed in Buffalo and a car was waiting to take West, Samuels and Barton to the Federal Center. Dan waited with his lawyer while West had his statement processed. Finally, he was presented with the statement for signature. The FBI Agent, Samuels placed some documents into another pile regarding his relocation to be read and signed. Dan's lawyer looked them over first and placed them in front of Barton. West handed him a pen. Dan read all the paperwork but before signing, he put the pen down on the table.

"Something wrong?" Agent West asked.

"Not with the paperwork. But before I sign, I want to make a phone call to my partner, Henry Reed."

"Why?"

"Because I need to talk to him before I leave for good."

"We told you we'd explain everything to him. You don't want to jeopardize your situation, Barton, so I suggest you leave it to us, sign the papers and get on your way," West said.

"I agree with that, sir," Agent Samuels added.

Dan sat back in his chair and folded his arms across his chest. "Look, I've complied with everything you've asked of me. Henry Reed and I have been partners and friends for twenty years. That means a lot me and to him. Now that Teslin is contained, I'm not jeopardizing anything. I'm asking you to be a little human here and not a suit. All I'm requesting is one phone call and some privacy."

The men looked at each. Agent Samuels nodded and stood.

"All right, one call. We'll have to take that cell phone when you're done," Agent West said. Everyone left the room and Dan stared at the phone. It wouldn't be an easy call. He pressed the programmed number and waited for Henry to answer.

"Dan? Where the hell are you?"

"It's not happening tonight, Henry. I couldn't call you until now."

"What happened?"

"Teslin's busted. It's all over that's what's happened."

"Oh shit. What about you? Where are you?"

Dan stood and paced the room. "Listen, I have to tell you something and please don't interrupt until I'm finished. That last job we did. The Asians? The feds were all over it. They were there that night and got the whole thing on tape. We were busted."

"What? Then how come we weren't arrested?"

"They picked me up that night as I got home. They wanted me to work undercover with them so they could nab Teslin."

There was silence at the other end of the phone. "Dan? You there?"

"So you're a goddam snitch. I can't believe it. You saved your own ass. And what about me? When are they coming for me?" Henry was angry and bitter.

"They're not coming for you, Henry. I refused them at first and they were going to charge you and pick you up. I made a deal with them. I'd work for them if they left you alone."

"And you think they'll honour that? I never took you for a fool until now. I gotta get out of here fast."

"No you don't. We wouldn't have gotten off, Henry. It was a sealed case for them. But the feds were more interested in Teslin than you and me. We're small potatoes compared to him. They put it into legal papers, signed and registered. I couldn't leave without explaining it all to you and saying goodbye."

"Goodbye? Why are you leaving if you have such a good deal with the feds?"

"Because I have to testify in court against Teslin. I'm in the Witness Protection Program and they're taking me out of state shortly."

"So I'll never see you again?"

Dan sat down again and tried to relax. "It sucks, but yes. It's goodbye friend. But listen up. You have to quit and go straight, you hear me? They won't honour the deal if they catch you doing anything illegal from now on. And the Tribal Police will be watching you. You know that. Are you hearing me?"

"Ya. I get it. This sucks all right."

"One more thing. Tomorrow, I want you to go to see the priest at the Catholic Church on the reserve. I told him I was leaving town and you were away and I wanted to give you some items from my house. I left a package with him for you. I told him I'd left a message on your phone to pick it up when you got back. I even gave him a donation for the church for holding it for me. It's enough to pay off your debts and then some. That's the least I can do for you."

"Thanks, Dan. You were a good friend and partner."

"I've got to go. Stay out of the casino, pal and take care of that family of yours. Bye."

"You too, partner. Bye."

Dan shut the cell phone off and placed it on the table. He picked up the pen and signed the documents.

The others returned a few minutes later. Dan said goodbye to his lawyer. Agent West put out his hand. "Good job tonight." They shook hands. "I'm turning you over to Agent Samuels. He'll get you settled in your new home and bring you back for court. Good luck to you, sir."

Agent Samuels led him back down to the parking garage. Once again, they headed to the Buffalo Niagara International Airport. They boarded a government plane for the flight to Louis Armstrong New Orleans International Airport. Dan tried to sleep but he was wound too tight.

Just over two hours later, they reached Louisiana. Another waiting vehicle picked them up and they continued their journey to his final destination. It was a little two-bedroom house with a detached garage, perfect for small engine repairs. There was a red SUV parked in the driveway. There were neighbours on the street but all the houses were well-spaced, affording privacy. Agent Samuels showed him around the house which was still empty. His furniture wasn't arriving for another day. There was a sleeping bag and a foamy on the bedroom floor.

In the kitchen, Samuels placed a folder on the counter. He opened it up and pulled out new ID. He placed them down one by one. "Driver's license, Social Security Card, Visa card, bank card, etc. We opened an account for you at the bank in the mall and deposited the monies you were paid as an informant and what you're entitled to under witness protection."

"Okay."

The agent held up two cell phones. "The black one is your new personal phone. The red one is to be used only to call me. My number is programmed into contacts. This is for emergencies or any questions you may have. It's a secure number. Carry it with you at all times, along with your regular phone. I'll be calling you occasionally to check in with you and update you on court proceedings. You can set your own phone to whatever ring you want, but the red one is programmed to ring to '*Find my Baby For Me*' by Roy Orbison."

Dan's eyebrows shot up. "I remember that song. Interesting choice."

Samuels smiled. "There's a line in the lyrics, *Call the FBI.*"

"Clever."

"We thought so."

Dan picked up the driver's license. "Darcy Watkins."

"Here's your house keys and vehicle keys for your new ride in the driveway. We stocked the fridge with some food."

"You seem to have it all cased. Thank you."

"I'll let you get settled in. Talk to you soon."

After Samuels left, Dan/Darcy went out into the back yard. It was a nice size, fenced all around with bushes and trees against the fencing. He sat at the picnic table on a cement deck and tried to get a feel for his new home. Living a normal life would take some getting used to. The privacy was great, not that he needed to hide anything from his neighbours anymore. But he liked his privacy all the same and this home suited him fine. He soaked up the warmth of the evening for awhile and went back inside. It'd been a long night. Darcy crawled into the sleeping bag and fell asleep almost instantly.

It was a beautiful day towards mid-July. Darcy had been in his new home for several weeks. The truck had arrived with his belongings from New York state and he'd been kept busy setting up his residence to his liking. He'd upgraded the detached garage and turned it into a work shop for small lawn mower and boat repairs. Painters repainted the house and out buildings. He'd even met a few of his neighbours who'd invited him over to a July 4th BBQ celebration.

He was up at the crack of dawn this morning, deciding it was time to try his hand at fishing. He knew of a great spot in the Sabine Lake area that he wanted to try out. He packed a lunch and a thermos of coffee. Darcy headed down Highway 73. By the time he reached Bridge City, Texas, his thermos was empty. He stopped at the cafe to refill it. He headed southwest towards the lake and crossed the Rainbow Bridge. Past negative memories crowded his thoughts, but he pushed them away. *It's all behind you.* Happier than he'd been in years, he whistled to the music on the radio.

Life is good.

Chapter 44

Detective Calloway parked his personal vehicle in the police garage. He had a feeling in his gut that something was going to happen today. And his gut feelings were always right. He grabbed his coffee from the cup holder and headed for the elevator. He was on his own for a few days. His partner had taken a week off. When he reached his office, his assistant stopped him.

"Good morning, Detective. There's a Cassie Turner waiting for you in Room 1."

"Thanks, Kelly." He changed directions and headed to the interrogation room. *I knew it. Something's up. Didn't expect it so early in the morning though.* He opened the door. "Good morning, Miss Cassie."

"Good mornin'."

He set his coffee on the table, pulled a pad and pen out of his pocket, and sat across from his visitor. "What can we do for you today?"

"I saw him, he came in the cafe this mornin'. I came straight here to tell y'all."

"And who might 'him' be, Miss Cassie?"

"That man, the one who was at the cafe the night that poor woman went into the river."

A feeling of excitement coursed through his body. "How long ago was this?"

"About twenty-five minutes ago. He only came in to get his thermos filled with coffee. So he was in and out within a few minutes."

"Are you sure it was him, Miss Cassie?"

"Absolutely. I wasn't his server, so I was able to stare at him and get a good look. I went to the window when he left. He was drivin' a red SUV, newer model. I did get the license plate number." She fumbled in her pocket and pulled out a piece of paper.

"Good job. Did you notice which direction he was headed?"

"West. So I told 'em at work I had to leave for a bit and jumped in my car. I thought if I could catch up to him, I'd follow him and see where he went. But I never saw him again and came straight here."

"Hold on a minute." Calloway left the room. He gave the paper to an officer. "See if you can get a name and address to go with this license number pronto, please." He went into his office and pulled the Charles-Dixon file. He found what he wanted and returned to Room 1.

"Here's the composite drawing we did five months ago. Is there anything you would change?" He handed her the picture.

Cassie studied the poster. "His hair is longer. Falls over the forehead. Otherwise, that's him."

"What was he wearing?"

"A plain black t-shirt, blue jeans, white runners."

Calloway stood, "Great job, Miss Cassie. You're a good citizen."

"Hope it helps."

He walked her out. "Thank you for coming in."

The owner of the SUV was identified and later that morning, Calloway called the FBI in Lake Charles, Louisiana. "Special Agent Samuels, please." He waited impatiently while on hold.

"Special Agent Samuels here, how can I help you?"

"Good morning. This is Detective Scott Calloway with the Port Arthur Police Department. I need your help on something. It's to do with the Georgia Charles-Dixon file."

"What do you need, Detective?"

"If you remember the aspects of the case, there was a man who stopped at the cafe around the same time as Miss Georgia. We've never been able to identify him until now."

"And how does that involve the FBI?"

"The man we've identified lives in Lake Charles, Louisiana. I can't find anything on him. It's like he dropped out of the sky recently. No history."

"Okay, Give me what you've got and I'll see what I can do."

"Address is 393 McClury Rd, Lake Charles. Drives a newer red SUV, licence number Buffalo Buffalo Apple Six Zero Nine, registered to one Darcy Watkins. Got that?" There was silence on the other end. Calloway waited. "You still there?"

Samuels cleared his throat, "I'll get back to you."

Calloway noted the agents voice had dropped to a lower tone and his answer was curt. "One more thing before you go."

"What's that, Calloway?"

"This man has only been seen twice in the past five months, no one recognized his composite sketch. He shows up twice at the same coffee shop, on the only two occasions that Georgia Charles-Dixon travels from Canada to Port Arthur. And that really bothers me."

"Leave it with me." Samuels hung up.

Detective Calloway stared at the telephone. His gut was talking to him again. *Something's not right.*

Calloway went to see his superior and filled him in. "I want to place an officer on the family while they're here. Just to be on the safe side."

His boss agreed. "We don't need any more negative publicity regarding this case. She's as good as a celebrity and a guest of the Mayor's. I suggest plain clothes. No sense in upsetting them at this point."

237

FBI, Lake Charles, Louisiana

Special Agent Samuels pulled the file on Daniel Barton alias Darcy Watkins. There were updates in the file he hadn't had time to read. When he was done, his blood boiled. He went straight to the Resident Agent in Charge, Cam Hutchins.

"We've got a big problem, sir."

"Fill me in."

"Something's come up with Darcy Watkins. Five months ago, he was in Lake Charles for his mother's funeral. Immigration Agents from his resident state of New York had us watching him while he was here. On one occasion I left my stakeout for a few minutes. When I returned he was gone. He returned to his mother's home around midnight. His time was unaccounted for approximately twelve hours."

"Yes, yes, I know all that. What's the problem."

"I just finished reading updated reports from ICE in Buffalo, New York. They cleaned out his property. In one of the outbuildings they found a vehicle registered to one James Draper aka James Pearson."

"The serial killer?"

"That's the one. Watkins must have smuggled him into Canada. His last victim was Georgia Charles-Dixon. Benjamin Pearson was stalking her and kidnapped her in British Columbia. She killed him."

"I remember it. Continue."

"Five months ago, Miss Georgia was in Houston at a conference. She came to lake Charles to visit an acquaintance and had an accident on the way back to Houston. We were briefly involved in the case until it was determined the accident happened back in Texas. The Port Arthur Police maintained control. This morning I had a call from Detective Calloway. There was a man at a Bridge City, Texas cafe at the same time as Miss Georgia on the night of her accident. This morning a waitress reported he came into the cafe, for the first time in five months. She wrote down his licence number. It's Watkins'. And the day of Miss Georgia's accident was the day he disappeared under my watch."

"Holy shit. You think he's the one who drove her off the road? But why?"

"I don't know but he was in Texas today and so is Miss Georgia with her family. I think we'd better pull him in and have a serious chat."

"This is bad. It could jeopardize the whole program and the ICE case. Bring him in."

An hour later, they had Watkins in one of the interrogation rooms. Samuels took his file with him and dropped it hard on the table in front of his charge.

"What's going on?" Darcy asked.

"Playtime is over, pal. We have some serious talking to do. So listen up." Samuels stood at the table and presented the facts to Darcy one by one, with each point he threw a picture from the file down in front of the man. When he was done, he leaned across the table and shouted. 'Why'd you do it, Darcy?"

Dan shook his head. "It was an accident. I didn't mean for her to get hurt."

"Who was Benjamin Pearson to you? Did you help him cross the border?"

"Benjamin Pearson and I were kids together. He was the only friend I had. And yes, I helped him cross the border."

Samuels raised an eyebrow. "You wanted us to believe you had more integrity than Teslin. You wouldn't traffic women and children because it crossed your line." He pounded his fist on the table. "Pearson was a fucking serial killer. He tortured women, raped and murdered them, and buried them in the desert. And you helped him cross into Canada so he could kidnap Georgia Charles-Dixon who most likely, he'd torture, rape, and kill as well. Luckily, she turned the tables on him. What were you doing that night five months ago? Finishing the job because she killed your 'childhood friend'?

"No. I didn't know he was a killer until after he was dead and they published the map of the bodies and the diary excerpts he'd kept about what he'd done. I was sick to my stomach. It ate me up that I'd help put that woman in danger. After my mother died, I knew I couldn't do it anymore. I had to change my life and decided to retire. I was going to when ICE arrested me."

Agent Samuels sat down and stared across at Darcy. "Why were you following her that night?"

"I'd seen in the papers that she was in Houston at some convention. That morning I'd gone to the mall and stopped at a coffee shop. There she was sitting at a table with another woman. I was pretty sure it was her so I sat down nearby and listened to their conversation. It's hard to explain why."

"Try."

"My mother and Pearson were my only friends growing up. Ben understood me because we both had abusive home lives. I'd go to school with bruises and kept to myself because I was embarrassed. Some of the kids thought I was weird and bullied me. He stood up for me. I survived because I had a mother who loved me and she took me and ran. James' mother was as bad as his father. I tracked him down when we were both adults and we stayed friends. But I had no idea what he'd become."

"So what's that got to do with you stalking Miss Georgia?"

"That wasn't my intention. My mother had died and I was in a bad way. I'd been drinking all week, but not that day. I was grieving and in alcohol depression—then there she was. This beautiful, strong woman I'd read about and admired. Pearson hated women—his mother, the women he killed, even his wife. But he told me he loved this Georgia woman. I think I wanted to see what it was about her that gave her a hold over Pearson." He shrugged. "It gave me something else to think about. Sounds crazy, I know."

"So how'd she end up in the water?"

"I sat watching them at her friend's house from the park across the street and followed her when she left. I didn't see any harm in it at the time. We spoke briefly as she was leaving the cafe. I left too 'cause they wanted to close up early due to the storm. I realized how ridiculous it was. It was time for me to go home. I decided to head to Beaumont and stay for the night, figuring the highway would be open by morning.

I followed behind her 'til I caught up to her. I tried to pass but I hydroplaned towards her lane. It all happened so fast. She went onto the shoulder and I skidded into her lane. I tapped the wheels to slow down and saw I was heading towards the bridge span. I hit the brakes hard and stopped. She'd slowed down and I figured she'd be okay. So I took off over the bridge. I saw her slide sideways towards that big rock. I thought it would stop her. I didn't know she'd end up in the water."

"Why on earth did you want to relocate here with that hanging over your head. What were you thinking?"

Darcy shrugged. "My mother lived here. She's buried here. I wanted to feel close to her. That woman was back home in Canada and I figured it was over."

"Why did you go to the Bridge City area today?"

"Fishing. I caught some bass."

"Did you know Miss Georgia is in Port Arthur with her family?"

Darcy looked shocked. "Shit, no. I swear."

"You weren't honest with us, Darcy. You've jeopardized your position in the protection program and the Teslin case. This is going to have to go to Head Office. Meanwhile, you're going to have to stay in custody until we figure this out."

Darcy stiffened. "Henry told me I shouldn't trust you. You're going to screw me aren't you."

"I don't make the decisions. It's out of my hands."

Chapter 45

Port Arthur, Texas

The synergy in the room was electrifying. Two hundred people filled the room. There was an open bar at one end, with a stage on one side. A three piece jazz group were playing background music. The twenty-five round tables with seating for eight each were covered with white tablecloths and a multi-coloured floral display sat in the centre of each. Some people were standing in small groups chatting, but most were already seated.

As Georgia and the rest of the family entered the room, a woman holding a folder approached them. She led them to a table in front of the stage. Georgia was pleased to see that they were seated with Dylan and Camilla Ortega and their two sons. After they acknowledged each other, Sean went to the bar to get them all drinks. The table behind them seated Dylan's parents and some of his old co-workers and friends.

Georgia looked around the room and was surprised to see a table with her medical team. At another table she saw the two detectives with their wives from Houston sitting with the Port Arthur detectives and their wives. She'd make a point of talking to them all sometime during the evening. Sean returned and sat down.

A woman from the table beside them approached and introduced herself as the Mayor of Port Arthur. "So nice to meet you all. We're pleased that you were able to come."

"It's a pleasure to be here. We wouldn't have missed it for the world," Georgia said. She introduced Sean and the girls.

She smiled at Sean. "Are you enjoying our fine state?"

Sean stood and shook her hand. He gave her one of his devastating smiles. The effect on the Mayor was obvious and Georgia suppressed a smile. 'We certainly are. Your southern hospitality definitely surpasses its reputation."

"Wonderful."

The woman with the folder whispered to the Mayor. "Everyone is here, your worship. If you'd like to welcome your guests, we'll serve dinner."

The Mayor smiled at Georgia and gave Sean an even bigger smile. She climbed the stage to address the room.

Georgia leaned over to Sean. "Well aren't you the southern gentleman. She's impressed with you." Three days of Texas sun certainly contributed to his good looks.

"Just warming up for my beautiful wife. You look gorgeous by the way."

"Thank you."

The microphone screeched and Georgia turned her attention back to the Mayor.

"Good evening, ladies and gentlemen. I'd like to welcome you all to our Hometown Hero Dinner Gala. If you could all please be seated, I have a few announcements to make." She waited until the tables were full. "First I'd like to introduce you all to our hometown hero, Dylan Ortega. Stand up so everyone can see you." *Applause.* She then introduced Camilla and the boys. Applause.

"Next I'd like to welcome and introduce you to our out-of-town guests from Canada. Georgia and Sean Charles-Dixon and their daughters, Kaela and Shelby. *Applause.*

The Mayor then introduced the special dignitaries and Council members. " As you can see, we have a silent auction set up on the far side of the room. If you haven't already placed a bid, the tables will be open until the end of the evening. Make sure to go back often and rebid to assure you get the item you want. All the proceeds from tonight's tickets and the silent auction will be donated to the Julie Rogers "Gift of Life" Program. Enjoy your dinner and after dessert, we'll begin our special presentation."

Dinner was delicious—a tender prime rib rubbed with garlic and rosemary, roast potatoes, carrots, broccoli, with a light gravy and mild horse radish, served with a dry red wine. Then came desert. Kaela and Shelby couldn't believe their eyes; a peach cobbler Texas style made with bourbon and not just one scoop of vanilla ice cream, but two. No one at their table could finish theirs.

"Omigod ..." Sean said, holding his stomach. "They'll have to roll me out of here."

The presentation began and the Mayor introduced the State Senator. He spoke about the area and the community, praised the Mayor and council, and commended Dylan Ortega on his bravery. The media had been allowed inside the door. Light bulbs flashed and cameras zinged. A TV crew were filming beside the stage. A number of other local dignitaries spoke next. The Mayor then invited Sean up to say a few words.

"I'd like to thank the Mayor, Council and the City of Port Arthur for inviting us here tonight for this happy occasion. When Georgia and I were here five months ago, it was our first trip to Texas. It wasn't the trip we have planned. The past months have been a difficult transition for Georgia and all of us, but she's doing very well. To return to the great state of Texas as your guests is such an honour for us. We can't say enough about your Texas charm and hospitality and we've taken full advantage of our trip to be tourists in your great state. First off, I'd like to take the opportunity to acknowledge Detectives Brian Castle and Alan Blake of the Houston Police Department, and Detectives Scott Calloway and Jarrod Brown from your very own Port Arthur Police Department for their diligence and continued work on Georgia's case. They're sitting right over there." Sean pointed to their table. *Applause.* "And, sitting to our right, I wish to thank Georgia's Medical Team, Dr. David Edwards, Dr. Nuri Benadie, Kelly Franco, Tara Viera and Samantha Cole." *Applause.* Sean turned his attention back to Dylan. "It means so much for me and my family to be here tonight to honour you, Dylan. For us, this is not only about your bravery in diving into frigid waters and giving Georgia life-saving CPR; it's about what you gave back to me and my children. You gave me back my wife and you gave Kaela and Shelby back their mother. We'll be forever in your debt. Your family have a lot to be proud of. Congratulations. *Applause.*

Georgia came to the stage next. "Since Sean's words voiced my thoughts and those of my family, I'll keep this short and not repeat them. Dylan, how could I possibly find the right words to express my gratitude to you. One of the positives that has come from my accident was meeting you and your family." She addressed the audience. "Over the past five months, we have corresponded with Dylan and Camilla through Facebook, emails, and over the telephone. Under normal circumstances, I doubt we would have ever met. But from my tragedy, we did meet and in spite of the geographical distance between us and the cultural differences between our families, we have found common ground, mutual values, and a warm friendship." Georgia looked at Dylan. "We're honoured to share this evening with you and your family. I thank you with all my heart and hope to continue our friendship as we move forward in our lives." *Applause.*

The Mayor asked Dylan to join her on stage. She spoke to the audience about his family and history in the community. She spoke of the things she'd learned about Dylan's character and his act of bravery.

"We're proud to say you are one of our community members, Dylan. First, I have a letter for you from Governor Bradley Stone of the great state of Texas." The letter was mounted in a silver frame and was typed on official state stationary with a stamp from the Governor's office.

"This is a letter from the city of Port Arthur honouring your bravery." It was also on official stationery and stamped with the city seal. "And finally, we'd like to present you with this plaque naming you our hometown hero. Congratulations."

Dylan stood at the podium. His face exposed his emotions. With tears in his eyes he spoke. "I'm a simple man. Speaking to this many people is not easy for me. I find it hard to think of myself as a hero. I'd like to believe that anyone would have done what I did that night. I just happened to be the one who was there to be the helping hand that Miss Georgia needed."

Georgia couldn't hold back the tears. She picked up her napkin and dabbed at her eyes.

"I really must share this with my wife, Camilla. She played an important role. If we hadn't had a husband/wife squabble that night, and if she hadn't lost her fiery Spanish temper that spurred me to childishly walk out into that storm, we wouldn't be having this gala and Miss Georgia wouldn't be with us." He smiled at his wife and held up the plaque. Everyone laughed and applauded. "I'd like to thank the City of Port Arthur, the Governor's office, and all the dignitaries here, and all of you for being here tonight. I'm humbled and honoured."

The Mayor said her final thank you to everyone. "The evening isn't over. We're going to push the tables into a horseshoe so we can have some dancing. Don't forget to check your auction items."

The rest of the evening was more relaxed and full of laughter. Georgia spoke with the medical team and joined the law enforcement table. She met the Chief of Police, the Fire Chief and a slew of other people, including the Senator.

Chapter 46

They'd slept in late the morning after the gala, having returned to their hotel around midnight. The girls and the Ortega boys had made it until about eleven-thirty and all seemed to hit a wall around the same time. The boys were seven and nine, and totally loved the girls, even with the three year age difference.

Dylan invited them to a Texas BBQ, steaks and chilli for that afternoon. The kids were swimming in an above ground pool and the women were in the kitchen organizing for their meal. Sean and Dylan prepped the BBQ and set up the picnic table.

Dylan reached into a cooler and handed Sean a beer.

"Thanks. You've got a great property here," Sean said.

"We like it."

"So how are things going, financially I mean. I know it's been a tough road for you and Camilla."

"We doing okay. She's working great hours at the accounting firm. She gets to see the kids off to school and I'm here when they get home. I make dinner and we have the evening together before I have to go to my security job."

"I'm glad. But it must be hard on you with your education, working nights at a security job."

"Sometimes, but I'm grateful that we're making our mortgage payments. There just aren't any jobs out there in my field right now. We'd have to sell the house and move away. That's not really an option with my elderly parents here. And the kids don't want to leave their friends. Besides, I do enjoy being here in the day to putter in the garden."

"I'm amazed with the draught and desert-like soil that you've managed to have such beautiful gardens."

Dylan smiled. "I love working with this type of soil. My grandfather in Mexico was a landscaper. When I was little, I'd spend my summers there and he taught me how to grow the right plants in areas with little water."

Sean studied Dylan. "Did you like your job in the computer world?"

"It was a good job, great pay. But I always wanted to be a landscaper like my grandfather. But when my parents immigrated here, my father said I had to go to college. He didn't bring his family to Texas so I could grovel in the dirt like his father."

"Your love of the land shows. You have a natural talent for landscaping." Sean looked at the big barn that sat on the property. "What do you use that for?"

"Storage is all. It came with the place but I haven't had a need for it."

"Is it usable?"

"I suppose. Wouldn't take much to upgrade it."

"Listen. I have a proposition for you. Next year, I'm going to have a whopper of a tax bill unless I invest some money somewhere. How about I invest it in you and help you set up your own landscaping business."

Dylan pushed his shoulders back. "I'm a proud man. I don't accept charity."

Sean laughed. "Who's offering you charity. I'm a businessman, Dylan. The important thing to me is you have the talent and the love of the land. My indigenous heritage and your Mexican heritage share common values when it comes to the land. I don't want to be involved in any way. I'm just the banker. You work out a business plan—what it'll take to set this property up as a home-based business, upgrade the barn, equipment needed, vehicles etc. I'm willing to loan you the money for it all, I'll pay you and Camilla one year's salary, and you don't have to start paying back the loan until your business is up and running and profitable."

Dylan looked perplexed. "Camilla?"

"Absolutely, you need to set up an office at home. Camilla has the skills to run the business side of things. All you'll need at year-end is an accountant to do your taxes for you. Camilla can be home for the kids too. It could be a good life. And I see a need for your talents as Texas struggles through draughts and water shortages. You know the business and you're smart." Sean grinned. "And you can use your new celebrity to obtain big accounts. You know people now who count."

"Wow." Dylan ran his hands through his hair and shook his head. "You'd do this for us?"

"Look, there's only so many times I can say thank you and shake your hand. It still doesn't feel like enough. This is like a paying it forward gesture. My family would be honoured to do this for you and Camilla and I need to move some money. I'd rather it be invested with you then anywhere else. Talk it over with Camilla if you like but I'd like to shake hands on this before we go home. What do you say?"

Dylan put his hand out. "I will discuss it with Camilla as soon as we've eaten. But I know what she'll say, so let's shake on it."

"Done."

After they'd eaten, Dylan insisted that Georgia and Sean relax while he and Camilla cleaned up. Georgia started to rise and Sean knew she was going to offer to help anyway. He placed a hand on her arm and held her back. She looked at him with a question in her eyes and he shook his head no. He knew Dylan wanted time alone with Camilla to discuss their deal. After they'd entered the house, he filled Georgia in.

She leaned forward and kissed him. "No wonder I love you. You're such a compassionate man."

When their hosts returned, Camilla walked over to Sean and demanded he stand up. She put her arms around him, kissed him on both cheeks and gave him a tight hug. "You're a wonderful man and a good friend. Thank you." When they parted, her eyes were filled with tears.

Chapter 47

Gibsons, BC

The flight home was uneventful. Once again Georgia was calm and relaxed on the flight, a phenomenon that Sean found mind boggling. They decided to stay home and maybe return to the cabin in August for a couple of weeks. They'd all had enough of travelling for awhile.

Georgia's parents were staying with her grandmother down the road. A few nights after the family had returned from Texas, they all came to visit with her ex-father-in-law, Frank. They sat outside on a beautiful warm night. Georgia had never seen her grandmother so up. She was bubbling over and giggling with Frank like a schoolgirl. Frank was Georgia's ex-father-in-law. Since he and his wife had separated four years previously and eventually divorced, he'd been living on the Sunshine Coast. Her Grams was nine years older than Frank. There was a discernible difference in age between Georgia's parents and her first husband's parents. Hers were teenage parents; Frank and Alice had started later than most couples, which put Frank closer to Georgia's grandmother's age than her mother's.

Her grandmother spoke out. "Everyone, could I have your attention, please. We have something to tell you."

They all stopped talking and turned to her. "Frank and I are getting married. He's moving into my house."

Georgia's mouth dropped open. No one spoke. Frank and her Grams were smiling at each other. Kaela and Shelby giggled like they did at most things. Finally, Georgia's mother spoke. "Now that was a bomb-shell. How wonderful. I'm happy for you both." She stood and walked over to them and gave each one a hug."

Georgia and Sean congratulated them and her father shook hands with Frank.

"Have you chosen a date?" her mother asked.

" We were thinking in August, right at the house. We want to keep it simple."

"Grams can Shelby and I be part of your wedding party?" Kaela asked.

"Certainly, one of you can be the flower girl, the other can carry the rings. You decide who's who."

The girls looked at each and shrugged. "We could do rock, paper, scissors, three out of five does flowers, the other does rings," Shelby said. In the end Shelby got flowers.

"Settled, Grams," Kaela said. "Omigod … we could wear our new dresses we bought for the gala in Texas. Wanna see them? They're pale pink."

"They sound perfect. Let's go have a look, shall we?" The three disappeared into the house.

Georgia and her mother followed them in to make coffee.

"Wow. I didn't see that coming," her mother said.

"I wouldn't have a clue since I'm still missing the past twelve years," Georgia said. "It's strange though, my ex-father-in-law and my grand-mother?" They both laughed.

"I suppose it's nice to have companionship when you're growing older," her mother said.

"I agree, Mom. And they do seem to really enjoy each other. They have fun together."

Grams and the girls returned. "The dresses are perfect."

"What are you going to wear, Grams?" Shelby asked.

"Oh, I hadn't thought that far ahead. Certainly not white. Probably champagne or a deeper pink than your dresses. We'll see."

"Uhh … I saw the most darling thing the other day in a magazine. They're called barefoot sandals. Just a piece of lace with glitter or jewels in various colours. They fit on the foot around one toe and your ankle. They're perfect for backyard weddings and they cost like under ten dollars," Kaela said, all excited.

"My dear, I'm sure they'd look adorable on your feet, but my poor arthritic feet wouldn't do them justice."

George and Sean cuddled in bed talking about their evening and her grandmother's news while touching each other in their favourite places until physical passion took over, and their thinking became more primal than practical. Sean's adeptness took Georgia beyond her expectations and when he entered her, their minds and body became one, rising as the waves of passion took them to the brink, the ebb teasingly pulling them back, until they exploded over the edge and were spent.

They lay quiet, happy and content, their bodies entwined. "You realize your grandmother is a cougar."

Georgia snorted. "What? At their ages, nine years means nothing. Companionship is wonderful for seniors."

"Companionship? Did you see how they were lusting after each other? Now I know where you get your appetite from."

"Oh, Sean. I can't think of my Grams like that."

"Why not? Seniors do it too, you know. Yup…your Grams is a cougar."

Georgia smacked him on the shoulder and giggled. "You know what I'm thinking?"

"What?"

"When my ex-father-in-law marries my Grams, he'll become my grandfather."

Sean laughed. "And not only will he be Kaela's and Shelby's grand-father, but he'll be their great-grandfather too."

"Omigod ... you're right. And he'd become my mother's step-father instead of mine."

"Just as I thought I had your family figured out. You're a weird bunch, aren't you?"

Georgia punched him. "And...my ex-sister-in-law would become my aunt and my mother's step-sister."

"And your ex-father-in-law would become your Dad's father-in-law."

They burst into laughter. "I'm immersed in a crazy family..." Sean mused.

Georgia hit him with a pillow.

"Ow... I think you've become more aggressive since your accident. I didn't know you were so violent. But you know what?" He started to stroke her face and she melted at his touch.

"What?"

"I'm in for the long haul 'cause..."

Georgia finished it for him, "...baby, you're worth it." They stared at each other in silence. "You said the same thing to me on our wedding night at the cabin when we slept in the meadow in the tent with the defender by our side...in case a grizzly paid us a visit."

Sean reached across her, turned the lamp on and stared into her eyes. "You remember our wedding night?"

Georgia couldn't speak. She knew he was waiting for her to say something but so many memories flew threw her mind, one after the other, crashing together and leaving her speechless.

Sean's eyes never left hers. "Georgia?"

She took a deep breath which was more like a gasp. A nervous laugh escaped her lips. "I remember everything," she said in a whisper. She wrapped her arms around Sean's neck and he pulled her close. To-gether they cried, then they kissed and then they laughed—and cried some more.

"Tell me something you remember, so I know it's real." Sean said.

Georgia tried to think of something obscure that hadn't been talked about in the past five months. "Okay. When you were a boy and staying with your grandfather at the cabin, you caught so many fish that your grandfather decided to smoke them. He told you the process would take about six hours. You didn't believe him. You thought the fish would be ruined so you tried to open the smoker and you burnt your fingers."

Sean kissed her again. "My sweet Georgia."

"I'm ba...ack."

She looked at the clock. It was just after eleven. "Let's wake up the girls. I don't want to wait until morning."

They slipped into the girls room and turned on a lamp. Sean woke Kaela while Georgia prodded Shelby. Two sleepy heads sat up in bed and stared at them. "Mommy, what's wrong? "

"Nothing's wrong, girls. Everything is right." She and Sean smiled at each other.

"Then why did you drag us out of bed?" Kaela asked.

"Come sit with me and Shelby and I'll tell you." Kaela joined her on Shelby's bed. "I couldn't wait until morning to tell you ... " Her eyes blurred once again. "... I remember."

"All of it?" Kaela asked, in a whisper.

"All of it, sweetheart."

Georgia looked at Shelby.

Shelby's eyes were huge. "Everything, Mommy?"

"Everything," she whispered. Both girls came into her arms. Georgia looked at Kaela. "I remember the night you were born, alone at the cabin. Suddenly everything I feared disappeared. I knew we would be alright and having you there with me took away all the loneliness. I was whole."

She turned her head and looked at Shelby "And I remember the day we were at the beach on New Year's Day to pay tribute to your mother. You asked me if Julie would mind if you called me Mommy too. I was so filled with love for you. I had my two girls and my husband of six months. We became a family that day" Georgia looked at Sean and smiled.

"And tonight we're a family again."

Epilogue

Special Agent Samuels sat down opposite Darcy Watkins. "Here's the deal. Since Teslin's arrest, a search of his place and new witnesses have brought more damning evidence against him. He's about to be indicted for murder. With your testimony, Teslin will never get out.

We believe you meant Miss Georgia no harm the night of her accident, even though leaving the scene of an accident is a criminal offence and a chicken shit action on your part. We've learned her memory has returned in full, except the night of the accident. And her Doctor doubts she ever will remember it because it is very common for victims to not remember incidents from head trauma. There's nothing to challenge your story in a court of law, so you'd probably get off on probation with a hefty fine.

The Teslin case is too important to lose. So we've decided to keep you in the program and move forward."

Darcy gave a big sigh of relief. "Does that mean I get to go home?"

Samuels pulled a document out of his folder. "Only if you agree to sign this."

"What is it?" Darcy eyed the paper with distrust.

"This states that you will never ever try to contact Georgia Charles-Dixon in writing, by telephone, or through a third party; nor will you ever follow her; and should you ever find yourself in proximity to her, you will turn and walk away. Should it come to light that you've broken the terms of this document, you will be automatically withdrawn from the Witness Protection Program and prosecuted for her accident. Now probation and a fine may not seem like something to be fearful of, but the publicity surrounding our celebrity victim would expose you to the world and I'm sure bring Teslin crashing back into your life. He has arms outside the prison system. And the FBI will not protect you. Do we understand each other?"

Darcy shifted in his seat. "We do."

"Do we have an agreement?"

"Absolutely. I'll sign it."

Samuels handed him the document and a pen. He witnessed the signature.

"We're done. You're free to go."

Darcy was hesitant. "That's it? I can go home?"

"You can, sir."

Both men stood. Darcy turned back at the doorway. "Thank you."

The agent returned to his office to find an angry Detective waiting for him. He knew why he was here. *Stay calm and professional.*

"Detective Calloway. I wasn't expecting you this morning. What can I do for you?"

"I think you know why I'm here, Agent Samuels. What's going on?"

Samuels settled behind his desk. "You want to know why you were pulled off the Charles-Dixon case. Am I right?"

"Damn right. I put a lot into this case and just as I think we've got a break, you come along and shut me down. Why?"

"You know I can't divulge FBI information to you. I'm bound by an oath of confidentiality, just like you are."

Calloway's fist came down on the agent's desk. "Don't play coy with me, Samuels. Tell me something."

The agent weighed the emotions on the detectives face. He knew what it was like to be involved in a case and have it yanked out of your hands. *It becomes personal. It shouldn't but it does.* "I'll tell you what, sit down and I'll tell what I can. But then you have to let it lie. Okay?"

Calloway nodded. "Do I have a choice?" He sat opposite the agent and waited.

"Darcy Watkins is in the FBI Witness Protection Program."

"I knew it was something like that," Calloway interjected.

"I can't give you the specifics of the case, but it's a big one, and important. It involves murder, and trafficking of women and children. Darcy is one of our star witnesses. Believe me, he's helping to take a bad man off the streets."

"But he's a scumbag if he's part of that scene and turning witness."

"Believe me, he's not a saint but he wasn't involved with these people until he was recruited by law enforcement."

Calloway sat back in his chair. "It's just not fair. Miss Georgia deserves to know what happened to her and why."

"I know she does. But she has fully recovered, has no memory of that night and probably never will have according to her doctor. You know as well as me that if Darcy Watkins goes to trial for leaving the scene of an accident, he won't do time. It's not worth blowing a big case. He's not the only witness but losing him and his credibility could open it up and bring it crashing down. You and I have both seen that happen with cases in the past."

"You're saying it was just an accident? Nothing to do with who Miss Georgia is or her celebrity?"

Samuels leaned forward. "We're convinced he meant her no harm. And there's nothing to challenge his story if it went to court."

"I hear you." Calloway digested the information for a few minutes. "Okay, I'll let the waitress who fingered him know he had nothing to do with what happened that night. And as far as the Port Arthur Police Department is concerned, the case is closed."

The two men shook hands and Detective Calloway left.

Special Agent Samuels swung his chair around and stared out the window of his office into the busy streets. He watched people passing by the Federal Building he worked in, all of them trusting he and his peers were doing their jobs to ensure their safety. He let out a long sigh and turned back to his desk. He picked up a new file from his in-basket and opened it.

Another day! Another compromise!

Dear reader,

We hope you enjoyed reading *Missing Thread*. Please take a moment to leave a review, even if it's a short one. Your opinion is important to us.

Discover more books by June V. Bourgo at
https://www.nextchapter.pub/authors/june-v-bourgo

Want to know when one of our books is free or discounted? Join the newsletter at http://eepurl.com/bqqB3H

Best regards,
June V. Bourgo and the Next Chapter Team

You could also like:

Woman in the Woods by Phillip Tomasso

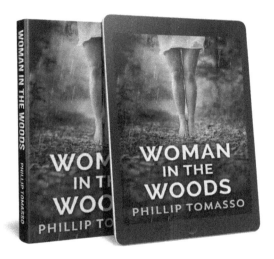

To read the first chapter for free, please head to:
https://www.nextchapter.pub/books/woman-in-the-woods

Missing Thread
ISBN: 978-4-82410-272-0

Published by
Next Chapter
1-60-20 Minami-Otsuka
170-0005 Toshima-Ku, Tokyo
+818035793528
16th November 2021

9 784824 102720